Maternal Instinct

A novel

by Rebecca Bowyer

Story Addict Publishing
Melbourne, Australia

First published 2019 by Story Addict Publishing.
PO Box 11, Croydon, Victoria 3136 Australia
storyaddict.com.au
Copyright © Rebecca Bowyer 2019

Publisher's Note: This is a work of fiction. Names, characters, places, and incidents are a product of the author's imagination. Locales and public names are sometimes used for atmospheric purposes. Any resemblance to actual people, living or dead, or to businesses, companies, events, institutions, or locales is completely coincidental.

Cover design: Gianfranco Piras
Cover images: Adobe Stock
Book Layout ©2015 BookDesignTemplates.com
Printed by IngramSpark
Maternal Instinct/ Rebecca Bowyer. -- 1st ed.

ISBN 978-0-6485323-0-9 (pbk)
ISBN 978-0-6485323-1-6 (ebook)

A catalogue record for this book is available from the National Library of Australia.

For every parent who has silently offered their child to the goblin king,

but regretted it a moment later.

"It is time, little one."

"Time for what, mother?"

"Time for you to go out into the world and be heard."

And so the little story went.

Thank you, dear reader, for listening.

CHAPTER 1

ALICE WOKE TO daylight and the sound of a fussing baby. The snuffling turned to huffy grunting and then a thin wail. "Sssssh!" A woman hissed sharply at the infant.

Alice smiled, reached for the remote hanging from her bed rail, and pushed a button to tilt the bed head upwards, allowing her to see past her feet.

"Hey, Monica," she said.

The young woman seated in the faded vinyl armchair looked up from positioning her son at her breast. She frowned.

"Sorry, Mum. I didn't mean to wake you."

"It's okay. Is it Sunday already?"

Monica blinked quickly and rubbed her shoulder against her cheek. The movement shifted the baby's head and it began to fuss again.

"No, only Friday. But I was bored and thought I'd come and see how you're doing—ow!" She pulled the infant away from her chest and clutched her nipple. "God, this breastfeeding thing sucks. Why can't they just use bottles? I mean, seriously." She scratched at her stringy red hair. It was banded loosely together and in need of a wash.

Alice sucked on her tongue and swallowed, feeling her jaw clench. Sometimes she still couldn't quite believe that she'd managed to raise a daughter so ungrateful, so oblivious to the privilege she enjoyed, living in this lucky country.

Then again, she mused, she hadn't actually raised her. Not really.

"Monica, your breast milk is specially designed—"

"—for my baby and reduces disease and is more efficient. For the sake of the children. Yeah, yeah, blah, blah, I know." She twisted her upper body around unnaturally, trying to get the writhing baby reattached before the wailing really got going. "It's just so... undignified." Monica pulled the baby's blue muslin wrap over his head and tugged it taut to cover her own chest, as though to prove a point.

Alice sank back into the pillow, feeling suddenly weak and trying not to laugh. She should know better than to try. Despite repeated lectures about communal responsibility and the crucial role of birth mothers in ensuring every child grows to become a well-adjusted and productive adult, her daughter had never hidden her deep resentment about being forced into compulsory National Procreation Service. In Monica's opinion, being required to birth and feed two babies over three years was an inconvenience which delayed her from following in her genetic father's footsteps as a molecular immunologist. She'd been doing her best to plead her way out of it since she was twelve, much to Alice's annoyance and embarrassment.

When Monica turned sixteen, she had written to the U.S. Department of Immigration pleading for political asylum from Australia's reproduction program. She received a prompt e-mail back, rejecting her application on the grounds that she was not being persecuted for political or religious beliefs. Alice suspected the rejection had more to do with the United States' perception of Australia as a rather promising social experiment.

Time would tell.

"Don't worry, the breastfeeding is only for six months, then you'll get your body back." Alice tried to keep her impatience out of her voice as she winced and pushed another button, releasing a cold liquid into her hand. It flowed up her arm and she lay, still and tense, waiting for it to course through her body and quell the sharp pains in her abdomen.

"Yeah, just in time to get pregnant again," Monica muttered to her tiny human bundle, frowning sourly at the lump where she knew his head would be. She peered through the muslin wrap to check if he'd finished his meal. "Two years, two months and one more baby to go, little one." She looked up at Alice. "He's gone to sleep again, damn it. How am I supposed to get anything done when he won't concentrate on taking a full feed and then thinks he should feed every two hours?"

"What did you expect, that he'd just lie in a crib and sleep for six months? Oh, and I'm doing fine after the surgery, thanks for asking."

Monica ignored her, extracted her nipple from the baby's soft, thick lips and flopped him down into the empty pram. Alice winced as the pram squeaked in protest and the little boy let out a single, startled cry before grumbling quietly and falling silent again. She forced her own eyes open and felt around for the bed buttons again. Pushing the remote with her thumb, she raised herself to a reclined sitting position.

"Could I have a hold?" she asked.

"Of what?" Monica sat at the end of the bed, legs crossed, stroking the metal tube hooked over her ear as she scrolled through the projected visuals only she could see. She blinked twice to clear her vision, then looked up at Alice and traced her gaze to the pram. "Oh, you mean the baby. Sure, please do, he might stay asleep longer if someone holds on to him."

"Have you given him a name?" asked Alice as she held out her arms to take the sleeping bundle.

"No. They're calling him Oscar. I suppose it suits. I just call him 'the annoying thing that wakes me up ten times a night and makes me soak milk through all my tops.'"

Alice sighed and shook her head as Monica took up a plastic perch next to the bed and continued flicking through her messages. She was accustomed to her biological daughter's disinterest in all things human and wasn't in the least surprised to find that birthing her own tiny human had made no difference to the status quo.

"Hello, little Oscar. It's lovely to see you again," she cooed.

Oscar yawned in his sleep, revealing a tiny pink tongue surrounded by matching gummy ridges. A drop of thick, white milk traced a line across his chin. She held him up a little, stopping as she felt a pull in her abdomen that the opiates couldn't mask, and rubbed her cheek against his. He responded by nestling ever so slightly in towards her neck.

Alice breathed deeply, inhaling the scent of memories more than twenty years old. She bit her lips—hard—as her tiny grandson scrunched up his perfect face and wriggled in her arms. He snorted, then snuffled, arched his back and considered crying. He opened his mouth and let out one short protest before changing his mind and settling down to continue sleeping.

Monica tapped the top of her ear and removed the metal tube. She stared, dazed, at the baby.

Alice watched her watching Oscar and smiled.

"He's got your hair."

Monica reached over and cupped her hand around Oscar's auburn down covered scalp.

"Yours too."

She pressed the backs of her fingers against her son's squishy cheek. He stirred and started to whimper again. She withdrew her hand and retreated into her chair.

"So... I've managed to get permission to continue my studies for a few hours each day," Monica said lightly. "I can do one unit stretched out over the next six months. But I have to give it up once I'm pregnant again. They're worried it might cause too much stress and affect the development of the foetus."

The words hung, sterile, in the quiet hospital room.

"Okay," said Alice hesitantly.

She looked down to find Oscar peering at her with curious blue eyes. His gaze moved from her face to her shoulder and back again, trying to focus. One tiny hand broke loose from his wrap and waved wildly in her general direction. He cried as his arm smacked into his own nose. Monica huffed impatiently and whipped the baby out of Alice's arms.

'There's just never a moment of peace with a baby, is there? I don't know why people choose to be a Mater or Pater."

Alice thought of the parenting professionals who had raised Monica. Mater Peta and Pater John were warm, but not intimate; strict but not cold; deliberate and informed but not prescriptive. They'd been fostering children together for fifteen years already—under the old system—when Monica came into their care. They were used to welcoming children into their home for short periods of time—a month while a parent was ill, six months while a mother kicked a drug habit, a few years when the drug habit kicked back. Monica had been part of the first wave of infants to be taken into mass permanent care in this new world order her grandparents had built.

Alice smiled inwardly as she watched her irritable daughter strap her reluctant infant into his bassinet attachment. Peta and John had done a good job with Monica. She was confident, internally driven to succeed, and had no inkling of the sacrifices that had been made to allow her generation to enjoy what no other country on earth had: Equality, Ecocentricity and Equanimity. She would go far in Australian society, though she certainly would not follow her adoptive parents in their chosen careers. At this rate, Oscar would be lucky if he saw his genetic mother a handful of Sundays each year.

"Your Mater and Pater must have been thrilled to meet him," ventured Alice.

"Um, they haven't met him yet."

"Oh?"

"No, I've only just been allowed out of the Birthing Home. He was six weeks old yesterday." She looked up at Alice, suddenly flustered. "I'll go and see them soon. I just figured I'd see you first because…" She faltered as she dropped the nappy bag. Rattles, wipes and dummies scattered across the floor. "Well, you're closer and… and you're sick. So—just get in there, will you?" she cried at the assorted jumble as she tried to stuff it untidily back into the bag. Oscar started to wail frantically. "Twenty more weeks," she muttered furiously. "Twenty more weeks and we're done, baby."

"It was lovely of you to come. The first time out with a new baby is always hard. You're doing a great job." Alice smiled weakly, saying the words she knew Monica needed to hear.

Monica continued to rock the pram wildly. Somehow, the motion worked to calm the infant and his wailing segued into an irregular squawk.

"Mum?" Monica looked up at her mother, bit her lip and frowned, regarding Alice as though seeing her properly for the first time.

"Yes?"

"Did they get all… the cancer?"

Alice nodded, her arms aching to reach out in comfort. "Yes. They got it all."

Monica sniffed and swallowed. She rocked the pram a little more furiously, as though she could shake the remainder of the noise out of the baby.

When she made no move to leave, Alice continued. "I'll come and take you out next Sunday. I should be out of here by then."

"Okay, great. See you then."

Monica hurled the nappy bag across the pram's handles and nodded in the direction of the hospital bed without making eye contact. Alice sank back into the pillows as Monica swung the door shut behind her, banging the pram into the frame several times in her hurry to leave with her screaming bundle.

CHAPTER 2

Twenty years earlier: 2020

ALICE AND OLIVER giggled as they made their way along one of the many bush trails surrounding their Birthing Home.

"I can't go... any further..." puffed Alice as she broke away from her sweetheart and sagged down onto a fallen tree. Her protruding abdomen rested heavily on her thighs. Together they sat in the soft late evening light of summer, watching the sun sink below the treetops and listening to the galahs screech their nightly bedtime rituals. The sky was a fiery half-rainbow of pink running into orange. Safely away from prying eyes, Oliver wrapped his arms around her and spread his fingers over her rolling belly.

"He's hosting his own football match in there tonight," he breathed into her ear.

"Mmm, no, not football. He was sleeping, dreaming of his future ballet career. The birds woke him up with their god-awful racket," she teased.

"Whatever he's going to be, he'll be ours."

He squeezed her and the unborn child tightly. Alice stiffened and fought back sudden tears. Oliver released his hold and she turned to face him.

"Don't start that again, Ollie."

"Hush," Oliver said, putting his hand to her face and wiping a single tear from the corner of her eye.

She grabbed his wrist and gently pulled.

"No," said Alice firmly. "You'll only make it harder. He's—"

"Don't." He shook his head.

"But, Ollie—"

"No!" He wrenched his hand free of hers as though breaking the physical connection could stop her words.

"He's not yours. He's barely mine," she whispered, the tears rolling down her face. "We have to remember that."

It was so much harder for him, Alice reminded herself. Oliver aspired to be a Pater. He loved being around children, teaching them, watching them grow.

It was a career that had never appealed to Alice, much to her own mother's dismay. Monique Mooney had worked hard to make sure her daughter had all the opportunities she felt her own generation had been denied. When the Equality Party rose to power on a combined tide of female fury, blue-collar disenfranchisement and general voter dissatisfaction two years ago, Monique—a founding member—had been triumphant.

Sixteen-year-old Alice had been horrified.

Growing up surrounded by idealists, she'd had the entwined principles of human equality and environmental sustainability drummed into her before she could say 'gender wage gap.' It wasn't so much that she disagreed with the overall plan. Of course, Alice was thrilled to see the mega-wealthy—the much-maligned one percent—stripped of their status and power (also their yachts and sports cars) so that parents of the poorest one percent could feed themselves and afford proper medical care for their children. She loved that the Equality Party had implemented a social system that meant every woman was supported through pregnancy and childbirth, every child grew up in a safe and caring environment, and men played an integral role in nurturing them both. It was a triumph, it was a victory. She was so very proud of her mother and all she had fought for.

None of this made her any happier to be eighteen and pregnant with a baby that was hers and not Oliver's. Not that she would ever admit her reluctance to her mother.

Pregnancy hadn't come easily to Alice. Each embryo was created and tested in a laboratory because of complications with her genetic profile. She was told the risk of damaged children was too high for natural conception. Oliver told her she was lucky; he hadn't been permitted to contribute genetic material at all. His genetic profile contained 'irregular anomalies.'

"What does that even mean?" Alice had asked, trying to decipher the government-speak in the brief rejection letter Oliver had received.

"Who knows? It doesn't matter. I'll just share your babies," he'd teased.

Oliver had come to every appointment at the local fertility clinic, holding her hand as she slid her feet into the stirrups and closed her eyes.

"I'm so sorry, I seem to have forgotten the shiraz and roses," he would joke.

As her belly grew, Alice kept to herself, quietly watching the other girls in the Birthing Home with their advancing pregnancies or newborns. She spent her days reading everything she could about what would happen after the birth. The first six months would be hers alone, then the child would enter a Home to be cared for by a professional Mater and Pater until the age of eighteen. She would be able to see the child every Sunday while she went back to her studies and entered the workforce.

Oliver passed the time joking around with the three other young men assigned to their Birthing Home to look after the expectant mothers and the infants. He worked equally hard, whether he was tending the vegetable garden of the large house, mucking out the chicken run or massaging aching pregnant backs and feet. He learned how to cook nutritious meals that were free from additives, soft cheese and runny eggs, and took turns pacing the Birthing Home hallways at night with unsettled babies.

Alice tried to accept what seemed to be the generally received wisdom, that it was best not to surrender to the pregnancy hormones which promoted bonding with the foetus. She distracted herself with facts, figures and instruction manuals.

Once her baby began to roll and kick inside her, that resolve had weakened.

And now she had to deal with Ollie's ridiculous daydreams about the two of them raising this baby together. Wonderful, gorgeous Ollie. Hopelessly romantic and pragmatically challenged. All he'd ever wanted was a three-bedroom house in the suburbs, a white picket fence and a wife and children to care for.

Alice's mother loathed him.

She took a deep breath as Oliver scraped at the dry, hard ground with a stick. He drew swirls through the dust, flicking up the occasional tiny stone in his wake. She rested her head on his shoulder.

"Ollie?"

He shifted away from her along the log and turned to face her. Picking up both her hands in his, he peered at her face and frowned.

"Alice, I don't want to talk about this again. Yes, I know that the baby is not genetically mine. Yes, I know we can't keep him forever. But we have the next three months or so before he's born. We get the next six months after that to watch him day and night and get to know him. And then we get to see him every Sunday for as long as he'll have us. If that's all I get, that's enough. He's growing inside of you, I'm going to be there for him. And that's enough for me. That makes him mine, too."

Alice pulled her hands back from his and placed them on her expanding belly, testing out this new theory in her mind. A baby of her own that she could claim but couldn't keep. She tried to glance at Oliver in her peripheral vision, imagining him as adoptive father to a child that would slip through both of their grasps. She shook her head.

"Okay."

"Okay?" he whispered raggedly.

"Yes. Okay." She pulled him towards her and placed his shaking hands on her belly. Time would break his heart; it didn't need to be helped along by her.

CHAPTER 3

2040

MONICA NESTLED INTO one of three specially designed breastfeeding chairs in the living room of her Birthing Home, holding Oscar to her breast with one arm and reading from her tablet with the other. It was an awkward position to hold for long periods of time, and she inwardly cursed the rules which outlawed earpieces in Birthing Homes. Something about airwaves and developing foetuses.

She absentmindedly rocked them both by gently pushing against the charcoal fabric of the ottoman with her feet. The room was warm but not hot. A Mozart sonata leaked softly from the speakers in the corner. Oscar sucked long and deep. Suck, swallow; suck, swallow. He stared up at her as he drank, watching her face intently as she frowned at the text on the screen.

The staccato bleat of a newborn infant could be heard faintly from a room down the hallway. A heavily pregnant woman lay sprawled in an armchair opposite—Angie was nearly at the end of her second pregnancy. She was cursed with big babies and pelvic girdle pain which had rendered her virtually immobile for the past three months. Sleeping upright was her escape from the discomfort of lying down.

Breakfast aromas wafted through from the adjacent kitchen. The vapours picked up the intoxicating scent of a milky baby before entering Monica's nostrils. The combination made her feel suddenly ravenous.

Joe, a short young man with a small nose and jet-black hair, appeared in the kitchen doorway. He was a genius in the kitchen and more than a little besotted with Monica. Babies, however, were not his forté. He kept his distance while she fed.

"Breakfast is ready," he announced, too loudly.

Oscar startled and bit Monica's nipple with his strong gums.

"Ow!" she shrieked, in turn waking Angie, who opened one eye, groaned and drifted back to sleep.

"Sorry," whispered Joe, slinking back into the kitchen quietly and banging plates and cutlery on the table.

Monica sat Oscar up and rubbed at his back. He burped loudly, giving her a look of great surprise as he did so.

"Well, that's you fed. Now it's my turn," she said as she lay him down on his stomach on the quilted mat at her feet.

Oscar's tiny fingers scratched at an image of a brown teddy bear with a red ribbon around its neck, perplexed that he was unable to pick it up. Monica ran her hands through her wild red hair, raking it into a rough ponytail. She slid her feet into her slippers and padded into the kitchen.

"Where is everyone?" asked Joe, presenting her with thick buckwheat pancakes lavishly garnished with cream cheese, walnuts, and syrup.

Monica ignored him and sat down to eat. Joe sat opposite her, hands wrapped around a steaming mug of coffee, and watched.

"Sorry. Hungry," she explained, looking up after several mouthfuls.

Joe smirked. "Coffee?"

"Yes. Thanks."

Three minutes later she'd cleaned her plate and sat, blowing on her coffee.

"I'm looking forward to inner-city coffee. This stuff's terrible."

Joe raised an eyebrow and rolled his eyes. "No offence, Joe," he mimicked in a higher pitch. "Oh, don't worry, Monica, no offence taken." He paused, waiting for a reaction. He was disappointed. "Yeah, okay, it's pretty awful. I've been petitioning for two years to get a proper machine in this house, but no one will listen to me. All I get is lectures about how caffeine is bad for babies and may damage sperm and I shouldn't be drinking it anyway."

"Well it's not like you're feeding it to the babies, are you?"

"No, Mon, I'm not feeding it to the babies." He sighed. Monica had a frenetic positive energy which drew people to her, but any time he tried to get closer to her, it was like she flicked a switch, reversing the magnetic poles and pushing him away again.

Monica leaned back on her chair and glanced through the kitchen doorway. Tummy time had become too much for little Oscar, who had fallen asleep on the mat, one arm under his head and three fingers in his mouth, his pink lips slightly parted.

"So, when's your time up?" she asked, referring to the end of Joe's mandatory National Procreation Service.

"Not long to go now. Two months and I'm done with all you pregnant ladies and the little crying babies." He grinned. "I'll put my chef skills to much better use in a traineeship at some fancy city restaurant. Feeding people who can appreciate the fine flavours of my dishes instead of you lot who wolf it down like it's beans on toast."

Monica rolled her eyes and sipped her coffee, screwing up her face in distaste as she did.

"Will you come and visit me when you're done?" he asked hopefully.

Monica held her breath and put on her best sweet and innocent I'm-sure-I-don't-know-what-you-mean face.

"Oh, I will have forgotten all about you after another bloody pregnancy and horrible labour and six months of sleepless nights." And then added, a little more softly, "I will, however, miss your cooking."

Joe stood up and returned to the stove, stirring the pancake batter and pouring another portion into the hot pan.

Angie hauled her enormous body through the doorway and sat down at the table.

"I'm going to a party at a fancy restaurant in the city in a few weeks, as it happens," said Monica, to nobody in particular.

"Half your luck," said Angie. "Are you taking the baby?"

Angie called all the infants, including her own, 'the baby.' No genders, no endearments, definitely no names. Rumour had it that separation from her first child had not gone well, though she refused to talk about it.

"No. Maddy's looking after it for me—I mean, *him*. She's got enough milk for five babies."

Maddy was cursed—or blessed, depending on your view—with a massive supply of milk to feed her thriving four-month-old baby. Her breasts had expanded five cup sizes during pregnancy and showed no sign of shrinking any time soon.

"What's the party for?" Angie picked at an indented circle melted into the table top by a long-gone mug of coffee.

"My mum's turning forty." Monica's explanation elicited no response from Angie. For some reason this irritated Monica, so she elaborated. "She's just come through a cancer scare so it's a pretty big deal. Her partner's invited half of Melbourne."

Angie stopped picking and looked directly at Monica. "Wow. What's your Mum do?"

Monica smiled involuntarily, then quickly shrugged. "She's some bigwig in government. Genetics and Reproduction Department."

"Not Alice Mooney?"

"Mmm-hmm, that's her."

Angie raised an eyebrow. "Kept that quiet, didn't you? You're practically part of a royal bloodline. Huh. I guess you'll be going to Melbourne University then. My mum's a cleaner in a restaurant, below average I.Q. I'll be lucky if I get a basic certificate spot at a local college," she finished glumly.

Joe flipped a cheese, chive, and bacon omelette and looked up.

"Which restaurant does she clean at?" he asked.

"Nothing so classy that you'd be interested," scoffed Angie. She closed her eyes and sniffed the air. "Man, that smells good, Joe. Is that one for me?"

Joe grinned. At least someone around here fully appreciated his culinary skills. "It sure is. Just how you like it." He slid it onto a plate and delivered it to the table with a flourish of his tea towel.

"Mmm, heaven." Angie dug into her meal with gusto. "We should totally hook up when I'm done popping out mini humans."

A slight girl with pure white hair appeared in the kitchen doorway, shifting her weight from foot to foot and staring at the sleeping baby on the mat in the lounge room.

"Hey, Sylvia," said Joe. "You want some breakfast?"

The girl jumped, as though caught with her hand in the cookie jar. She tried to meet Joe's eyes but kept getting drawn back to baby Oscar, who was now snoring softly, cheek smooshed against the mat.

"Oh. Um, no, I'm fine," she said, her voice barely audible.

"You gotta eat something, girl," said Angie. "You'll never get a baby to stick inside that scrawny little belly. The longer it takes, the longer you're stuck here."

Sylvia crossed her arms over her stomach. "Maybe, um, some toast and a cup of tea, then," she said to Joe.

He nodded, popping two slices of multi-grain bread into the toaster.

Sylvia had arrived a week ago and seemed constantly embarrassed and surprised at talk of her becoming pregnant. Monica chewed on the last of her pancake, using it to mop up the remaining syrup. She wondered if the girl was as clueless as she seemed or if her Mater and Pater just hadn't prepared her very well for her national service.

"Come and sit down," said Monica, patting an empty seat at the table next to her. "Joe'll bring it over when it's ready."

Sylvia scuttled around the edges of the kitchen, giving Angie a wide berth, and came to rest on a wooden kitchen chair. She perched on the edge, as though she might jump up and run away at any moment.

"So, you going treatment or natural?" asked Angie.

"Um, I don't know," Sylvia said, looking confused.

"It's all treatment now since the G.D.S. came in," Monica reminded the older girl.

"Oh, yeah," said Angie, nodding. "What can I say? I've been here too long." She looked Sylvia up and down and then managed to catch her eye and keep it. "Trust me, natural conception is highly overrated. My first was natural and treatment is much better. You're lucky." Angie sat back and drummed on the table, waiting for Joe to bring her fresh coffee.

When Monica had first been assigned to the Birthing Home, Angie had spent all her time in her room with her three-month-old son, refusing to speak to anyone. Joe had told Monica the story of Angie's betrayal by her lover in hushed tones.

Angie and Nathaniel had arrived at the Birthing Home together, very much in love and looking forward to conceiving their first genetic child together. Before the G.D.S. was implemented, couples who were genetically compatible were allowed to try natural conception for three months before they had to undergo fertility treatment.

Angie and Nathaniel had conceived immediately.

Their relationship had been hot and steamy throughout the pregnancy, but things started to fall apart in the final month or two as Angie's belly grew, her pelvic girdle pain became more pronounced, and her interest in passionate pursuits died a swift death. Nathaniel started to pursue his own passionate interests elsewhere. On the day she went into labour, Angie marched into the Birthing Home a few doors down and discovered her lover engaging in an attempt at natural conception with a short, dark and slender girl named Mai.

Angie screamed abuse at both of them throughout one particularly nasty contraction before storming back to her own Birthing Home to pack Nathaniel's belongings. By the time she was five centimetres dilated and her contractions were fifteen minutes apart she had thrown a dozen bags out the front door and demanded he not be allowed back in or she would drown their baby in the bath.

The midwives were used to hearing such extreme threats issued during the heat of labour but never carried out, but deemed it in the best interests of the mental health of the mother that Nathaniel be transferred immediately.

Angie never spoke of him again. Fortunately, the baby was born looking like neither of its parents. Angie opted to have her second baby conceived in a laboratory.

Sylvia sniffed and chewed on her thumb.

"You'll be fine," Monica reassured her. She patted Sylvia's hand. "People almost never die during the procedure anymore."

Sylvia regarded her with alarm.

Joe sighed and shook his head, accustomed to Monica's failed attempts at empathy.

"Well, I think the whole thing's bullshit," Angie burst out.

"Now, Angie, don't get started. The midwives'll be here soon." Joe placed buttered toast and tea in front of Sylvia, a frothy cappuccino in front of Angie, and removed Monica's empty plate. "More?"

Monica shook her head. "No, thanks."

"Seriously, though, it's just not natural. Treating women like bloody baby factories and then taking their babies away from them. What kind of society does that?" Angie rubbed her massive belly vigorously and clenched her teeth.

"What, you'd rather go back to the way it used to be?" Joe asked as he sat down at the head of the table. "When women were expected to cook, clean, hold down a job *and* raise several children? When children were ignored, beaten or even killed in their own homes? When five-year-olds arrived at school not even knowing how to open a book?"

Monica took a deep breath and considered leaving. She'd heard their arguments before and none of them were particularly rational or well thought out. She glanced at Sylvia. The poor girl looked like a deer caught in the headlights.

"None of that warranted turning child-rearing into a freaking military operation. They could have put more resources into helping women, made men do more work around the house, made the workplace more flexible," Angie shouted, warming to her cause and waving a fork in the air.

"Seriously? Have you even read any history? Can you imagine how disruptive it would be to have a woman taken out of the workforce for a whole year, not knowing when she was coming back or how many babies she was going to have? Women at twenty-five, even thirty-five, opting out of society to have babies! Then stuffing six-week-old infants into institutional 'day-care' centres with fifteen other babies in the room because their mothers can't afford to take time off work to look after them. Is that what you want to go back to?" Joe spat the last sentence out at her, rising from his chair.

"Have you ever had a baby taken away from you? A baby you've grown inside you for nine months, that you've rocked and fed and spent every moment with for another six months? To have someone come in, tear them away from you and then implant you with a substitute, which you know you'll have to give up again? Do you? Do you know what that feels like, Joe?" screamed Angie, playing her usual trump card.

Joe shook his head. "You're just not being reasonable, Angie. It's the hormones. You'll feel better when it's all over and you're out of here and back to normal." He stalked away to the sink and started stacking dirty dishes in the dishwasher.

Angie picked up her coffee, dragged her body up out of the chair and staggered slowly out of the kitchen.

Sylvia pulled her hand out from under Monica's and stared at her.

"I have to go to the hospital today. Does that mean I'm having a treatment?"

Monica wondered, not for the first time, whether the girl was quite the full quid. She thought for a moment about how to explain the process and wondered where Sylvia was up to in the treatment cycle.

"Well, have you been to the hospital before?" she asked.

"When I was little I broke my arm."

"Okay, and since then?"

"Um, I went a few weeks ago and they gave me a needle and put me to sleep."

"And you'd been taking medicine before that?"

"Yes!" Sylvia nodded enthusiastically, as though they might be on to something in this vast mystery.

Monica tried not to roll her eyes. "Okay. That means they've taken eggs from your ovaries. They're growing a tiny baby in the laboratory, called an embryo. Today is probably so they can put the baby back into your uterus and it can grow into a bigger baby." Monica shook her head. "Didn't your Ma and Pa explain all this to you?"

Sylvia nodded, her eyes wide. "Can't they just keep growing the baby in the laboratory?"

"They could," said Monica impatiently. "But then they lose the psychological benefit of creating a shared societal experience that leverages the emotional connection between parent and child and ensures the ongoing wellbeing of the children, the future of society, and the system in general. Got it?"

Sylvia remained glued to her seat, staring up at Monica. Monica tried to picture this slip of a girl with a swollen belly, in the first pains of labour.

Her face softened and she spoke in an even tone, feeling strangely protective of this guileless newcomer. "You'll be okay, Sylvia. Really, you will be. Everyone will be here to help you through it. After a few years you can go back to your other life and forget all about it if that's what you want."

Sylvia nodded.

Monica stood and turned her back to the girl, resumed her position on the breastfeeding chair, picked up her tablet and continued to read about the intricacies of germ theory.

CHAPTER 4

ALICE SWIPED AT the tablet on her lap and silenced the screen on the living room wall. She sighed. She'd been watching re-runs of *Mad Men*, a drama of 1960s entrenched sexism and fast money. A time when people still abandoned their kids to unknown fates and proof of paternity was actually an issue. Another swipe at the tablet screen and a wall of drapes began to move silently, revealing full-length windows in the high-ceilinged apartment. She squinted in the late afternoon autumn sun and looked across at the Melbourne city skyline. In the foreground were wide, green spaces crisscrossed and enclosed by high canopy trees, a buffer to the harsh sight of the trams which headed in and out from among the tall, grey buildings. Heritage architecture huddled up to sleek glass buildings, trying to escape the slight embarrassment of the brightly coloured apartment blocks left over from a period when architects were a little too enthusiastic about their primary-colour palettes.

Gingerly, Alice touched her stomach. It was still sore, but she was bored. The apartment seemed so cavernous from her vantage point on the sofa: the double-storey ceiling with a sweeping iron staircase leading up to the mezzanine bedrooms; an open kitchen nestled under the upper storey. Oliver had kept her well-stocked with new books and magazines, a trail of which appeared to have followed her around the apartment. And yet the walls still felt pale and too close together after three weeks spent in their confines.

It was time to go out.

She checked her messages. Scrolling through, the last one was from Monica: *Baby fine. Starting study again. Much more interesting than spew and poop.*

Feel like a visitor tomorrow? she tapped out.

Sure. You can even come inside this time if you like. I finally told them about my famous mother. You allowed to come on Thursdays? came the reply.

Alice laughed. *Sunday rules don't apply in Birthing Homes. See you in the morning.*

The next day Monica sat cross-legged on the rug in the living room, her back against the sofa, when the doorbell rang. Soft music filled the front entrance and the kitchen for a few seconds to announce the arrival of a visitor. There were no jarring bells here—sudden, loud noises could wake sleeping babies. She took an earbud from her ear and paused the lecture video on her tablet. Introduction to immunological principles would have to wait. She'd been only half-listening anyway, distracted by the scent, squirms and gurgles of the infant waving his arms on the rug in front of her. She smiled as she placed her fingertip on his tiny palm. He gripped it tightly and beamed back at her. Her stomach clenched and she held her breath.

"Monica, there's somebody here to see you," called Gertrude, the Birthing Home's junior maternal and child health nurse on rotation. She regarded Alice with awe, hovering just behind her shoulder as they both entered the living room. Gertrude was young, straight out of nursing school and still that strange combination of over-confident and nervous.

Alice sat on the sofa and placed a hand on Monica's back.

"Oh, he's even more gorgeous than when I last saw him," said Alice, grinning at Oscar.

Monica picked him up and handed him to Alice.

"Here, you take him then. I get far too much time strapped to him as it is."

"Um, can I get you a tea or a coffee?" asked Gertrude, still hovering.

Monica huffed and muttered something about groupies. Alice frowned at Monica then smiled at Gertrude, shaking her head.

"I'm fine, thank you. This is a lovely Birthing Home you're keeping. I'll look after Monica while you tend to your other charges."

Gertrude wrinkled her nose and shifted her weight from one foot to the other, then back again.

Alice tried again. "She's in good hands, I promise."

"Oh, of course, yes." Gertrude nodded and backed out of the room. Her footsteps could be heard scurrying down the hallway to the front living room. Monica sent up a silent apology to Angie, who she knew was trying to nap in the front room.

"Your celebrity precedes you," noted Monica. "It's all those press conferences."

"Oh, everybody loves a life-and-death drama, especially when it's someone they feel like they know. They're probably terribly disappointed the cancer surgery didn't kill me. A funeral would have brought much fanfare and festivity." Alice tickled Oscar gently. He gave her a gummy grin. A raspberry blown on the sole of his bare foot elicited a deep baby chuckle.

Monica shuddered. "Don't say that. You're fine now. The hormone therapy and surgery have worked."

"Yes, for now. They'll have to settle for mobbing me at my birthday party instead. Don't worry, they'll lose interest soon and go back to attacking me personally for every perceived flaw with the new Genetic Diversification System."

"Not so new anymore. And it's not like the G.D.S. was even your idea."

"No, it wasn't. But they see my face on the screen every time something goes wrong with it." Alice tried to lift Oscar and winced as she flexed her abdominal muscles. "You'd better take him back. I don't want to drop him."

Monica reached up to take Oscar from her mother's lap and placed him on his belly on the floor. He held his head up as high as he could, looking mildly surprised and jerking occasionally when the effort of supporting his own head became too much. Monica leaned back against the sofa and accidentally touched Alice's leg with her arm. She instinctively moved away at first, but slowly, drawn by the warmth and a need she barely understood, she allowed her elbow to rest against Alice's calf.

"Mum, what happened to your mum?"

Alice stiffened. "She's in Sweden, you know that. She's... unwell."

"Did you miss her? After you had me, I mean. Did you want her there?" Monica tickled Oscar's bare heels and watched him kick her away.

Alice stilled and held her breath. Monique had left Australia before her granddaughter—and namesake—was born. By the time Alice gave birth to Monica she'd run through the full gamut of emotions: disbelief, anger, devastation, worry... and was left with a shopping list of questions for which the answers were out of stock, and a locked compartment in her heart for which she'd burned the passcode.

"I had plenty of support around me, from professionals who knew what I needed. They looked after us well," she said carefully. "But, yes, I missed my mother."

"What about Uncle Pete? Was he there?"

"No, he left before that. About a year before I went into the Birthing Home. He absconded before they could make him start his National Service."

"Smart guy, wish I'd thought of that."

"A few years later, I got a cryptic e-mail from him, from Sweden. He said he'd gone to see our mother. He appears to have been travelling the world ever since, if his postcards are anything to go by. I suspect his nature is better suited to wandering the globe than living a quiet life here in Australia." She smiled, then shrugged. "Besides, he's on the deserters list now. He can't come back or he'll be arrested."

Monica looked up at her and frowned. "Do you ever hear from your mother? Does she know about me? And Oscar?"

Alice swallowed, trying to weigh the memories back down before they came shooting to the surface again. Monique had tried to contact her, through Pete, several times. Each time she'd refused, preferring to keep the distant past exactly where it was. But looking at her own daughter now, with *her* grandson, the locked compartment felt leaky and insubstantial.

She'd reached out to her mother to tell her of her own second pregnancy. She'd left three messages on her mother's voice service and, after a week, had tried visiting her apartment. She'd pushed the doorbell again and again but there had been no answer. Later that day an e-mail had arrived. Monique Mooney had been sent abroad to Stockholm, Sweden, for urgent medical treatment. She had an unspecified illness which prevented her from communicating with anyone before she left. It was not known when she would return.

"No, I don't hear from her," Alice finally answered, the words coming out thickly through her dry mouth. "Pete keeps an eye on her though. It's very different in Sweden, not like here. There are no Homes to care for people who are seriously ill. They live in their own houses and... fend for themselves mostly, I suppose." She paused. "Mothers and fathers fend for themselves, too, over there. They raise their own genetic children."

Monica stared at her silently.

Alice shook her head suddenly and nodded towards the discarded tablet at Monica's side. "So, tell me, how are you finding getting back into study?"

"Hard to concentrate. My brain feels foggy."

"I told you it was too early." Hunter waltzed into the living room and casually dropped himself into an armchair. "You must be Alice." He smiled, then shook his head at Monica. "You girls never listen. The first three months is hard. It's madness to try and attempt anything beyond eating, sleeping, feeding and watching mindless home renovation shows."

"Or gardening shows, game shows or educational mother craft programs," added Monica, flipping the lid of her tablet closed and tucking the earbuds in its pouch.

"Ah, so you have been listening." Hunter crossed his long legs so that his ankle rested on his knee. He placed his hands on the arms of the chair and leaned his head back. "Rough night. Maddy's little one looks like he might be teething, poor chap. And Angie's been getting nasty Braxton-Hicks contractions. I hope she pops a couple of weeks early, for her own sake. I reckon her babies are so big they'd quite happily come out at thirty-six weeks if they could."

Both women remained silent. Monica had explained to Alice that Hunter would continue to preach his vast knowledge of midwifery as long as he had a responsive audience. The less they said, the more likely he was to leave them alone. Monica knew she should be grateful for all the advice and assistance he'd given her, but she'd be even more grateful when he left in a few months to take up his university place in a medical course. He planned to do obstetrics and Monica mused that at least this would provide a finite period during which he could talk the ears off of each patient.

"Well, I'd best leave you to it and have a shower and breakfast so I can get on with the day. But think about giving up the study for now, Mon. There'll be plenty of time for that later. You only get to live these precious months with little Oscar once." Hunter stood, clapped his hands together and, Alice thought, bowed ever so slightly before leaving the room.

Alice waited until he was out of ear shot before opening her mouth. "Maybe he should stop lecturing you if he's so hell-bent on stopping you from learning."

Monica snorted. "Nah, he's harmless. He means well and he's kind of got a point. The days are long, but the years are short, as they say. Or half a year, in our case."

"If you want to get technical, it's more like a year and three months. You've already carried him in your womb for nine months."

"Mmm," replied Monica, not really listening.

Alice smiled at her daughter's obvious distraction and marvelled at how far she'd come. She remembered being horrified by Monica's pre-schooler fits of perfectionist rage. Torn, half-coloured pictures of unicorns hurled at the floor because the pencil marks had strayed the wrong side of the right line. An entire pot of dove-white paint flung across the kitchen bench when it became irrevocably contaminated with a spot of cerulean-blue paint.

Monica's perfectionism had eventually found more constructive outlets and morphed into a calm, unshakeable task-focused mindset. Her Mater and Pater were thrilled, attributing the change to intense cognitive therapy.

Alice hadn't been so sure of the success of the sessions. She shuddered now as she remembered the last time she'd taken Monica to a playground. Monica was seven years old. Alice had been watching a game of football being played on the distant oval, had taken her eyes off her daughter for just a moment.

"Oh my god! Oh my god! Get away from her!" The hysterical shouts had come from a woman sitting on the bench next to Alice as she bolted towards the swings, where a girl lay on the ground, unmoving. Alice went cold as she realised the child standing over the girl was her daughter, Monica.

Later, after the girl had been whisked away in an ambulance, reports to the appropriate authorities had been made, Alice asked Monica why she'd done it. Why she'd picked up a discarded baseball bat and hit a young girl in the back of the head with such force that she'd fractured her skull.

"She was in my way," Monica had explained, in what the psychologist later described as a droll manner. "And then she wasn't."

Her behavioural management plan was modified after the incident, and the frequency of sessions increased.

That driven, task-focused Monica had very little in common with the woman sitting in front of her now. Alice watched as her daughter and grandson locked eyes. She glanced down at the discarded tablet and back at the baby. Her heart sank as she acknowledged the dark side of her daughter's newfound maternal bond. She'd convinced herself that handing over Oscar would be easy for ever-logical Monica. If you'd never wanted something to start with, you couldn't very well mourn its loss. But now—maybe abbreviated motherhood wasn't going to be as simple for Monica as she'd hoped.

After the midwives had left for the day and the residents had retired, Monica stepped lightly into the darkened hallway of the Birthing Home. She glanced briefly back into the room she shared with baby Oscar. The dim outline of the cot's bars was visible thanks to the moonlight shining between the cracks of the window's heavy burgundy drapes. Not quite closed. She needed to get out, to breathe some air that didn't smell of milk, vomit or dirty nappies.

Angie and Maddy assured her the nappies got worse once the babies started eating solid food around five months of age. Monica thanked the universe she would be almost rid of her first burden by then. A few more months. Then hopefully a quick fertilisation, nine months of pregnancy and another six months of this. Of being a corralled milch cow. A total of twenty months; two years at the most, she calculated.

She froze just outside the door as she heard a small cry, a soft snuffle. Then silence. She clenched her fist around her tablet, digging her nails into the black leather cover, willing the digital portal to suck her in and away from this soul-destroying monotony. She should be filling her brain with new information, making discoveries, not treading water while her mind turned to mush. Her free fingers traced the wall lightly as she floated in the dark towards the back door. Inching the lock open, holding her breath for the click, she swung the door inwards and slipped through the gap into the cool night air.

Monica's stomach flipped and a pleasant sensation rippled through her lower abdomen as she felt the breeze in her hair and lifted her eyes to the stars.

"Shit," she whispered furiously, grabbing her left breast as a stabbing pain shot from the centre of her chest outwards to the tip of her nipple. Her pyjama top was already drenched with milk as her body's let-down reflex kicked in. "Shit, shit, shit." The cool breeze whipped up again, making her damp breast even colder. She hugged her arms around her chest and sat down on the back steps, flipping her tablet open and scrolling through to her lecture videos with fierce determination.

"Bit cold for star-gazing, isn't it?" murmured a deep voice behind her.

Monica whipped her head around, dislodging the earbud she'd just fitted. She swore again.

"You'll never be able to be a Mater with that vocabulary," laughed Hunter, planting himself next to her and handing her the lost earbud.

Monica scowled at him. "Can't think of anything worse than being stuck with a house full of feral kids for the rest of my life," she said, eyes glued to the starting video as she fitted the audio attachment neatly back in her ear canal.

"Really? Imparting your wisdom, helping the next generation of scientists, doctors, and teachers form the building blocks for a successful future? Not to mention fun games and sticky cuddles." He grinned, lightly flicking her earlobe so the bud jiggled precariously.

Monica lifted her hand to shove the bud back in without taking her eyes off the talking head on her screen. She waited for Hunter to leave, but he didn't.

Hunter had been at the Birthing Home for two years now and had earned the title 'The Baby Whisperer.' The other girls at the Birthing

Home swooned for him, though it was unclear whether it was because of his piercing blue eyes and tousled blond hair or his ability to settle babies and allow their mothers a good night's rest.

Tonight, Monica didn't particularly care about either. She hazarded a sideways glance at his knees. Her eyes alighted on his hands, which he held, one on each knee, tapping each finger slowly and methodically in a silent rhythm. Her stomach bottomed out again, an involuntary tug at her groin caused her to shift uncomfortably as her right breast started to twinge. The baby had better wake up for a feed soon or she would end up the victim of her very own waterfall.

Hunter placed his hand over hers, knocking the tablet screen and pausing the video as he did so.

"I'm worried about you, Mon."

She met his eyes. "I'm fine. The baby's fed and growing, I'm managing to get some studying done, everyone's happy."

"Don't you *feel* anything?"

"Cold, Hunter. I feel cold."

She snapped her tablet shut and stood. He let his hand fall from hers.

"It'll come," he warned softly. "It always does. And when it comes, I'll be here for you. If you need to talk, I mean."

Monica glared at him before opening the door and heading back to her room.

Sitting on her bed and pulling on a fresh pyjama top, Monica peered through the crib bars at the baby's pursed lips. Oscar twitched his head suddenly and snorted, then sighed heavily and started making sucking motions, his tiny mouth working away furiously at an invisible dummy. The actual dummy had been released from his gummy jaws soon after he'd fallen asleep. Now it lay on the mattress next to his right ear, a slight imprint on his cheek where he'd lain on it.

Monica held out a hand tentatively to the nearest upright crib slat, running her fingers down the dark wood. She smelled the sweet new-baby perfume, as though the aroma of previous tiny inhabitants had embedded themselves into the framework, layering their scents over the top of each other. The baby stirred and started fussing, rubbing his face with balled-up fists and snuffling. Monica rose and leaned over the crib rails, frowning down at him.

It had been so easy to tell herself, 'No, motherhood is not for me,' when the babies belonged to someone else. Through nine months of pregnancy she'd cursed the discomfort, the inconvenience, the delays in her career. She'd watched the other girls in her Birthing Home coo over their offspring and secretly rolled her eyes.

She had dismissed them as weak and irrational and so she had not been prepared.

The smell of her own baby after he was born was different, primal. The way he somehow recognised her above all others. It was just the smell of the breast milk, she told herself. But the other mothers smelled of milk too. He didn't recognise them. Only her.

Still she steeled herself against becoming attached. Just a few months and then it would be over. She would go back to her studies and forget all about him.

Then, at four weeks old, he learned how to smile. And she was lost.

Oscar opened his eyes wide and locked onto hers now, desperately trying to focus.

"Hey, baby," Monica whispered, stretching her arm down into the cot and stroking his warm cheek with her forefinger.

Oscar looked surprised. Then his mouth opened in a gummy grin. It lit up his whole face, this smile of his. He waved his arms and kicked his legs, frowning and then smiling again. Teardrops fell onto his nose and slid down his cheek. Monica wiped her eyes with her shoulder as she reached in to pick him up.

"Don't tell Hunter, but it's too late, little one. It's already come, hasn't it?" She sat back down onto the edge of the bed and unlatched her bra, letting the cup drop open. She positioned Oscar in the crook of her elbow, aiming his mouth at the outer edge of the dark circle surrounding her nipple as she'd been taught. As he closed his mouth over her and started to drink, she let her tears fall freely onto his blue-striped sleeping wrap and cupped her free hand protectively over the top of his head.

"I don't want to feel like this," she whispered. "But I do."

CHAPTER 5

"ARE YOU SURE you're ready to go back to work?" asked Oliver, watching her with sleepy eyes from their tousled bed. Alice struggled to poke a silver bird-shaped earring through her earlobe. The hole had nearly closed over after four weeks of lying around the apartment.

"Ow!" She cried out as she missed the opening altogether and stabbed fresh skin. "Pass me a tissue, will you?"

She pointed at the box sitting askew on Oliver's bedside table. He pulled out three and handed them to her. She pressed them against her ear, but not before a drop of bright, red blood had landed on her clean, white shirt.

"Dammit!"

"Why don't you take another few days off? You're meant to take six weeks. The department won't collapse without you," Oliver pleaded half-heartedly.

Alice smiled to herself at his obvious defeat. He would know from long experience that he wouldn't be able to persuade her otherwise once her mind was made up.

"I can't sit around here any longer. I'm turning into a potato." Alice slid the last tiny satin shirt button out of its hole.

Oliver edged towards her across the bed and tugged at her collar, bringing the billowing shirt cascading down her back.

"And a lovely potato you are, too," he said, kneeling and kissing her neck. "On the plus side, if you're well enough to go to work, I guess you'll be well enough tonight to…"

Alice laughed. "No, tonight I'll probably be too exhausted to say boo to a kitten. I have, after all, just had major abdominal surgery and am returning to work early, against doctor's orders," she said sternly, turning to kiss him but wincing mid-pucker. "Mmm, note to self: no bowing, twisting, scraping or yoga permitted on the first day back."

She braced her legs to take the pressure off her still-healing abdomen and stood up, carefully keeping her back to Oliver so she didn't have to confront his worried frown.

"I'll be fine. All I do is sit at a desk and sign papers all day, anyway, right?" she teased. "Are you on overnights this week or will be you be home for dinner?"

"Just evenings this week, so home for a late dinner. Overnights next week. This week is bath-book-bedtime week," said Oliver, referring to his work as Pater to four kids ranging in age from three years to fifteen. "I've got my days all to myself this week. I had planned to spend them with you, but sadly I forgot that I'm married to a masochistic workaholic." He sighed dramatically, burrowing back down into the covers and rolling to face the window.

Alice shook her head as she pulled on a teal silk camisole and shrugged her charcoal suit jacket over it. A red, blue and green rosella flashed past their second storey apartment window and landed in the uppermost branches of an apricot tree. It pulled at one of the ripened fruits with its claw and ripped off a chunk. Breakfast.

"Don't forget to eat, yeah?" Oliver mumbled sleepily from his doona hideout.

Alice rubbed her stomach gingerly and flinched. As if the pain from the surgical wound wasn't enough, her nausea had returned during the past few days. It was worse now that she was moving around more. She would have to remember to stay seated as much as possible if she was going to last the day.

It wouldn't be hard. Today was the annual strategic review and planning day for the Department of Genetics and Reproduction. Mostly it would involve sitting around an enormous table in a stuffy room and listening to the directors drone on about the wonderful things they had done this year and fight about what should go in the annual report. A firm hand was needed to prevent the directors drifting off course and steering away from cold, reliable statistics, straight into a storm of emotional propaganda and chest bumping. What they needed for the annual report was a balance between what they wanted the general public to know and what they couldn't avoid telling them. This year there were certain strategic directions that had proven unpopular with the media and—consequently—the general public. The most problematic, by far, was the G.D.S.

Oliver's soft snoring broke into her thoughts. Alice picked up her satchel, checked her tablet was safely inside, tapped it gently to flick off the bedroom light and headed out the door.

2020

Twenty years earlier

"Is he okay?"

Alice turned to Oliver from the operating table, her hair slick with sweat and her eyes wild with fear. No sound came from the baby boy they had just cut from her belly. No one would speak to her or even look her in the eye.

"Ollie? Ollie?" Alice started to cry. Her whole upper body shook from the after effects of the drugs which had numbed her body from her chest down to her toes. "I'm cold. I'm so cold," she whimpered. "Where is my baby?"

"She's bleeding out. Get a transfusion ready," came the order from behind the screen set up across Alice's chest, blocking her lower body from view.

Oliver watched the medical team work on the tiny, silent body in the corner. He looked down at his lover as her eyes fluttered. He pressed his cheek against her forehead and let his tears fall.

"You hang in there, my love. The baby is just fine," he lied.

CHAPTER 6

2040

❝ WE SHOULD CONGRATULATE ourselves on another year well done," said Graeme Smythe, Departmental Secretary, to the eight bleary-eyed directors gathered in the board room. "The budget is back under control; birth complications are continuing to decline, and the new Genetic Diversification System is resulting in healthier babies and a stronger generation."

"Except that the public hate it," muttered Mary, Director of Communications. Her team had borne the brunt of community outrage through social media when the G.D.S. was implemented.

Graeme ignored her. "Before this year, couples entering National Procreation Service could choose to reproduce naturally, provided there were no genetic incompatibilities likely to result in a sick or disabled child. However, as we know, creating embryos in a laboratory is, by far, a preferred method as it provides greater certainty in avoiding genetic diseases."

Mary rolled her eyes and exchanged glances with Alice. Alice shook her head and frowned slightly. Now wasn't the time to fight this. Mary and Alice both knew the Australian public had not been entirely persuaded to embrace the G.D.S., despite Graeme's contrary—and delusional—narrative. The problem was that most people were fairly content to take a small health risk to preserve the traditional romance of a natural conception.

"You'll never get Graeme Smythe to empathise with people enough to understand the deeply ingrained prejudices against the Genetic Diversity System," Alice had said to Mary after her hot-headed colleague had received the news that the decision had been made to go ahead with the program despite public resistance.

"You mean he's an unfeeling dick without a romantic bone in his body," fumed Mary.

"That too," she'd conceded.

Alice picked at her fingernails while she stared at a point just above Graeme's forehead. He continued to drone on about the success—in dollar terms, not human—of his pet program.

"New technology recently developed has made the old I.V.F. look like high school biology. Successful implantation rates of our new cheaper, less invasive, method are now ninety-seven percent. Screening means that embryos can be selected to maximise their future potential for health and productivity. We want a society of healthy, gainfully employed professionals, not sickly idiots."

Mary yawned. She'd heard it all before. Seeing vast opportunities for increases in efficiency and decreases in costs, the government had quickly funded the expansion of the new technology and forced the G.D.S. on a reluctant population, requiring all conceptions to be performed in a laboratory. Natural conception became a criminal offence on the basis that the parents were endangering the future health and wellbeing of society's children. They'd tried to sell it as a positive reallocation of public funds to child welfare and education. It hadn't worked.

"Every month a woman spends in a Birthing Home, without conceiving, costs the government money. Every baby born that is sick or disabled, costs our society precious resources and causes the parents unnecessary grief," said Graeme. He glared at Mary, who had gone back to doodling spiral patterns in psychedelic colours on her tablet. Graeme sipped from a glass of water and coughed, his bulky frame shuddering from the effort. He changed the image again. The words 'G.D.S. Improving Our Future' appeared in shimmering blue.

"The Genetic Diversification System leaves nothing to chance. Genetic partners are matched based on a range of relevant factors including intelligence, health, diversity and appearance. Eggs and sperm are extracted and up to six embryos created."

The wall display flicked to a Petri dish containing five putative children. Alice's drifting mind threw up a picture of caviar. She mentally slapped herself and tried to concentrate on Graeme's long and waffling introduction.

"All embryos are screened, and the highest quality embryo of the desired sex is implanted back into the genetic mother." The display blinked again and showed a graph; the line sloped gently downward from left to right. "The immediate savings in accommodation costs— an average of one month per woman—is significant. The long-term benefits to society of a healthier, stronger and smarter population are immeasurable."

He'd clearly missed his calling, thought Alice. His empty rhetoric would have been better tolerated in the political arena, not the administration. She glanced at Mary. Mary ignored Graeme and continued to doodle, inserting cartoon birds at the centre of each spiral.

"Graeme, are we planning to report on complaints this year?" asked Mario, Director of Reporting and Statistics.

Graeme nodded.

"Even the handling of the, uh, recent incident?"

Mary put her stylus down and eyed Graeme, waiting. Everyone else in the room held their breath.

A week earlier a seventeen-year-old girl had tested positive to a routine pre-Birthing Home pregnancy test. The media had been churning out alternately outraged and salacious headlines ever since.

Initial investigations revealed the putative child had been conceived naturally with her biological father's gardener, a man considered genetically inferior and, at forty-six, well past his reproductive prime. The day after being interrogated by Compliance Officers, the girl miscarried. The girl's genetic father was loudly proclaiming the miscarriage to have been brought on by stress at the hands of the government's 'brutal' new G.D.S. policies.

It didn't help that the girl's genetic father also happened to be the political leader of the conservative party. In federal opposition for twenty years and seeing a chance to use public outrage at the G.D.S. to return to power, he was willing to use anything to erode confidence in the government. Including his own daughter.

"We will report on complaints as an aggregate, as we're required to, as we do every other year. And Mario, remember to put in a paragraph or two about our improved response times and how we brought that about." Graeme waved a hand grandly in his subordinate's direction.

Mario nodded and scribbled something on his tablet.

"What's our position on accidental conceptions, then?" Mary asked, without looking up. "We've been deflecting queries but we can't keep it up forever. We need to put out a statement, particularly in light of last week's debacle."

Graeme stopped and looked out the window, his jaw noticeably clenched and his eyes squinting. After a long and awkward silence, he turned to Mary, who met his steely glare with a blank stare of her own.

"I would hope as our Director of Communications that you don't use that sort of inflammatory language externally. I would thank you to refrain from using terms such as that internally as well. We can take this discussion offline. Today we're here to establish an overarching narrative for our annual report."

Mary raised one eyebrow. She shrugged and returned to her tablet, doodling a broad top hat and long cane for each bird to dance in their merry spirals.

"Oh, look, the croissants have finally arrived. Perhaps it's a good time to break for coffee before we get into the nuts and bolts of the day?" suggested Damien brightly. Graeme's nervous executive assistant jumped up to greet the caterer like a dear old friend, grabbing the tray laden with breakfast pastries and shoving him out the door again.

Without waiting for further encouragement, the general noise level rose as staff started to mill around the espresso machine and load up their plates.

Alice found herself smiling at Mary across two empty seats. "Did I miss much while I was away?" she asked.

"Nothing you wouldn't have already read in the online rags. The good people of Australia still hate the G.D.S. and want to go back to the reproductive status quo," answered Mary. "What can I say? They like sex and babies. Should've phased in the G.D.S. gradually—but no, his precious budget was more important. Now people are starting to rebel against the whole system thanks to Richard White and his conservative party stirring up trouble." Mary glanced in Graeme's direction and shook her head. "That man is going to inadvertently bring down Australia's entire reproduction program in the name of the G.D.S. before he's happy. The rest of it was working just fine, but he's taken it that one step too far."

"Oh, but it's saving plenty of money, Mary. And it's terribly efficient," Alice said in a gruff voice.

Mary hooted with laughter. "It's so good to have you back. How are you feeling, anyway? I thought you weren't coming in for another couple of weeks."

Alice tried to stand, winced, and changed her mind. "Well someone had to keep you all in line before Hercules over there decides to wipe out half the population in the name of the national surplus. Children are so expensive to feed and house, you know—does terrible things to your bottom line. Now, be a good girl and get us some caffeine, would you?"

Mary snorted. "Get it yourself if you're so well."

"Well, I would, Mary, but that wouldn't be very efficient, would it? Seeing as how you're going over there to get one yourself. Think of the composite energy that would be saved. Why, perhaps I'll even drink out of your cup, too, to save on recyclable materials. Remember, Ecocentricity is part of our mission!"

"You'll keep." Mary smirked. She stood and stretched before swaggering over to the coffee corner, slapping Damien on the back and somehow talking him into making two cappuccinos for her.

"Alice," said Graeme, perching on the seat next to her, a distasteful look on his face.

"Graeme," she replied, turning her body gingerly towards him.

"I didn't think we'd be having the pleasure of your company here today."

"I'm here mostly to observe. Don't want to get out of the loop entirely. I've missed so much in just four weeks, from what I hear." She smiled sweetly.

He frowned. "Yes, well, don't exert yourself too much. We wouldn't want you relapsing, would we?"

Did he look hopeful, Alice wondered, or was that just sunbeams bouncing off his shiny forehead?

"Oh, I'm fine," she replied. "I might take it easy for a week or two, but modern medical technology is doing wonders for our health these days, isn't it, Graeme?"

"You'll be needing more time off for chemotherapy, of course," he said, uncrossing his legs and leaning forward slightly.

Alice stilled, resisting the invasion of her personal space. There was something about conversations with Graeme Smythe that made her want to take a long, hot shower afterwards.

"No, actually. I managed to get into a trial of a new pre-operative hormone-based therapy program. It makes the chemotherapy unnecessary." She paused. "Isn't that wonderful?" she prompted when Graeme continued to glare at her.

"Fabulous," he said, standing abruptly and moving away.

"What's his problem?" asked Mary, returning with their steaming caffeine doses.

Alice slumped slightly in her chair and rubbed her temples. "You, of course."

"Here, have some coffee," said Mary, placing the cup straight into Alice's hands. "He still hasn't forgiven you for nearly busting him with pornography on his laptop last year. Jenny—the new graphic designer, I don't think you've met her—she says she heard from a friend that he used to go to these weird sex parties."

Alice scrunched up her face as though in pain. "Oh, Mary, gross. I really don't want to know. The thought of that man... please, I already feel nauseous. You're not making it any easier."

Mary peered into her face, taking in the dark circles and sunken eyes. "They give you any good drugs? You look like you could use some."

Alice didn't move.

"You can't leave now. He'll eat you alive," Mary said softly.

"I shouldn't have come," said Alice. "I'm just so tired. It's so frustrating. There's so much to do and I can't let *him* walk all over..."

Mary put a hand on her arm, a warning. Alice sighed.

"Yes, you should have. Now sit in the corner like a good mushroom and remind him you're still around. He's got the rest of the drones so scared of him they'd agree to round up and shoot anyone with an I.Q. under eighty if he showed them a graph to prove the economic efficiency dividends." Mary picked up Alice's handbag from underneath her seat, rummaged around for a moment and pulled out a bottle of pills. She held it out to Alice. "Take two, they'll get you through the next few hours. You can take tomorrow off if you need to, tell him you're out of the office at meetings with external stakeholders or something."

CHAPTER 7

SAFELY BACK IN her apartment, Alice collapsed onto the corner couch and slept deeply. Mary had been right, whatever was in those tablets had given her the extra boost she'd needed. Once they'd worn off though, she'd paid the price of her earlier exertion.

She woke to the sound of morning chat show conversation and the sight of Oliver sitting on the couch at her feet, sipping green tea with jasmine.

"Morning, sleeping beauty. Rough first day?"

"Yeah, you could say that," she lisped, her mouth dry from sleep and thirst. She considered moving, but decided against it.

"Coffee?" asked Oliver, placing a warm hand on her knee.

Alice's stomach turned at the thought. "No. That tea smells good, though."

"Green tea it is, then," he said, holding out his steaming mug.

"Thanks for the blanket." She sat up and adjusted the soft, mint green throw rug around her waist.

"Ellie said 'Pater' for the first time last night," said Oliver, grinning as though he was personally responsible for her newfound eloquence.

Ellie was a three-year-old girl in Oliver's charge who had been slow to talk. Nobody was particularly worried about her progress for she came from a long genetic line of late talkers, but it was still a relief that it was more a case of later rather than never.

Alice sipped her tea and gazed blankly at the television until she caught a flash of Mary's familiar, sharp face. She grabbed the remote and turned up the volume just as the footage switched back to the news studio.

"The Department of Genetics and Reproduction has confirmed that no enforcement action will be taken against Charlotte White, daughter of Richard White, leader of the Conservative Party, for her unauthorised conception. Ms. White has agreed to refrain from relations with any man for a period of six months while her body recovers from the miscarriage," said the news anchor with a flick of her dark hair.

The picture moved to Mary standing next to a contrite and pale Charlotte White at the entrance of the Department of Genetics and Reproduction's head office.

Mary spoke clearly and without emotion. "After a period of six months, Ms. White will commence her National Procreation Service in a Birthing Home of her choice. No further action will be taken by the D.G.R. at this time."

The camera followed the grim pair as Mary guided Charlotte White through the media throng to a waiting dark sedan.

"Why are they black? Why do people always get into black cars after press conferences?" Oliver wanted to know.

"Huh?" Alice asked, staring at him blankly. "Oh." She looked back at the screen, just in time to see the ubiquitous black car drive away, narrowly missing an outstretched microphone. "Yes, they are always black, aren't they? I don't know."

"Forty-six-year-old gardener, hey? Lucky bugger," Oliver said, stretching and getting up. "I'll go and make another tea. You want something to eat? I feel like bacon."

"Just some Vegemite toast would be great, thanks."

"Okay." He hauled himself off the couch and started assembling the meagre meal in the kitchen.

Alice sipped her gifted tea and watched a panel discussion about the pros and cons of the Genetic Diversification System. A large, feisty woman from the Coalition for Free Love argued that it was barbaric. People should be allowed to conceive their children in a loving and natural environment if the genetic combination posed no threat to the health of the child. She pitted her fierce arguments against a slight, pretty scientist from Greyson Laboratories.

"Oh, for goodness' sake. Nobody's denying people the right to have romantic sex, just not for a couple of months while impregnation takes place," said the scientist, pursing her bright red lips. "The procedure is simply giving nature a helping hand to get it right."

Alice flicked the screen off. Into the silence wafted the sound and smell of sizzling bacon from the open kitchen.

"Oh, hey, I meant to say, you've got a couple of messages. Your earpiece was buzzing when I got home last night but I didn't want to wake you." Oliver pushed down on the bacon strips with a spatula. One popped loudly and he jumped backwards and yelped.

Alice nodded, fighting waves of nausea to reach down and pick up her earpiece from the low coffee table. The first message was from Mary, warning her about the media statement the next morning. Alice deleted it. The second was Monica, left at 3.00am.

"Mum?" Monica's voice broke and she sniffed. "How did you do it?" she whispered, audibly gulping back her tears. "How did you give me up?" She paused. "Mum? I don't think I can do it. I can't leave Oscar. I can't."

A baby gurgled in the background and the message ended. It appeared that the maternal love bug had finally bitten her stubbornly rational daughter. Hard.

Alice stared at the blank screen as Oliver slid a plate of toast onto the coffee table, loudly scraping the glass surface.

"Everything okay?" he asked.

Alice frowned. "Um, yeah. Just Mary, letting me know about her media stint this morning."

Oliver nodded and returned to the kitchen.

Alice thought for a moment. "Hey, Ollie."

He popped his head up above the countertop, his face disembodied. He poked his tongue out, crossed his eyes and bounced his head slowly up and down.

Alice smiled. "You're crazy."

"Yes, my love. You knew that when you married me, all part of the package deal."

He pulled his head in again and appeared moments later carrying a plate of toast, bacon and eggs with thick brown sauce layered on top.

"Mmm," he said, waving his nose back and forth through the fragrant steam and flopping himself down next to Alice on the sofa.

Alice made gagging noises. "I never can get used to the smell of bacon. It's revolting. How can you stand it?"

"How can you live without it?" Oliver picked up his tablet and started flicking through channels on the wall screen, coming to rest on Play School. "I've got a surprise for you," he said.

"You've decided to give up Paterdom and dance and sing with Big Ted on Play School?" she guessed.

"Ha! I wish. Those guys are awesome. Nah, I'm far too tone-deaf." He let out an operatic screech, accompanied by sweeping hand gestures, to demonstrate his defect.

Alice cringed and stuck her fingers in her ears, laughing. Oliver checked his watch, an antique curiosity he insisted on wearing so he didn't have to carry a tablet or wear an earpiece to tell the time when he was at work.

"The sky is falling in five minutes?" Alice tried guessing again, becoming impatient.

"Pfft. Still a few minutes to go," he said, watching the presenter paste red cardboard onto an egg carton. He put down the remote and picked up his fork, lifting great mouthfuls of bacon and sauce into his mouth, eyes glued to the wall screen.

"Anyway, Ollie, I was wondering if I could come and visit you at work this afternoon?"

Oliver stopped chewing and looked at her.

"Really?"

Alice squirmed a little. As passionate as Oliver was about his work and as often as he encouraged Alice to come and get to know the kids in his care, she usually found a reason not to come. Important meetings, media checks, a head cold, yoga class, dinner with friends... She certainly had never asked outright before.

"I thought maybe I could invite Monica to come as well. You know, to get an idea of where Oscar will be going soon. She, um, sounded a bit down when I last spoke to her."

Oliver's face fell, as Alice knew it would; as it did every time she mentioned her daughter.

"Oh. Yeah, sure. The Home is only a few blocks away from her Birthing Home," he mumbled through a mouthful of bacon, turning back to the screen to watch the presenter cut out a green paper beak for his egg carton toucan.

Oliver had never warmed to Monica. Alice never questioned him, knowing how badly it hurt him to be unable to have a child of his own.

After the stillbirth of her son, Alice fell apart. She was allotted six months by the specialists to recover from the ordeal, both physically and emotionally. She spent most of it either shut in her room or wandering among the bushlands close to the Birthing Home, trying to avoid the psychologist who visited intermittently.

Oliver dealt with his grief by moving on. He re-applied to contribute genetically to his own child. Again, he was refused. He avoided Alice during her second pregnancy, instead helping to bathe and settle the other babies in their Birthing Home. He volunteered for emergency relief at other Birthing Homes whenever possible but stopped short of actually requesting a transfer.

Once Monica was weaned and their National Procreation Service ended, Oliver and Alice moved into an apartment together in the city. Alice had braced herself for the inevitable relationship breakdown, but it never came, and after a while she stopped expecting it. On the surface, they were a happy couple—and just like any other young couple they went through all the usual motions of being in love.

Except on Sundays.

Each Sunday morning Alice would slip out of the apartment before Oliver woke. She would spend as much of the day as possible with Monica while Oliver spent the day visiting children abandoned by their own genetic parents. Each Sunday evening they would sit together on the corner couch and sip a glass of Riesling (in the summer) or Merlot (in the winter). They never spoke a word about their day.

Six months after baby Monica had settled in with her new parents, Oliver proposed to Alice. Alice accepted, thus sealing her decision to compartmentalise her life into separate loves: her lover and her daughter. Their Maters, Paters and Oliver's genetic parents attended a small ceremony where they pledged their everlasting love to each other. Over time the fragmentation of her heart became normal; it became—almost—easy.

But now Alice needed Oliver's help to show Monica that everything would work out fine—that Oscar would be well cared for in a home like Oliver's.

"Ha! Look!" Oliver sat up straight and bounced on the couch in excitement. "There it is!"

On the screen the Play School presenter sat down on a comfy armchair with a tablet. She smiled at the camera.

"Today we're reading a new story called 'Bears Don't Like Toilets'. It's by Oliver Mooney," she said, swiping to the first screen and beginning to read. Oliver turned to Alice and pointed at the screen.

"See? See? It's my story! On Play School!' Alice pushed aside unhappy memories and smiled.

"That's so exciting." Her flat tone failed to match her bright expression. She took a breath and tried again. "You're an international success story. Move aside Roald Dahl, here comes Oliver Mooney!"

Oliver waved her away and turned back to the screen.

Alice picked up her tablet and tapped out: *Meet me at 93 Cochrane Street, Mitcham at 3.00pm today if you can get away. I want to show you something.* She scrolled through her contacts, selected Monica's name and hit *Send*.

She sat back and watched the familiar pages of Oliver's debut children's book roll by. It was illustrated by his Mater partner, Margery. Apart from being a wonderfully warm and generous human being, Margery was also a talented painter. Alice smiled as the presenter held up the final screen for a camera close up. It depicted, in beautifully detailed watercolours, a toddler bear, finally sitting on the toilet and happily straining away.

Her earpiece buzzed softly. She tapped it to bring up the message suspended in front of her eyes.

Ok. Will b there. Here's pic of Oscar being happy today. Hope it lasts. Last night not so good.

Alice resisted the urge to show Oliver the image of a smiling baby Oscar. She began to hope that Monica's hysterical message was a once-off, brought on by weeks of sleep deprivation and easily cured by a few words of encouragement and a dose of common sense.

Oliver flicked off the screen, put down his empty plate and turned to Alice.

"So. Now that you've given up this ridiculous charade of good health, shall I take you out for a mountain drive, fine wine and a gourmet lunch?" he asked.

"Sure. Why not. Olinda?" she suggested, naming a picturesque hillside town known for its log fires and gourmet food.

"Where else?" he said, standing and holding out both hands to her.

CHAPTER 8

OLIVER AND ALICE'S idle chatter turned to silence as their silver sedan turned off the main road and down Cochrane Street. The tick, tick, tick of the indicator pounded at the same speed as Alice's racing heart.

The brunch had been glorious. The creak of old, well-polished floorboards, the gentle lilt of international tourists discussing the day's itinerary, the intoxicating wood smoke smell of the first log fires of late autumn in the chilly hills.

But as they descended along the winding mountain road the temperature in the car seemed to drop. Alice wasn't sure if it was the prospect of her coming to Oliver's workplace or Monica seeing Oliver for the first time in four years. Monica's opinionated entrance into teenagedom hadn't done anything positive for Oliver's perception of her.

"You have reached your destination," the car politely informed them as it pulled over to the curb and slowed in front of number ninety-three. Oliver watched the buxom, red-headed young woman standing against the trunk of a massive ghost gum. Alice half expected him to turn around and leave again. Instead, he waited for the seatbelt to retract into its compartment, then opened the car door and unfolded himself.

"Hey," he called out over the roof of the car.

Alice waited and watched Monica through the car window. Monica looked up, cradling her baby's head as he slept in a burgundy pouch attached to her chest. Alice thought she looked pale, thinner and with grey shadows under her eyes. Her skin had broken out in patches around her cheeks and her hair needed a wash. The broken sleep of new motherhood was starting to take its toll. Yet, somehow, she glowed as she rubbed baby Oscar's back and pressed her cheek against the top of his head.

"Hey," Monica called back, nodding in Oliver's direction. Her gaze drifted back to the park across the road, where pre-schoolers swarmed like excitable ants over the play equipment. Maters, Paters, Aunties and Uncles chatted to them and each other, smiling, waving and wiping tiny tears when grand expectations didn't quite bridge the gap between the third and fourth rungs of the ladder to the big, spiral slide.

Alice opened the car door and swung her legs out.

"Hey," she said.

"Pater, Pater, Pater!" came a duet of childish voices from behind the screen front door of Oliver's Home.

Oliver grinned. "Come and meet Ellie and Tom," he said to Monica, raising his hand next to her arm to guide her, falling short of actually touching her.

"Stop banging on the door, you two, you're going to break it," chided a warm voice from behind the screen.

"Pater's here! Pater's here!"

"Yes, I can see that. Are you going to move out of the way so I can actually let him in?"

A lock clicked and the door swung open. A tiny scrap of a girl with impossibly tight, golden curls launched herself at Oliver and clung to his leg. A taller, dark-haired boy hurtled after her and tried to push her out of the way, wrapping his arms around Oliver's waist. The girl screamed indignantly and slapped him on the arm. Alice peered behind them but couldn't see any sign of Margery, who seemed to have disappeared.

"Ooof!" exclaimed Oliver dramatically, hoisting the boy sideways onto one foot and giving the little girl space to reposition herself at his other. "Goodness me, I'm quite sure you've both grown since yesterday. And... what, wait... how can this be? My legs have suddenly become... ooof!... very, very heavy."

Oliver slowly marched through the doorway, holding on tightly to the two giggling kids attached to his legs. Their joy was infectious. Alice smiled at Monica, shrugged, and followed them into the house.

"Hi, Marge!" Oliver called out.

"Hey, Ollie!" came the voice from the kitchen. "I see you brought reinforcements. We'll need them today, these two have not stopped since they woke up this morning!"

A short, round, grinning figure appeared bearing a plate of fresh, round buttermilk scones with raspberry jam in one hand and scraping long, wispy grey hair back behind her ear with the other.

"Alice, sweetheart, it's so good to see you. Sit down, sit down, you must be tired. Ollie told me you tried to go back to work yesterday, you silly thing, what were you thinking? Here, sit over here on the sofa and I'll get you a cuppa." Margery herded Alice over to a recliner seat and gently pushed her into it. "It's white with none, yes? And have a plain scone, they're fresh out of the oven, butter arrived just this morning and homemade raspberry jam from our very own backyard. The older ones helped me boil the fruit for the jam. The younger ones tried but, well, you know."

Alice sat as she was directed and let Margery's kind words envelope her with their warmth. Monica remained standing, swaying slowly from side to side and patting the pouch where the baby's bottom would be. The please-stay-asleep-baby waltz.

"I have one too!" yelled the little girl, jumping up and down at Margery's feet, threatening to upend the entire plate, her curls waving frantically.

"Ellie! You have to sit at the table and be patient or you won't get any scones at all," said the older boy, crossing his arms and shaking his finger at her from the moral high ground of his dining room chair.

"I have one too! I hungry!" Suddenly Ellie flopped herself down on the carpet and burst into tears.

Margery chuckled and bent down to scoop her up in her free arm.

"Come here. There's plenty of scones for everybody here and it'll only take a minute to rub some flour and butter together to make more if we need them." She deposited Ellie onto a free chair at the table and placed the scones down, just out of reach of both children. "I'll get these hungry hippos sorted first, shall I? Anyone would think they didn't eat every other minute of the day! Ollie, put the kettle on, will you, love? And you must be Monica, my dear, and what a gorgeous little baby you have attached to you there. How old is he?"

Margery somehow managed to spread thick layers of jam on the scones, keep eager little hands at bay, issue gentle orders and welcome strangers all while keeping a grin on her creased and wrinkled face.

Monica opened her mouth to reply.

"Not that one!" shrieked the little girl. "Don't want that one! That one Tom's!"

Margery placed a calming hand on Ellie's back. "It's okay, I wasn't going to give you that one. That's already on Tom's plate. This one is for our visitor. This one over here is for you, there you go. And maybe this one could be for the baby, what do you think?" Margery whispered this last sentence conspiratorially while sneaking a peek at Monica over her shoulder.

Ellie looked around with wide blue eyes, scone possession issues momentarily forgotten.

"There baby?" she asked, looking from Monica back to Margery.

"Yes," whispered Margery. "See in that little pouch that lady's carrying, there's a teeny tiny head poking up over the top?"

Ellie nodded, her curls bouncing up and down.

"That's a baby," whispered Margery.

"Baby need scone?" she held out her own plate to Monica, tilting it as she swung around and spilling the scone on the floor, homemade-jam side down.

"Whoops!" said Margery, picking up the scone and plate, and turning Ellie back to the table. "Ollie, dishcloth, please!"

"Coming!" called Ollie, appearing a moment later carrying two cups of tea in his hands and a damp blue cloth in his teeth.

Margery plucked the dishcloth out of his mouth and he placed the steaming cups on the low table in front of Alice. With the kids settled into their afternoon snack, Ollie perched on a chair next to Ellie, and Margery sank down on the sofa patting Alice's knee.

"So, this must be your lovely daughter and grandson," beamed Margery, nodding at Monica.

"Margery, this is Monica and baby Oscar," said Oliver. "Monica, this is Margery, Mater-extraordinaire and expert on removing stains from any surface in the house."

Margery hooted. "Yes, that's me! Twenty years on the job and another twenty before that as an early childhood educator. Though I'm getting a bit old for the little ones I think. These two little rascals will be my last before I head off into retirement. Oh, how rude of me.

Monica, the little rascals are Ellie, three years old, and Tom, not long turned four."

Monica nodded and smiled slightly, still swaying but edging closer to the table and the heady scent of freshly baked scones. Ellie tried to stand on her chair to peer at Oscar. Monica wrapped both arms around her baby and stared down the toddler. Ellie backed away and sat down.

"So, the hormones are wearing off and it's all starting to become a little too real, is it, love?" Margery patted the empty cushion next to her. "Sit down, your back must be killing you. He looks like he's a good size, there."

Monica eyed the scones longingly before coming to sit on the sofa, carefully spreading her knees to make room for Oscar and his pouch.

"Pater, may I please have another scone?" asked Tom politely.

"I have more scone too!" shouted Ellie, brushing her half-finished snack aside with a sticky hand.

"But you haven't finished your first scone! And you didn't say please! You have to say pleeeease!" whined Tom, bouncing on his chair indignantly.

"All right, all right, calm down," said Oliver with mock exasperation. "Tom, you may have another scone, and well done on your lovely manners. Ellie, you can have another scone when you've finished eating your first one. And remember to say 'please.'"

"Ta," mumbled Ellie, taking another bite of her reclaimed scone.

Oliver moved to the table to sit with the children, hoping to preempt further disputes.

"Don't mind them, love." Margery addressed Monica quietly. "You tell me, what's on your mind?"

Monica stared out the window at the extensive, lawned backyard. A set of swings and a slide stood next to a large, wooden sandpit.

"I only have a few months left with him, then he's gone," she whispered.

Margery put an arm around her. "Oh, love, he won't be gone. He'll be a hop, skip and a jump away. He'll be in good hands with a Mater, Pater, Aunties and Uncles who've been specially trained to know what's best for him from toddlerhood to teenagedom. That's not a small commitment, you know."

Monica remained silent, stroking Oscar's soft downy hair.

Margery gave a barely perceptible frown and continued. "Besides, you'll always have your Sundays with Oscar. Believe me, us Maters and Paters look forward to our free Sundays!"

"But I'll miss him so much. I just wish... I wish I could keep him with me every day."

"Be careful what you wish for, my dear," said Margery, quietly enough that Oliver and the children could not hear her words. "My generation wished for things, too. They wished for equality for all and a safe, caring and stable home for every child." Margery sat back and nodded towards the table, where Oliver was dishing out another scone to Ellie. "We got what we wished for. I'm not so sure it's worked out quite the way most of us expected, though."

Monica appealed silently to Alice. Alice shook her head and looked away.

Margery patted Monica's knee again and continued in her usual, jovial manner. "Before you decide what it is you really want, make sure you think it through to its natural conclusion first. That's all I'll say on the matter. Now, you look thirsty."

Alice's earpiece vibrated and she swore softly, berating herself for not turning it off before coming inside. She made a small movement with her hand to activate the display: Mary.

"Sorry, I have to take a call." Alice slowly pushed herself up off the sofa with one hand and swiped at her ear with the other. "Hey, Mary," she said. "Just a minute."

Margery pointed to the playroom through a pair of folding doors. "You head in there, love. I'll keep Monica company."

Alice stepped through and pulled the doors closed. "I'm here," she said.

"Charlotte White's killed herself," said Mary flatly.

"What? When?"

"Not sure. Body found in her room by the Mater, overdose. Two hours ago."

"Note?"

"Yep. It says..." Alice heard the tap of a stylus on a tablet. "Here it is. 'I can't live in this world anymore without my lover's baby. I refuse to bear the fruit of any other man. Goodbye, my lover.'"

"That's it?" said Alice. "She ended her life over the matter of a few genetic markers? That's ridiculous."

Alice glanced at Monica through the frosted glass of the folding doors. Monica was still Alice's own genetic material, regardless of whether she'd inherited anything from Oliver. That didn't make her less loved.

"That was enough, apparently. I need your permission to broker a gag order. The Conservative Party doesn't want this to get out any more than we do. Richard White is smart enough to know he won't get any public sympathy for a selfish kid destroying a life that society invested heavily in—even if it was her own life."

"Sure. What are they offering?"

"They'll put out a statement that Charlotte White died of 'complications relating to her former pregnancy' but stop blaming the miscarriage on us. In return, we'll drop the whole matter and seal the autopsy results."

Alice peered through the glass doors to where Ellie was standing on tiptoe next to Monica, trying to poke a sticky finger into baby Oscar's cheek.

"Okay. Do it. Does Graeme know?"

"No. I wanted to clear it with you first."

"He won't argue. Make the deal and inform his office. Don't leave a written or video trail. Voice calls only, secure lines."

"Got it. You coming in today?"

"No. I'll be there first thing in the morning. Call me tonight if there are any developments."

"Okay. See you tomorrow." Mary ended the call.

Alice paused and ran her hand across her stomach, her nausea returning. Young love. Teenagers. They just weren't rational. She was grateful Monica hadn't formed any romantic attachments yet. It was so much simpler this way. She watched as the young mother tried to fend off a determined toddler from her sleeping baby. No lover, perhaps, but a mother's love for her baby complicated everything.

On the footpath outside Oliver and Margery's Home, Alice awkwardly embraced Monica, unsure whether to hug her straight-on against the baby pouch or sideways. She settled for a sort of neck-hug, reaching over the top of the infant's head to press her cheek briefly against her daughter's. Monica seemed a little less tense than when they had first arrived.

"Better?" asked Alice.

"A little."

"Good."

They stood together in companionable silence for a moment, staring at baby Oscar. Before long he started to fret.

"I should go now or they'll wonder where I've gone on my mega-long fake walk," said Monica. "And before His Majesty here decides it's snack time again."

"You'll be okay," Alice said quietly. "You won't lose him. Not completely."

"I know."

"It's for the best."

"Yes." Monica started to walk away. She turned back. "Mum? See you Sunday?"

Alice smiled. "Of course. I'll be there."

She stood on the grassy verge, watching a disorderly line of uniformed children approach from the distance, their school day over. As the yellow-shirted, green-legged boisterous pack came closer, Monica and her baby melted into the crowd.

CHAPTER 9

❝ IT TURNS OUT she used the window between having her contraceptive implant removed and going into the Birthing Home to deliberately get herself knocked up," said Mary, sifting through a folder of print outs on the Charlotte White case.

Alice held out her hand for a document and started reading.

"She published a blog? How have we kept that quiet?"

"Pseudonym," said Mary.

"Still. Looks like lots of European followers? How did she get past the international firewall?"

"She was the genetic daughter of the leader of the opposition. She had privileges."

"Equality, ecocentricity, and equanimity, hey?" Alice raised her eyebrows at Mary.

Mary shrugged. "Old habits die hard."

A tall, dark man with glasses and a walking stick hobbled through the door and sat heavily on an empty chair next to Mary. Alice looked up from behind her desk.

"Is this whole department falling apart? What happened to you, Chu?"

"Skiing accident?" Chu Long, Director of Intelligence, looked suitably embarrassed.

"In autumn?" Mary snorted.

"Sure. Why not?"

Alice looked him up and down, raised an eyebrow and smirked. "We should be so lucky to get another ski season in Australia in our lifetime. The snow's melted before it hit the slopes for the past three years." She slapped the folder shut and held it out to Chu. "What do you make of this one? The lover's coming in to talk to us. Says he's got some information."

"Paper?" Chu picked up a single sheet and held it up to the light as though expecting to discover it was embedded with something more interesting.

"No electronic trail. Paper doesn't leave this office." Mary snatched the single sheet from him, united it with the others in the folder and held the package out to him again.

Chu shrugged and started reading. "Young girl, falls in love with Dad's gardener, romantic notions of old-fashioned parenting. Deliberately gets pregnant, gets found out, miscarries. Kills herself." He grimaced and turned the page. "History of depression and dissociative episodes... Dad makes a deal to suppress the evidence in return for shutting up about everything and getting on with his life." He looked up. "What did I miss? Why does lover-boy want to talk to us? Daddy didn't lean on him hard enough?"

"That's what we're trying to figure out. We thought you might have some ideas." Alice glanced at the screen on her desk, which had begun to flash. She pushed a button on the keyboard and a female voice spoke.

"Alice, Mr. Johnston is here for his appointment. Do you want me to show him in?"

"Yes, Olivia, please do." Alice tapped the screen to terminate the connection and turned to Chu. "I guess we're about to find out."

A messy crop of dirty blond curls appeared in the doorway of Alice's office, atop thick, stocky shoulders that looked as though they could fell a tree in one almighty charge.

"Mr. Dean Johnston?" Alice assessed him from behind her calm, professional demeanour. What had Charlotte White offered him that could persuade him to risk his entire future on a brief affair with a pretty girl? She figured he must be either a pushover - able to be bullied into submission by a young woman made powerful by her father's position – or a brave man who resolved to stand by his lover regardless of the consequences. Knowing what she did of Charlotte White, Alice didn't for a moment believe the version of events suggested by some media outlets, which portrayed Dean Johnston as a cradle-snatching predator.

The man in question raised his head and glanced briefly at her with wary eyes before nodding and lowering his chin.

"Sit down, please." She indicated an empty chair near the door.

There was an awkward silence as the gardener sat carefully and pressed his large, rough hands together in his lap again and again. His gaze darted from person to person like a new puppy, unsure if it was about to be befriended or beaten.

"You don't look forty-six," said Mary in her usual abrupt fashion.

The gardener frowned, the action barely making a line in his forehead and not reaching the edges of his eyes at all. Alice frowned slightly too. This young man seemed to better fit the pushover theory, much to her disappointment. In those brief minutes she'd become quite attached to the idea of two young lovers standing against the world. How old-fashioned of me, she thought.

"I'm not forty-six." Dean Johnston spoke quietly but without hesitation. "I'm twenty-six."

"That's not what the report says." Mary took the folder from Chu and flicked through the pages, frowning.

The gardener shrugged. "Can't help that."

The identity of the genetic father in the Charlotte White case had generated little interest next to the high-profile political infighting and the dramatic figure of a beautiful young woman, grieving for her lost child. It didn't surprise Alice to learn that the news websites had profiled him so poorly. Her own department hadn't even spoken to him.

"I'm sorry for your loss, Mr. Johnston." Alice tipped her head slightly and considered him, intrigued. Perhaps this situation had little to do with love or power. He fit the profile of neither downtrodden fling nor devastated lover. "No action will be taken against you for the unauthorised pregnancy as long as you agree to silence. Has that been made clear to you?"

The gardener nodded.

"What is it you came here to tell us?" Why are you here? This was what she really wanted to ask him.

He leaned forward and rested his elbows on his knees. Alice noticed Chu lean in slightly to mirror him.

"Charlotte and I were friends. But we weren't lovers," said Dean Johnston.

A silence descended on the room as the listeners processed this news.

Chu was the first to speak. "But the foetus she miscarried contained your genetic material. How do you explain that?" He tapped his fingers and raised an eyebrow at Mary.

The gardener glanced at the bookcase over Alice's head and back down at his rough, dirt-stained hands.

"I agreed to lie with her. To conceive. But only to conceive."

"Why?" asked Mary, looking up from the notes she had started to write.

"She found some... information. One Sunday at her genetic father's house." Dean Johnston leaned back in his seat and spoke in the manner of a person about to recount a long story. "They were papers which described a bunch of genetic experiments, modifications being made to embryos as part of the Genetic Diversification System. She didn't want it to happen to her baby."

"Modifications?" asked Chu, leaning even further forward as though he might reach out and grab the rest of the story directly from the mouth of its teller.

The gardener looked directly at Chu for the first time. "To make the embryo... better. I'm not sure, I didn't understand it all." He shook his head and looked at his hands. "But Charlotte seemed to understand. And she didn't believe it was right."

"What, like Franken-babies?"

"I don't know. She wouldn't say. She hoped conceiving naturally would help her bypass the G.D.S. Charlotte couldn't go to her father for help. She told me he supported the G.D.S. But when her plan didn't work..." he trailed off and turned his head.

Alice was finding his stilted way of speaking difficult to follow. What he said seemed implausible but felt somehow familiar. What confused her most was the way he delivered his message – he seemed even-tempered and direct, not over-eager and slightly crazed like your usual conspiracy theorist.

"Okay." Chu drew in a breath and stretched his shoulders back. "So, what you're telling us is you think there's a bipartisan government conspiracy to alter the genes of future generations of Australian babies. Where's your proof?"

"No proof," he said, shaking his head and staring at his feet. "She just wanted me to come to you, Ms. Mooney. She said Ms. Mooney could help. That you would... know."

Chu and Mary looked at Alice expectantly. Alice fixed her gaze on the top of the gardener's head and rested her palms in her lap, gripping them to stop them shaking.

"Thank you, Mr. Johnston. Is there anything else?" Alice asked quietly.

He looked up then, into her eyes. "No. I know it's in good hands now. She didn't die for nothing." He said it with a firm nod. "Thanks for your time." Without invitation, he stood, half-bowed, opened the door and slipped out of the room, closing the door after him.

"Well, that's ten minutes of my life I'll never get back," said Mary, tossing the file onto Alice's desk.

"Sounds like no real loss to the gene pool there," agreed Chu. "So, can we get back to some real work now that you're back on board, *Ms. Mooney?*"

"Sure," said Alice, clearing her throat and pressing her hands against the desk to stop them trembling. She fought down her desire to follow Dean Johnston out of the room and interrogate him further. Why her? What did he mean – *what* was in good hands now? But running after him right then would have made her look as mad as her colleagues believed Dean Johnston to be. Instead, she turned to Chu and nodded.

"What have you got for me?"

Chu handed her a thick manila file with a single piece of paper clipped to the front.

"I need you to sign off on our sentencing recommendation for the Garth Campbell case."

He pointed to a line at the bottom labelled 'Authority to recommend' and handed her a pen.

Alice gripped the pen while the words swam in front of her. "Is this the Pater and the teenage girl?"

"Yep. Seventeen-year-old girl says she fell in love with the new twenty-five-year-old Pater at her Home. She'd been meeting him in an empty bush block behind the Home—no cameras—when he was off duty. The Pater's defence lawyer is claiming we hold some liability for placing a parental-figure in the Home with less than a ten-year age gap between him and his eldest charge."

Alice pretended to read the words, wondering if Dean Johnston had left the building yet. She pictured him handing his security pass back at the desk downstairs and walking out the revolving door. She blinked a few times and reprimanded herself. This was unprofessional, she was letting ghosts from her past get the better of her and cloud her judgement. Chu and Mary were right to be sceptical. Charlotte White and Dean Johnston were simply a couple of young adults with overactive imaginations and too many hormones raging around their systems. She resolved to put it out of her mind and focus on the real work she needed to see through.

"What are we recommending to the Court?"

"He pleaded guilty, but we're considering mitigating circumstances and reducing the penalty to ten years in prison and a lifetime ban from contact with all minors."

Alice frowned, her full attention on the case now. "That seems a little light, don't you think? It's still interference with a minor in his charge. Do we have a psychologist's report about anticipated long-term effects on the minor in this particular situation?"

Chu leaned over and flipped open the manila folder in front of Alice. He turned it around and rifled through a few pages before finding the one he wanted.

"Psych reckons long-term negative impact is close to nil. Minor was only a few weeks away from her eighteenth birthday. She didn't identify with Campbell as a paternal figure in any way. Was already sexually active and she claims she initiated the relationship," he said, scanning the twelve-page impact report.

"Okay, just make sure the non-parole period is no less than eight years. We can't have young Paters preying on teens in their care," said Alice as she signed. "Anything else?"

"Just a status report on the offshore detention facility. The latest inmate has perished."

"Cause of death?"

"Taken out by an Irukandji box jellyfish sting."

"Ooh, nasty," said Mary, shuddering.

"Better than being torn to shreds by dingoes like the last guy," said Chu.

"Yeah, but he died pretty quickly from his wounds. That dingo went straight for the throat, didn't you see it?" Mary's eyes shined as she rubbed her own neck. "Irukandji syndrome leaves you in agonizing pain for days before it kills you. I watched the live footage of Byrne last night and it was hideous. He was screaming in pain, sweating like a pig and dry retching. They reckon a brain haemorrhage took him in the end. I almost felt sorry for him."

"Really?" Alice asked. "After he'd sexually abused seven children in his care over the course of twelve years? He had them so petrified we only cottoned onto him when one of his victims left a suicide note pointing the finger at him. I'd say he got exactly what he deserved."

"Yeah, okay," said Mary, shifting uncomfortably in her chair.

"You're not old enough to remember the purges that happened after the safety cameras were installed," said Alice quietly.

"They were nasty." Chu picked up the signed recommendation and manila file from Alice's desk and sat back in his chair.

"Is there anything else we need to talk about today?" Alice was already scanning the screen in front of her for other matters that needed her attention.

"Nope, that's it," said Chu, standing.

"Ugh, I feel dirty now. I feel like I need a good scrub," said Mary. "Or maybe just a quick vomit."

Alice looked up. "The good news is, it works as a deterrent and the children are now safe."

"Good," said Mary. "Kids need to be protected."

"Yep. Protected, nurtured, and raised correctly. That way we end up with useful, functional adults," said Chu. He looked at Mary and raised an eyebrow. "So, what went wrong with you?"

"Oh, haha, you're so funny. Why don't you go and... surveil someone or something, Mr. Surveillance Director?"

"All right, children. Shut the door on your way out, will you?" said Alice, trying not to smile.

CHAPTER 10

BRUNCH THE NEXT day was a bayside affair for Alice and Oliver. Winding through cross-city peak hour traffic was never fun, but this morning it made Alice's nausea almost unbearable.

"Open window to half. Raise internal fan speed to full," she commanded. She turned her face to the window and waited for the fresh air to buffet her face. Tapping at the armrest, she relieved them both of the punk rock music Oliver had chosen and sat back to the dulcet French tones of Edith Piaf, who was apparently loving Paris in the winter. She closed her eyes and let the strange combination of tram bells and rising violins wash over her.

"When are you going back to the specialist?" Oliver glanced at her as the car executed a right-hand turn from the left side of the road. The tyres skidded briefly on the slippery tramlines. Oliver cursed softly.

"Friday," she said.

"Will you be well enough for the party on Sunday night or do you want me to cancel?"

"I'll be fine."

"Really? You seem to be getting worse. Maybe you need to take more time off work."

"I'm fine," she insisted, opening her eyes and trying to attract his gaze from the road. "Really. I'm just tired. I'm doing alternate days at work. It'll be fine."

Oliver took manual control of the car and pulled into the beach-front café's car park, chosen because it had views over the bay and no walk for Alice, who was moving more freely now but still tired easily.

Forty years of life. It had snuck up on her. A cocktail party had seemed like a great idea at the time—a couple of weeks after her actual birthday but still enough time after the surgery that she would have recovered. Given her health scare it felt more important than ever to celebrate the milestone.

"Okay, then. It'll be fun to see everyone." Oliver grinned cheekily. "I feel like we've been living in a cave for the past few months."

"*You* feel like you've been living in a cave?" she scoffed. "How do you think *I* feel? At least you've had work to go to."

Oliver put his hand over hers and planted a lingering kiss on her cheek.

"I'm just glad you made it to forty."

They had spoken little about the worst possible outcome of the cancer surgery, as though by speaking its name it would gain power. Alice chose to trust in medical science and the ingenuity of the researchers. She had seen firsthand the miracles they'd wrought in all areas of medical science during the past two decades, especially with the money poured into prenatal and early childhood treatments. Her last scan had been clear, though there was still a long road of remission ahead of her.

"You're just glad I made it to forty so you can come to the party," she teased.

"Nah, I've got my own birthday party coming up next month. It'll be bigger and better than yours, I'm sure," he said, climbing out of the car and coming around to open her door. "Your Majesty." He bowed and swept his arm to the side.

She smiled and pretended to curtsy, which was rather difficult to do from a sitting position.

"Why, thank you." Alice stepped out carefully and pulled herself up by holding onto the car roof. She paused for a moment and looked out over the green lawn, the palm trees, the sparkling bay. Seagulls squawked angrily at each other, picking through the remnants of last night's socialites, hoping for a few soggy chips. She gave Oliver her outstretched hand and let him lead her into the café.

CHAPTER 11

THE FOLLOWING DAY found Alice at an early check-up at her specialist's consulting rooms on her way to work.

"The great news is your scan is still clear," said Dr Barnardos. "We just need to keep an eye on things now and check in every couple of months for the next year or so."

He turned away from the screen and looked her up and down cheerfully. Dr Barnardos had been instrumental in ensuring Alice had the latest in medical treatment when the bowel cancer first appeared. He was personally involved in the hormone therapy trials that had helped Alice avoid lengthy bouts of postoperative chemotherapy. He'd found a way to slot her in a month after the trials had officially begun.

Alice smiled weakly. "Wonderful."

"You'll be ready to go back to work soon. How are you feeling?" Dr Barnardos picked up the blood pressure cuff and waited for Alice to roll up her sleeve.

"Um, not bad," she said. "Tired. Nauseous. Not in so much pain now."

Dr Barnardos frowned. "Still nauseous?" He wrapped the cuff around her bare arm and started to pump air into it. "We might do another blood test and just see how those hormone levels are going. Each patient reacts differently but the side effects should have diminished substantially by now."

He turned to the screen and tapped a few times. "Okay, there we go, all done. See Jim before you go, he'll take some blood from you and upload it to the lab for testing. We'll let you know when the results are in. Any questions at this stage? Concerns?"

"I'm okay to be back at work, right?" asked Alice, somewhat sheepishly.

'Maybe hold off until we have the blood results back. We don't want you passing out all over the Minister, now, do we?" Dr Barnardos chuckled at his own joke.

At twenty-three minutes past nine o'clock, Alice sat uncomfortably in the executive office of the Honourable Barbara Mathers, Minister for Genetics and Reproduction. As Ms Mathers tapped a stylus with her painted talons on her leather-bound desk, Alice began to wish she'd followed the doctor's orders and driven home instead of to the office. Australia hadn't had an official prime minister for twenty years now. The Equality Party manifesto asserted the glories of working as a team, in true egalitarian fashion, but everyone knew Barbara Mathers was in charge.

Graeme glared at Alice, who looked down at her folder of papers and then out of the window.

Barbara narrowed her eyes at Graeme. "You're telling me that Charlotte White's boyfriend has disappeared now?"

Graeme shifted in his seat and straightened his back.

"Yes. He met with our officers just a few days ago and appears to have been a little—ah—unstable. That's how you described him, isn't it Alice?"

Alice paused and attempted to conjure an answer that would be true to her observations and also align with what Graeme wanted her to say. Despite Chu and Mary's opinion, the gardener had seemed entirely of sound mind to her, just a little unnerved at his surroundings. Though his story of embryos being genetically modified en masse was, perhaps, a little far-fetched.

"He seemed nervous," she conceded.

"Well, he's gone now," snapped Barbara. "Charlotte White is dead and not talking. We've all agreed to let the matter rest and not take it any further. I'd say that's case closed, wouldn't you?" Barbara slammed the folder shut and pushed it back to Graeme. She swiped at her tablet leisurely but with purpose.

The Honourable Barbara Mathers was the only person Alice had ever met who could make Graeme's hands shake. She worked tirelessly and ruthlessly for efficiency and the common good, which she viewed as one and the same thing. In her mind, Equality meant every person should receive exactly the same thing, Ecocentricity meant they should get it while consuming minimal resources and Equanimity meant that everyone should shut up and do what she told them to, if they wanted to keep the peace.

The Genetic Diversification System may be Graeme's favourite program but it was Barbara's brain child. Mass public backlash and demonstrative suicides would not deter her, they simply demanded more creative solutions.

"We need more carrots, a few sticks. People need to understand the G.D.S. is for their own protection," Barbara continued, tapping and swiping at her tablet. "Ah, here we are." She projected an image and, with a flick of her hand, rotated it to face Alice. "This. You need your communications people to make more use of it. Fabulous resource, see if you can organise a campaign around it."

Alice scanned the shimmering headlines as they scrolled slowly.

Father used barbed wire and chainsaw to torture daughter during assaults.

Domestic violence rates soar as inequality reaches highest level in forty years.

Twins found dead in cribs, starved by their own mother.

Alice felt sudden hot pricks at the back of her eyes. Her throat closed over as she stared at pictures of two happy nine-month-old boys together, adjacent to photographs of two tiny black coffins seemingly adrift in a sea of flowers. Next to them, a mug shot of a limp-haired obese woman with a vacant stare. She looked across at Barbara, who nodded towards the images.

"People need to be reminded of what the 'good old days' were really like. These are the sticks," she continued. "The carrots: throw in a bunch of statistics about the drop in congenital birth defects and genetic diseases since the introduction of genetic compatibility matching. Conflate this with the idea of a laboratory, lots of pictures of Petri dishes, embryos, scientists with goggles and pipettes, that sort of thing. Find some good news stories. Let people think they've reached their own conclusion about the need for the G.D.S."

Graeme nodded enthusiastically.

"Anything else?" asked Barbara. It was a rhetorical question. She had already returned to her tablet, swiping with her long fingers and tapping with her stylus.

Graeme picked up the folder and rose.

Alice sat, thinking. "The Charlotte White boyfriend. The gardener."

Graeme shook his head at her in an unspoken warning and motioned towards the door. Barbara stopped mid-tap and looked up, frowning. She folded her fingers together.

"I thought we agreed that matter was closed, Alice."

Alice met her gaze levelly. "He mentioned something about genetic modification. It might be... useful if I could know more about what exactly the G.D.S. is testing for and what changes are made during the process."

Barbara's thumb and forefinger gripped the stylus but her expression warmed. "Oh, come on, Alice. Modifications? We're not into designer babies here in Australia. We're just giving natural selection a hand, you know that. There's no *modification* happening, just choosing healthy embryos over... not-so-healthy ones. You, of all people, understand the advantages of that, surely?"

Alice met Barbara's stare, blinking rapidly and swallowing, suddenly afraid that she might start crying. Memories started to leak into her consciousness. A silent room. A cold baby. She breathed shallowly and forced a smile.

"Of course," she said, finally. "I'll have my communications team get to work on a new campaign immediately."

Barbara nodded. "See you next week, then." She turned to Graeme, who was opening the door and on his way out. "Graeme, stay. We need to talk."

He stopped and turned on his heel, as though snapped back by an invisible string.

Alice stood and paced quickly out of the door, past the secretary, through the fire door and down one flight of stairs before she crumpled on the landing, breathing heavily. She put her head in her hands, leaned back against the cold, concrete wall and let out a low, primal moan. Tears welled up and launched themselves from her eyes as she gasped and sobbed. The familiar ache started in her fingertips and worked its way up her arms. An unfillable emptiness, even after all these years, left by her baby boy who had never really lived.

CHAPTER 12

ALICE WOKE ON Sunday to the early morning sun sneaking in underneath the blinds. The room had warmed considerably after the overnight chill and she sweated through her green silk pyjamas. On the empty pillow next to her sat a card. 'Happy 40th Birthday Soulmate' was emblazoned across the front, underneath a misted photograph of herself and Oliver smiling giddily on their wedding day. Most of the background had been cropped but a pair of arms restrained a toddler dressed in pink tulle off to the side. The little girl tugged at her frilly hem with a determined frown.

Pushing the heavy coverlet off her overheated body, Alice picked up the card and rolled onto her back.

"My darling, my love, my soulmate," Oliver began in the inscription. *"Wishing you a happy 40th birthday. Looking forward to celebrating your special day with our growing family and friends. All my love, Ollie."*

Our growing family.

Alice let the card fall onto her chest and closed her eyes. It seemed baby Oscar had a new fan.

In the midst of her immediate shock over losing her baby son, Alice had fantasised about escaping Australia altogether to avoid repeating the devastation that followed her first pregnancy.

"Elope with me," Oliver had suggested one evening as they sat together in their favourite spot outside the Birthing Home, looking up at the stars.

"To where?" asked Alice, her voice hoarse from crying.

"Anywhere. Away from Australia. Somewhere we can be together properly."

"We are together properly."

"You know what I mean."

Alice thought of leaving Australia to make a new home somewhere else, perhaps near her mother. A letter had arrived a few days earlier from Monique, postmarked from Sweden. She wanted to speak to her, asking if they could arrange a time on a safe line away from prying ears?

Alice had burned the letter. Monique did not deserve her forgiveness—nor her understanding. Monique had abandoned her, and a mother should never abandon her child.

Alice had no idea where her son's grave was, or even if it existed, but she sometimes visited the hospital where she had given birth, hoping to catch the sense of him. Walking thirty minutes from her Birthing Home just to stand in the car park and watch the sliding doors as they opened and closed, sucking in pregnant girls and spitting out mothers and babies.

The midwives had sent her out a different door when she'd failed to produce a living child from her womb, a back door for not-mothers. She told herself it was a small mercy they permitted her, so she didn't have to see the mothers and babies. But it felt like a rejection, a punishment. No longer was she good enough to use the front door.

"I'm staying here," she'd told Oliver firmly. "It's obviously for the best, they've said our genes are incompatible. I can't take the risk."

He dropped her hand and sighed in frustration. He didn't ask again.

Oliver was polite during Alice's second pregnancy. He asked her all the usual questions—how was her blood pressure, was she feeling nauseous, were her feet swollen, weight gain normal? But anything relating directly to the baby was off limits.

Eventually, Alice stopped trying to involve him in her pregnancy. She took the obstetrician's advice when the scan showed her daughter was likely to tip the scales at more than four kilograms. She booked in for a planned caesarean birth and arranged for Veronica, another girl at the Birthing Home already several months pregnant, to be her birth partner.

Compared to the traumatic stillbirth of her son, Alice's daughter arrived into the world with little fuss. Veronica held Alice's hand while the anaesthetist put a needle in her spine; while the orderlies set up a screen across her chest; while the surgeon cut along her existing abdominal scar. It was Veronica who smiled kindly at Alice when she was shaking violently again from the after-effects of the anaesthetic; Veronica who called out the already known fact— "It's a girl!" —as baby Monica screamed her way into the cool hospital air.

With the help of the hospital midwives, Alice cared for her warm, impossibly soft—and too often, cranky—little bundle of joy through-out that first day and night, constantly fearing this baby might sicken and die, too. As she pressed the button to release another timed dose of pethidine into the drip attached to her hand, she waited for Oliver to visit her and her baby.

She waited three full days before he came.

"She looks just like you," he had said as he peered into the bassinet. He didn't ask to hold her. He left after a few minutes and didn't return.

By the time she was discharged back to the Birthing Home, Alice had accepted that Oliver and baby Monica would occupy two complete but separate sections of her heart. As she cuddled and rocked and suckled her own flesh and blood, she decided to devote the next six months wholly to this new gift of life. Oliver could wait. If he still wanted her in six months, she would gladly have him back... but she would not put him before her daughter. This baby girl was more important than anything—or anyone—else.

Alice would snatch an hour or two of sleep whenever she could. Monica had seemed to think sleep was highly overrated. The midwives assured her it was a good sign. Sleeplessness in infancy correlated strongly with increased intellectual ability. Alice nodded her weary head, sure she would be grateful for this fact later in life, but just wanting a solid eight hours of rest right now.

She'd spent hours at the local park, lying under a tree, reading a book or just gazing at baby Monica as she lay on her stomach picking at the blades of grass or trying to eat a beetle. Monica learned to roll at four months and excelled at disappearing under items of furniture, causing great panic. Her squeals of delight as she kicked at the bottom of a table or dresser, rocking it and trying to upend it, usually gave away her location eventually. Once, Alice had found her impossibly wedged beneath a low sofa, fast asleep.

By the time six months came around, Monica was pushing herself up on her knees and rocking. It wouldn't be long until she was crawling around the house and getting into everything.

"It's time, Alice," the head midwife had said one afternoon. "You need to choose a Home for Monica. We'll take her there on Monday."

"I know," Alice had whispered, looking down at her little girl, who had fallen asleep at her breast. She wanted to scream and scream until they all went away and left her alone with her daughter. Instead, she nodded and spent the weekend researching, sorting and ranking the available Birthing Homes.

Once Monica was settled in with her Mater and Pater, Alice moved into a residential college adjacent to the University of Melbourne and began her studies in law and politics. Every week from Monday to Saturday she attended lectures, spent hours in the library reading case law, and listening to loud music at local pubs to drown out the screaming in her head each night.

Sunday was the day she rested from her own fraught mind. Sunday was her day with Monica.

Oliver had started popping up at the pubs she frequented, buying her drinks and talking about his studies in child development. He was studying to become a Pater. They discussed the legalities around child support, argued about the ethics of surveillance in the name of safety—Alice had thought it too intrusive, Oliver found it essential to the wellbeing of the children—and slowly they began to warm to each other again.

Alice never mentioned Monica. Oliver never asked.

Now Alice felt the surge of old anger rise in her chest. Pure fury on behalf of her scorned daughter. Frustration with Oliver for his refusal to allow them to share their grief over her first child. Blind rage at the universe for letting it all happen. She closed her eyes, bit down on her tongue and carefully slotted her anger back into the box in her mind marked *Irrational Thoughts*. Her daughter could not be hurt by the neglect of a man who meant nothing to her; it wasn't reasonable to blame Oliver for the form his grief took. Stillbirths happened. Not often, but they did. For no particular reason. It wasn't anybody's fault. It just was. Her heartbeat slowed back to normal as she taped up the box in her mind and pushed it further back into the recesses of her memory.

Alice opened her eyes, picked up the screen next to her bed and tapped out a message to Oliver: *Thank you. Love you too xxx.* She pressed *Send* then rolled over and stared at the fly crawling around the back of the blind until she dozed off again.

Haunting melodies sounded throughout the apartment, intruding into Alice's dreams. The unicorn that was trying to fill her champagne glass, while explaining why privacy laws needed to be overhauled, suddenly pulled out a pan flute and started to play. A mist swirled around them both and Alice gasped as she woke suddenly.

The pan flute stopped, then started again, accompanied by sharp knocking. Alice huffed irritably. They really needed to replace their doorbell. Harking back to romantic, ancient gods was all well and good, but it just wasn't practical when you wanted to be alerted to visitors, divine or otherwise.

Alice threw back the covers and swung her legs over the side of the bed. The pain from her surgical scar had dulled to a slight twinge. The miniature golden analogue clock on the bedside table told her she had slept past midday. She padded across the plush pile carpet of the bedroom, down the stairs and into the entrance hall.

She pushed a button at the side of the door and the security screen came to life, showing a distorted picture of Monica: a massive head on tiny shoulders. Her nose took up almost a quarter of the screen.

Alice pressed another button and a buzzing noise was followed by a click. She pulled the door open and smiled broadly, feeling thoroughly refreshed by sixteen consecutive hours of sleep.

"Hello, I can't believe it's Sunday already! You're early." She peered around behind Monica. "No baby?"

"It feels weird," said Monica, wrinkling her nose and gripping her handbag and backpack as though they might stop her free-falling.

"He's with one of the other girls at the Birthing Home. She's going to feed him and one of the guys will put him to bed and look after him until I get back and..." She trailed off mid-sentence, looking mildly panicked.

"He's in good hands. He'll be fine," Alice assured her. "Come in. What brings you here? I thought you were coming straight to the restaurant."

"Oliver came to visit me yesterday."

"Really?" Alice raised both eyebrows, stunned.

"He's a man of few words or many, isn't he? There's no in between."

Monica told Alice how Oliver had shown up at the Birthing Home, unannounced, and sat with Monica, staring at baby Oscar for a long time without speaking. How he'd finally gazed intently at Monica and noted that the child had the same hair colour as his mother, and the same hair colour as Alice. How the intensity of the moment quickly dissolved as Oliver had started to speak excitedly of his plans for Alice's birthday and asked Monica to be a part of them.

Alice sat quietly with her hands in her lap, staring at a picture on the wall and nodding occasionally while Monica recounted Oliver's visit. Oliver was funny when it came to talking about serious things. A joker and a fabulous Pater to all the kids who had passed through his care, he'd always left the deep and meaningful conversations to someone else. Alice figured this was probably the closest she was going to get to an apology and acceptance. She could only guess at his explanation for nearly two decades of silence. Whatever the initial reason was, avoidance became a deeply ingrained habit after a period of time, especially when both parties were complicit.

"Well, then," said Alice. "I'd best go and have a shower so we can head off to our first appointment."

"I'll make coffee-to-go." Monica jumped up from the sofa and headed into the kitchen.

As the burning hot water streamed down her long hair and body, Alice's stomach started to turn over again. She washed the conditioner out quickly, turned off the water, and stepped out of the shower. Her world started to spin and her stomach convulsed. She sat heavily on the shower mat, leaning forward with her knees up and feet planted on the cold tiles. Breathing shallowly, she gagged again, quickly calculating whether she could stay where she was and ride out the wave of nausea, or whether she needed to make a play for the toilet bowl.

She stayed put.

Minutes passed, or seconds. Alice closed her eyes and tried to regulate her breathing, calm her abdominal muscles. She placed her hands on the cold tiles, then on her cheeks, then back again, transferring the cool to her face and beating back the fuzziness.

"Mum? You nearly done in there? The taxi will be here soon," Monica called through the door.

Alice lifted her head and tried to focus her eyes. The fog was beginning to lift.

"Almost," she managed, feeling her stomach lurch. She forced herself to stand up and dried off quickly with a heavy white towel. She opened the door and stepped out to the relatively cool bedroom with relief, flopping down onto the unmade bed, wrapped only in a towel, and closed her eyes.

The smell of coffee intruded.

"Mum? You okay?" asked Monica, setting two travel mugs of coffee down on the dresser.

Alice groaned. "No coffee," she mumbled into the pillow, rolling over and burying her nose to get away from the smell.

Monica paused, unsure what to do.

Alice tried to sit up. "Please, take the coffee away. I can't stand the smell."

"Okay," said Monica, picking up the mugs and disappearing through the doorway.

She returned with a glass of water. "We don't have to do this if you're not up to it. We can just stay here. I'll do your hair, get them to deliver the dresses." Monica held the glass while Alice took short sips.

"No, it's okay," said Alice. "I'll be fine in a minute. Green tea helps."

Monica nodded. "Green tea it is, then. I'll go and pop the kettle on."

Alice lay back against the pillows, waiting for the world to right itself again. She imagined chemotherapy would have been pretty awful, from what she'd read about it. But the side effects from the hormone therapy weren't so terrific either. She listened to the birds outside the window, tweeting busily. From the kitchen came sounds of ceramic canisters being opened and closed while Monica searched for the green tea. The kettle reached its crescendo just as a crow gave an almighty squawk and frightened the quarrelling birds away. A small click and the kettle started to deflate, along with Alice's thumping pulse.

By the time Monica came back with the steaming mug of yellowy-brown liquid, Alice was able to sit up normally and hold it herself. She inhaled the gentle scent and started to feel better.

"You're still very pale."

"It's okay, it'll pass. It always does." Alice took a sip of the tea and winced as she burned her tongue.

"When was your last checkup? Is this normal?"

"They took blood on Friday. I'll be fine."

Monica peered at her mother suspiciously. "Hmm," was all she said. She shook her head and got up to check Alice's closet. "You stay there. I'll find you an outfit to wear."

Alice didn't argue as Monica flicked through endless hangers in the walk-in robe, pulling out one in five, holding it up to the light, replacing it on the rack. Within a few minutes she had assembled on the bed a phantom woman wearing a loose, flowing maroon dress, black boots and a chunky charcoal knit cardigan which would reach Alice's knees when she stood.

Monica paused, looking uncertainly from the pile of clothes to Alice, whose red hair hung damp and frizzy around her pale, drawn face as she sat, hands cupped around the tea, sipping frequently.

"You need to eat something," Monica declared at last. "Toast?"

Alice nodded.

"Vegemite?"

Alice nodded again. The salty black spread was always a perfect remedy to a queasy stomach.

"I'll leave you to get dressed then."

"Thank you," Alice whispered weakly.

CHAPTER 13

MOTHER AND DAUGHTER waited silently in the warm sunshine as the limousine pulled up to the curb. Monica opened the rear passenger door and shepherded her mother in. She jumped in herself and turned to Alice, ready to offer her assistance.

"I'm *fine*," said Alice. "I can buckle my own seatbelt. I'm recovering from surgery, not sliding into dementia."

Monica narrowed her eyes and pursed her lips in mock annoyance then smiled, relieved to hear the firmness return to Alice's voice.

"You have started to get a few curves back on your body recently, I suppose. Your cheekbones don't seem quite as... pointy. Maybe you are recovering after all," Monica conceded. She gave the driver the address and they pulled out into the early Sunday afternoon traffic.

Weekday rush hour confined itself to discrete periods in the mornings and afternoons. Sunday rush hour lasted all day, with genetic mothers and fathers heading in and out of the city at various times to visit their offspring at whatever time of day suited their age bracket best.

First to leave were the parents of toddlers, sometimes relieving Maters or Paters of their lively bundles as early as 6.30am. Late morning and early afternoon saw the parents of teenagers off in their cars to pick up monosyllabic boys and melodramatic girls after allowing them a long, much needed, sleep-in.

"Are your Mater and Pater coming to the party tonight?" asked Alice.

"No."

Alice watched Monica, waiting for her to elaborate.

Monica glanced at her quickly and continued. "Um, Pater is unwell. Mater couldn't get away."

Monica's Mater and Pater were kind, generous people who had always encouraged her in her interests and passions. But for some reason, Monica had just never connected with them. She waited until Sundays to confide in Alice that Sally at school said she was a virgin and what did that mean, was it a bad thing—she'd said it like it was? And how did you know when you needed to get a bra?

Alice sometimes wondered if she had done the wrong thing, getting too attached to Monica. Had she interfered in the relationship between Monica and her Mater and Pater? She watched Monica as her daughter dug her phone out of her bag and checked for messages, then started scrolling hungrily through photos of baby Oscar. Alice shrugged off her doubts and resolved to enjoy the afternoon of pampering.

"No, hon, you should cut it all off. It would look fabulous," said the hairdresser, tucking Monica's hair up and under to help her picture a shoulder-length bob.

Monica frowned and turned her head from side to side, checking in the mirror.

"I like it the way it is."

Alice sat back with her feet up and eyes closed. A black cape covered her upper body and her hair stuck out in all directions, little tufts wrapped in silver foils. A tin head alien and a stinky one at that, thought Alice as the scent of the hair dye clouded around her.

"Shave it all off, Connie. Let her start again. Maybe it'll grow back more manageable," suggested Alice, not moving. She smiled, waiting for the expected reaction from her unbending daughter.

"Mum!" said Monica, clamping both hands over her stringy mop of red hair.

Connie burst out laughing. Alice grinned and lifted her head lazily. She hadn't felt this relaxed in months.

"Seriously, don't cut it too short," said Alice. "You want to be able to throw it back in a ponytail while you've got babies. Too much effort to style it every day."

Connie arranged her scissors on a plush black towel on the bench and huffed.

"Tish. Babies. They ruin every ounce of a woman's style, hon. You wait 'til you get out of that Birthing Home. Come back and we'll cut you up a right royal classy hairdo."

"Maybe just put it up for the party tonight?" Monica asked doubtfully, twisting the top half of her hair and piling it on top of her head.

"Plus, a colour and a nice long conditioning treatment," said Connie firmly, picking up long, wiry lengths and letting them fall again.

"Hi there! I'm Rita. Would you like a cup of tea?" The apprentice, a dark-haired girl in her early twenties, bounded into Alice's peripheral view with a cart full of potions, foils and combs.

"Green tea, please."

"Coffee? Do you have proper coffee?" Monica asked hopefully.

Rita looked perplexed. "It's high-end organic coffee from Costa Rica, freshly brewed. Is that what you mean?"

Connie laughed. "Hon, this chicky's been let out of a Birthing Home for the day. For Christ's sake, just get her a proper coffee, and be quick about it."

Rita nodded at her boss and scooted back behind the black velvet curtain.

"And some of those gorgeous chockies we got in from that boutique place yesterday," Connie called after her.

Monica settled into the chair and watched in the mirror as Connie sectioned off a line of copper hairs, pasted them with white goo then wrapped them in a piece of baking foil and folded it back up onto her scalp where it stayed suspended, as if by magic.

"How old's your little one, then?" asked Connie, kick-starting the stream of small talk hairdressers were famous for.

"Three months."

"Boy or girl?"

"Boy."

Connie paused. Monica shut her eyes, hoping to shut down the chatter and enjoy the pseudo head massage in silence.

"Boobs hurting yet?"

"What?" Monica's eyes snapped open.

"Yer boobs, love. First time away from a three-month-old, they're likely to be full and leaky by now."

Monica discreetly pressed her upper arms into her breasts underneath her cape. Oh yes, they were bursting and painful all right.

"They're a bit tender."

"You'll be wanting to express a bit before too long. Take some of the pressure off. When we're done with the colour here you can nip out the back and use the sink if you like. Plenty of privacy in there." Connie expertly flicked up four layers of silver foil hair packages with the end of her comb and inspected them. They cascaded back down like an aluminium waterfall.

"Um, thanks," said Monica, feeling bewildered.

"Did you bring a hand pump?" asked Alice softly, opening her eyes and reaching over to put a reassuring hand on Monica's arm.

Monica shook her head.

"I'll come and show you how to express manually. It's not hard when you're full. Ask someone to show you how to use a hand pump when you get back to the Birthing Home. It'll help... later."

"Just like milkin' a cow!" Connie shrieked with laughter.

Monica blushed, wishing she could sink through the floor. Motherhood had put the spotlight on her body, which she much preferred to keep to herself. Life had been so much simpler as a high school student when she could focus on her books and ignore the crowds. Irritated, she reached up under the cape and carefully touched her breasts. They were sore and lumpy around the edges. It seemed that wherever she went, she would still be a mother, baby or not.

Monica watched Connie scrape the last of the goo out and paste it over her hair.

"Alrighty then, that's you all wrapped up," she said, spinning the dial on a timer and setting it on the bench. "Just need to cook for a bit. You okay for drinks? Want another coffee?"

Monica peered into the mug which Rita had snuck onto the table in front of her. It was almost full. She shook her head at Connie.

"No, I'm fine, thanks."

"Lovely. Just sing out if you need anything." Connie wheeled her trolley around to the other side of the salon where an older lady sat, her short hair in wet clumps, watching a projected video.

Monica picked up her coffee and sipped slowly, savouring the smooth richness of freshly brewed. No bitter after taste. No weird chemical kick. Just beautiful, velvety coffee. She made a note to tell Joe and smiled as she pictured his wistful jealousy. Maybe she would bring him into the city next Sunday to get his caffeine fix.

She wondered how Oscar was going. Suddenly her arms felt empty, light, as though she'd forgotten something. There was a sharp twinge deep in her left breast and she felt the pad against her nipple start to soak with milk. She looked down in annoyance to check it hadn't come through her top. All dry, for the moment.

Monica glanced over at Alice, who seemed to have drifted off to sleep in her chair, feet propped up on a purpose-built metal rack. She tapped her earpiece lightly and smiled as she read a message from Maddy:

Proof of life attached. Figured you'd be freaking out by now. He's fine. Have fun. xxx.

Attached was a photo, date stamped fifteen minutes ago, of Oscar sleeping soundly in Maddy's lap, his arms crossed over his chest and his mouth wide open. Maddy had clearly taken the picture herself. Her naked breast had managed to protrude its way into the shot. Monica laughed to herself. At least she knew Oscar was being well fed, though she felt mixed emotions—at best—that he hadn't been fed by her.

"Do you want me to show you how to hand express now?" asked Alice.

"Oh, um, I guess so," said Monica, nervous but eager for some relief from the pressure building up in her breasts.

The two women made a strange parade of black capes and tin-foiled heads as they headed into the back room. It was a jumble of boxes and jars, a seat and a small shelf which housed three handbags. A stark contrast to the minimalist luxury of the salon proper.

Alice found the sink and summoned Monica with a sideways nod.

"Okay, so Connie wasn't far wrong. It is actually pretty much the same as milking a cow, except horizontal instead of vertical. Have you ever milked a cow?"

Monica shook her head, feeling like she might cry.

"Ever seen one milked?" Alice asked, more gently.

Monica nodded.

"Okay, so you get the general gist. You need to start at the base of your nipple and firmly brush outward, sort of pulling as you go. You'll get a feel for it after a while."

Monica stood, looking at the sink helplessly, not sure where to start.

"Do you want me to go and wait in the salon?" asked Alice, turning to leave and give her daughter some privacy.

Monica grabbed her arm. "No. Stay. Please."

The young mother lifted her shirt and unhooked the cup of her maternity bra, wincing as her rock-hard breast was released. She squeezed the base of her nipple but didn't move her fingers forwards fast enough. The nipple flicked upwards and squirted the mirror with a fine spray of milk. Mortified, she looked to Alice for further instructions. Alice stood in front of her, shaking with silent laughter as several drops of breast milk dripped down her face.

"Oh no, oh no, I'm so sorry, Mum. Oh, let me get you a tissue."

Monica grabbed a handful of tissues from a nearby box and tried to dab at Alice's face but found herself facing the top of her mother's head. A terrible wheezing sound emitted from Alice as she doubled over.

"Are you okay, Mum?" Monica put a hand on her shoulder.

Alice's whole body shook as the built-up laughter finally came out in great gusts of sound. Alice threw her head back, the tears rolling down her face as Connie stuck her head around the curtain.

"How are you girls going in here?" she asked.

Monica stood, petrified, forgetting she had one breast hanging out of her top.

Connie looked from one to the other and winked. "I'll have a latté while you're back there, hon. Plenty of milk, couple of sugars." She withdrew to the salon, letting the heavy black curtain drop back into place.

Alice had seated herself on the chair and was coughing, trying to stop laughing and get her breath back.

Monica relaxed a little and smiled. "Okay, let's try that again. You might want to stand a bit further back this time."

Two hours later, Monica was feeling a whole lot more comfortable, having mastered the art of hand expressing, and both women were starting to look rather stunning. Alice's shoulder-length hair was cut, coloured with light red hues and strawberry blonde streaks and pinned up in soft curls. Monica's long, wayward hair had been tamed into an elaborate French roll.

"No, no. Bill's taken care of," said Connie, waving Alice away as she stood at the counter, ready to sync her earpiece with the payment system. "Where to next for you girls?"

Alice looked at Monica expectantly.

"Oh, um, dresses next, I think," said Monica, swiping at her earpiece and checking the detailed schedule for the day.

"I'll call the limo back for you," said Connie. She tapped the screen on the counter, scrolled a little and tapped again. "There you go. Shouldn't be long."

"Thanks," said Alice, taking a seat on the plush lounge in the waiting area at the front of the salon.

"I'll leave you to it. You two have a fabulous night," said Connie.

Monica sank down next to Alice and leaned gently on her shoulder, taking care not to crush either of their elaborate hairstyles.

Alice smiled. "Don't worry too much. I've got so much product in here I'm not sure you could mess it up if you tried." She patted her hair tentatively, testing its resilience. "Yep, tough as nails."

"Hmm," said Monica distractedly, not really listening.

"So, what's the deal with the dresses? Are they already chosen? Or do we get to watch a fashion parade and then pick one out?" asked Alice, rocking her shoulders from side to side in a poor imitation of a catwalk model.

"Hey? Oh, sorry. I'm off in another world. I'm just so tired."

"Can't imagine why. Waking up to feed a baby every few hours for the past couple of months. Really, where's your stamina?" Alice teased.

Monica raised an eyebrow. "Dresses are pretty much ready. They're just doing a fitting to check if any alterations need to be made."

"This'll be interesting. Did you get to help choose them or is this all Ollie's planning?"

Alice loved Oliver dearly, but his dress sense sometimes left a little to be desired. It tended towards bright primary colours and loud patterns. Perfect for small children. Not so great for grown-up cocktail parties.

"No, he left it to the designers. He just sent photos of us—I gave him my measurements and they've guessed at yours. He let them know that you might have, um, lost weight recently, too," said Monica. "There'll be a make-up artist there to do our faces once the dresses are on, too. Oh, and shoes. They've organised them as well."

"Wow, he really thought of everything," said Alice, impressed.

"Either that or the designer did," said Monica, smiling. Her earpiece vibrated. It was another message from Maddie.

Mummy, Mummy, mean old Maddie won't let me stick my finger in the power sockets! Wish you were here xx.

Monica laughed at the picture of Oscar lying on his back and chewing on the plastic cord of a toy iron.

"How're you doing?" asked Alice, peering over her shoulder at the image. "Still okay to keep going? Not missing him too much?"

Monica stared at the picture of her son. "Missing him terribly. Looking forward to the party."

Alice nodded.

"Mum, how did you cope with letting me go?"

Alice smiled sadly. "I never let you go, sweetheart. I never will."

"I don't mean..." Monica shook her head, embarrassed. "How will I... hand him over?"

"You'll do what you have to do. Because it's best for him and it's best for you. And he'll have the best possible care," said Alice firmly.

Monica looked into her eyes, searching for evidence of a lie. She found none. She looked back at the image of baby Oscar, silently counting the hours until she would be with him again.

"And after you hand him over to his new Mater and Pater you'll go home and cry yourself to sleep every night and wonder why every day isn't Sunday. But after a while you'll be fine." Alice put her arm around Monica's shoulders. "You'll see him grow and you'll be jealous of his Mater and Pater. But hopefully, in time, you'll see that they know what they're doing, they care for him and they have his best interests at heart, always. And soon enough you'll be busy with another pregnancy, another baby."

"And what happens if I don't?" Monica pulled away. "What if I refuse to give him up?"

Alice withdrew her arm and looked at Monica, frowning.

"You won't. You'll do what's best for him. And for you," said Alice flatly.

"But what if...? I mean, would they take him anyway?" Monica persisted.

Alice looked past Monica and out of the window, searching the busy the street. She sighed and mentally put on her government regulator hat.

"First, you would be offered counselling. Then you'd be diagnosed with postnatal depression and offered medication. If you continued to resist you'd be charged with endangering the welfare of a minor. Depending on the manner in which you resisted you may be committed to a psychiatric hospital for treatment for suspected postnatal psychosis. Your rights to future reproduction may be revoked. Your access to your baby would be restricted on the grounds that you were a danger to its wellbeing and emotional development. This would continue until you could prove you were stable enough."

Alice turned back to Monica, took both of her hands and stared earnestly into her face. "Either way, they would still take him. Do you understand?"

Monica nodded, swallowing back tears. A horn sounded outside the window. She stood up, pulling her hands away from Alice and hurriedly wiping at her eyes.

"We should go. We don't want to be late."

CHAPTER 14

THE DRESSMAKER SEEMED to have jumped straight out the nineteenth century, with a mouth full of pins, hair piled messily on top of her head, a plain, grey A-line dress and flat, lace-up boots. She fussed silently around Alice as she gathered in the hem of the blue satin cocktail dress. Suffering from sudden vertigo on her low-rise pedestal, Alice blinked slowly and looked straight ahead, into the mirror. Dark smudges of purple brushed against the tops of her cheekbones, hollowing out her blue eyes in the fluorescent lights.

A young man in black leather pants and a tight checked shirt sat on a stool in the corner dabbing away at Monica's face. A small case containing six brushes, three palettes and a range of bottles lay on a table next to him. Alice hoped he was as expert as he seemed, or she risked looking like a cadaver with a shiny dress and a great hairdo.

Monica had barely spoken a word to her since they left the hair salon. It was a normal part of parental pre-separation, this grieving for anticipated future partings. Alice remembered spending many nights at university studying the intricacies of constitutional law while wondering whether Monica had taken her first steps without her there, whether she was sleeping through the night yet, whether Mater would pat and rock her back to sleep just like Alice used to.

Even if she had decided to run away with her baby, as Monica was fantasising about doing with Oscar, there was nowhere to go. She would have needed to work to feed and house them both and there was nobody she could have left Monica with during the day, except a Mater and Pater. Which kind of defeated the purpose of trying to keep her close.

Monica's genetic father hadn't been interested in children. With high connections, he'd managed to negotiate his way out of National Service altogether and had instead spent three years travelling the world, attending immunological symposiums as the assistant of a professor in the field.

Even if he had been interested, with both of them attending university for four years there was no way to earn an income to support a baby. Even in full-time work, with a tax rate of sixty percent to support the Mater and Pater system, there wasn't a lot left over for anything past the essentials. Then again, with only one person to support per full-time wage, most people didn't need very much. An apartment in the inner city, a meal delivery service, Internet connection and bit left over for eating out and entertainment. There was no need to pay for nappies, large backyards or hefty tuition fees.

Too many ifs, buts and maybes with no solutions.

Alice closed her eyes again and wondered how much longer the dress fitting would take. She needed to sit down soon. The nausea was rising again. She swayed slightly and jolted back upright. The dressmaker stopped and looked up at her pale face.

"Nearly done. You should eat more," she said.

Alice clenched her teeth and said nothing, pulling a face at the top of the dressmaker's head as she bent down again to insert one final pin. Alice chose that moment to glance at Monica. Monica smiled conspiratorially, then seemed to remember herself and snapped her head back to the make-up artist, face closed.

Alice sighed. Monica was kind-hearted but stubborn when it came to getting her own way in something she considered to be right and just. She was, however, also deeply rational. Alice was certain she would see sense soon and accept her and baby Oscar's fate.

"Did Ollie mention when we would see him?" Alice called out across the room, hoping to force a conversation. No response. "Is he meeting us here or at the restaurant?" The make-up artist paused mid-stroke, looking from Alice to Monica.

"Restaurant," said Monica tersely.

"Did he tell you he's ordered ice sculptures?"

The dressmaker looked up at Alice, frowned and shook her head, mumbling something about ridiculous ostentations.

Alice tried again: "He wouldn't tell me what they were going to be, though. I'm thinking maybe swans. What do you reckon?"

"Doves. He said they're doves, something about you being set free and at peace now you're forty and well," said Monica.

A full sentence, thought Alice. Progress. She waited, willing Monica to take the next step. Monica turned to face her, causing the make-up artist to swear under his breath as the brush swept wide of its target.

"I told him doves were a bad idea. The way he explained it made it sound more like you'd died. Set free? At peace? Pfft."

Alice smiled. "Swans would have been better."

"So, who's going to be there?"

"Oh, you know, everyone."

"Work colleagues?"

"Yep."

"The *hoi polloi*?"

"Specifically?"

"Politicians? Celebrities?"

"Um, politicians, yes. Celebrities, depends on your definition. Technically Ollie's a celebrity. His book was read on Play School the other day," said Alice.

Monica laughed. Alice inwardly breathed a sigh of relief.

"Do you have to make a speech?" asked Monica.

"Probably. I haven't really planned anything. It won't be long or poignant, that's for sure."

"Is *your* Mum coming? Uncle Pete maybe?" She added the last name cheekily, angling for another of her mother's unlikely stories about her mysterious uncle.

"Mum, no, of course not. Uncle Pete... I haven't heard from him in a while."

"Where is he now?"

Alice laughed. "Arrested in Madagascar; discovered a cure for cancer; sailing the seven seas with pirates. Who knows? He could be living around the corner for all I know."

Alice imagined the elusive Uncle Pete with a red beard, an eye patch and a brightly coloured parrot on his shoulder. She wondered if Monica held a similar image in her mind, because at that moment she finally grinned.

"Pirate," Monica said quietly. "Definitely pirate. But a friendly one who robs from the rich and gives to the poor."

"That's Robin Hood. He was land-based. Pirates just rape, pillage and murder."

Monica looked disappointed. "I'm sure Uncle Pete could turn them around."

Alice smiled tightly. Monica had always seen Alice's younger brother as a hero of sorts. He'd shown up at random intervals during her childhood—always unannounced, always fleeting visits. He would leave again before he could be discovered by the authorities.

The truth was, she hadn't seen Pete in nearly ten years. She had no idea where he was, other than he made sure their mother was well cared for in Sweden. Her stories of the adventures of Uncle Pete had become more elaborate as the years went by. Originally spun to keep Monica entertained, her yarns had taken on legendary status. From time to time she received a cryptic postcard in the mail, simply signed 'P xx'. She assumed they were from her little brother and that he was, at least, alive.

As for what his line of work was, Alice had asked him once, long ago. He gave some vague answer about 'keeping the bastards honest', whatever that meant.

"Pirates are the devil's work," muttered the dressmaker.

Monica stifled a laugh and snorted instead. Alice forced herself to frown seriously as the dressmaker looked admonishingly from mother to daughter and back again.

"Yes, they do dreadful things. Just dreadful," Alice assured her.

The dressmaker narrowed her eyes and stood up.

"You are finished," she announced, with a flick of her nose. "Take the dress off. Her turn now."

The make-up artist smiled at Monica, who looked slightly alarmed.

"Just a few more minutes, Magda, she's almost ready for you," he sang out in a sweet falsetto. In a low voice he continued, "Don't worry, she's harmless. Just don't mention the war." He winked as he brushed out Monica's eyebrows and gave a final touch up to her cheeks. "There, stunning. Off you go."

Alice stumbled slightly as she dismounted from the low podium. Magda helped her out of the dress and into a warm, soft pink robe. She took a few shaky steps and sank into the make-up chair gratefully. Monica took her place on the podium.

"Clothes off!" declared Magda.

Alice closed her eyes and luxuriated in the soft, cool strokes of the make-up brushes tickling at her sensitive skin. Monica fell silent under the steely ministrations of Magda. Soft folk music intruded into the room with sharp horn notes and plucked strings, adding to Monica's tension.

Twenty minutes later both women were sitting in robes with cups of tea, waiting quietly while Magda stabbed away at Alice's dress, adjusting the waistline, which had finally started to expand a little. She'd spent so long losing weight during her illness, it was nice to feel like she might finally be coming out the other end. Magda, however, was not so impressed with Alice's new curves. Monica had received grunted approval for managing to remain the same body shape since her measurements were taken.

"How are you doing?" asked Monica.

"I do wish you'd stop asking me that." Alice sipped her green tea. "I'm fine."

"Okay, just checking, no need to get your knickers in a knot."

"How are *you* doing?"

"Fine, too. I keep forgetting all about Oscar and having fun. Then I remember him and feel guilty. And miss him terribly," said Monica. "It sounds crazy but my arms feel... empty. God, that's such a cliché, sorry. But it's true."

"Clichés are clichés for a reason." Alice watched as Magda picked up her dress, shook out the material and hung it on the door of a dressing cubicle. Monica's dress already hung on the door of the next cubicle.

Magda turned to the women and stared at a point just above their heads.

"You may dress," she said, bowing stiffly. She picked up her measuring tape, turned on her heel and left the room, allowing the door to close slowly behind her.

Alice turned to Monica. "You heard the boss. Get thee dressed." She shook her finger at Monica, who snorted with laughter.

"Ah, but such finery is devil's work. I'd prefer a simple frock, thank you."

"Potato sack? A shroud perhaps?"

Monica frowned. "Shroud? Not funny, Mum."

"Sorry," said Alice. "Forgive me?"

Monica shook her head, smiling. "Let's get this show on the road, hey?"

"Two cheeseburgers, large fries, two bottles of water and an apple pie, please!" Alice shouted at the face on the screen.

"That'll be twenty-three dollars ninety, please. Drive through to the next window," came the crackling reply.

"Careful! You'll mess up your hair," said Monica irritably as Alice banged her head on the window frame trying to get her head back into the limousine.

"I could have concussion and all you care about is my hair?"

"I can't believe you're getting takeaway when we're about to head to the fanciest restaurant in Melbourne."

"For a cocktail party, my darling uninitiated daughter," said Alice. "Not dinner. You must learn, if you're going to be a famous immunologist, that cocktail parties do not equal substantial food. If you want to last the distance, you have to eat first."

"Immunologists work in labs, Mum, they don't swan around at *parties*." She spat the last word out with a sour face.

"*Famous* immunologists need to learn how to network." Alice stuck her hand out the window again to take the paper bags and bottles from the attendant. "And cranky adolescents need to learn how to take advice from their wise forty-year-old parents and eat when they're told."

Monica took the proffered cheeseburger after draping her comfortable jumper across the chest of her *haute couture* dress.

"Fine, but did you have to get cheeseburgers? With sauce?"

Alice ignored her and took large bites of her own package of hot, salty goodness. The taste of pickles, sugar and fat all combined to somehow quell her unhappy stomach. She munched it down quickly and started on the fries.

"Careful. You'll be busting out of your designer stitches if you eat too much," said Monica, taking petite nibbles from her own burger. After a few dainty bites she gave a lusty sigh and chomped off half the burger in one go. "Yeah, okay, I was hungry," she said, her mouth full.

Alice smirked. "Breastfeeding will do that to you."

"So will being stuck in a Birthing Home with nothing but healthy food allowed. The midwives would be horrified to see me tucking into this lot."

"We should start up Burger Joint Sunday. I had no idea you were feeling so deprived."

Alice started to feel much better as she chewed slowly on her crunchy deep-fried apple pie and sipped from her water bottle. Outside her window she watched the bay come into view. The dark water stretched away endlessly in the cloudy night. If she looked only to her left, she could pretend there was no civilisation at all, just the sand and the water and the stars, hiding away behind the smoky mists. To her right the car sped past ever-more elaborate waterfront mansions as they hurtled towards the city centre.

When she looked left again, her view of the water was obscured by restaurants, yacht clubs and car parks. The limousine slowed and pulled up in the circular driveway of the restaurant. Guests in smart tuxedos, colourful dresses and impossibly high heels milled around the entry. Alice spotted Oliver kissing newcomers on the cheek. Eschewing formal black, he stood out in a maroon lounge suit with a checkered neckerchief. She wondered if he'd brushed his shock of peppery brown hair at all or if he'd just relied on his hands that were constantly running through it, to keep it in order.

"Ready?" she asked Monica.

"Ready."

Alice steadied her breathing as she waited for the driver to open her door. The past few hours of casual fun dissolved and her official mask slotted back into place. She took Monica's hand and squeezed.

"Just follow me and stay close. Try to smile," she said. As she stepped out of the car, the sky-blue silk of her dress shone in the bright lights. She fixed her eyes on Oliver, but he quickly disappeared amid a cluster of photographic flashes in her face. Questions were fired at her by the barely contained pack of media behind the ropes.

"Has the cancer gone, Ms. Mooney?"

"Do you feel guilty about Charlotte White's death?"

"Who designed your dress?"

"How does your daughter feel about Charlotte White's death?"

"Do you feel bad that you're forty and Charlotte White is dead?"

Alice kept smiling, said nothing, and walked sedately into Oliver's arms. Readers of tonight's news would see the photographs but would not hear the unanswered questions. Politicians may have agreed to stop discussing Charlotte White's death, but the public was still chewing over the mysterious early demise of the beautiful, young and, apparently, star-crossed lover. Judging by the tone of their questions, they hadn't got wind of the fact that Charlotte White had taken her own life.

They would move on to something else soon enough when speculation ceased to be fuelled by new comments.

"Well, it's lovely to meet you, beautiful lady, but I'm afraid I'm married and waiting for my wife to arrive," Oliver murmured into her ear, placing his hand on her lower back in a loose hug for the benefit of the photographers.

Alice looked into his eyes and grinned. "Thank you," she said. "For everything."

Oliver rested his chin on her head. "Too little, too late. But I'm trying," he whispered. He gestured to Monica to join them. He put his arm around both women and faced the flashes of light. "Say cheese!" he muttered from behind clenched, smiling teeth.

CHAPTER 15

INSIDE, MONICA BLINKED furiously and shook her head.

"I can hardly see, I literally have stars in my eyes. I had no idea you were so popular," she said to Alice.

"I'm not. They're here for the ministers, but they'll try their luck on anyone who dares to tread the red carpet."

"Oh, wow, this is so beautiful," said Monica, finally clearing her vision and looking around. The entrance opened into a room filled with wrought iron, glittering chandeliers, and sumptuous chambray. Floor to ceiling windows lined the curved bay-side wall and the water stretched away from the beach just beyond the glass. Everything about the classy decor showcased the bay, with nary an anchor, captain's hat or seashell in sight. The rear wall held enormous mirrors. Even guests seated with their backs to the bay couldn't escape seeing it.

The ice sculptures rested on a long table, front and centre next to the windows. Transparent doves weaved through an archway of ivy atop an iceberg of massive proportions.

"Ollie, this is wonderful. Thank you." Alice kissed him gently on the cheek.

A waiter approached them with a silver tray and three glasses of sparkling wine. Oliver took two and handed them out, then held up his own.

"To fabulous, fit and forty," he said.

"To forty," agreed Alice and Monica, raising their glasses and taking a sip.

Monica looked at her glass curiously. "Hmm. Sweeter than I imagined."

Oliver frowned. "Oh! This is your first glass?"

She nodded. Mater and Pater suburbs were dry areas, and the Birthing Homes were strictly no-alcohol zones. Alice had complied with the recommendation that children not drink alcohol until after their National Service was completed. It made sense to keep reproductive bodies as healthy as possible.

"Oops. Now I'm in trouble," said Alice, taking Monica's glass from her. She beckoned the waiter back and handed him the glass. "Sparkling water for my breastfeeding daughter, please."

The waiter smiled, nodded and retreated.

"It's not like anyone would have known," grumbled Monica.

Alice raised an eyebrow. "So. When are you letting the rabble into the main event?" she asked Oliver. On their way into the restaurant they had passed a side room where a few punctual guests milled about.

"Soon." He smiled. "I wanted you to enjoy the scenery in peace for a few minutes first."

"Oh, yes, and did you see that photo of the little boy strapped in his booster seat in the back of the car while his parents were slumped over in the front?"

"Oh, that was awful!"

"It was heroin, wasn't it?"

"Yes, and he was so skinny and malnourished. Looked more like a two-year-old than four."

"Then there was that seven-year-old girl who told her school bus driver she couldn't wake her parents up and they were starting to change colours. Turns out they'd been dead for days."

"No! What happened?"

"Drug overdose. Again."

"I saw that. Poor child had been looking after her sisters for days. Five years down to just nine months."

"Just awful."

"Dreadful. That's America for you, though, isn't it?"

"This is what we've saved our children from in Australia, thanks to the Equality Party. We're so lucky. Don't you think so, Monica?"

Monica heard her name and shook her head slightly, trying frantically to figure out what was expected of her. Her mind had wandered off while listening to the circle of exquisitely-preened women regale each other with the latest international horror stories of parental failures. She found it harder to listen to the stories these days, imagining a grown-up Oscar in the place of every neglected and abused child, fighting back waves of bile and tears. Usually she simply switched the news off or left the room.

"*Your* baby, for example, Monica. He'll always be well cared for by responsible adults who actually know what they're doing," said a tall, blonde woman standing opposite Monica, waving her champagne flute passionately in the air. Liquid sloshed inside the crystal, threatening to escape over the lip at any moment.

"Yes. It's wonderful," agreed Monica, spouting the socially acceptable line while wanting to shout at them all: *But I am a responsible adult! And I don't know what I'm doing but I'm sure I can learn. Why should I be punished just because a bunch of other parents are doing a crap job?* Instead she stood and sipped her sparkling apple juice from her wine glass and looked around for an escape route.

A jab at her left side, in her ribs, made her jump. She swung around and found herself looking up at a tall, middle-aged man with shoulder-length black curls and a handlebar moustache.

"Look at you—little Mon, all grown up." He grinned.

Monica frowned and stared at him. The eyes, that grin, were familiar...

"Uncle Pete?" she yelled in a stage whisper. "Is it you?"

"Sebastien tonight," he whispered into her ear. "But you can call me Baz," he said, releasing her and speaking in a normal voice, albeit with a perfect French accent.

Monica raised her eyebrows. "Does Mum know you're here? What are you *doing here*?"

"I wouldn't miss my big sister's fortieth birthday for the world. It's my sacred duty as her little brother to tease her for becoming an old, old woman two years before me."

Monica returned his embrace enthusiastically, but then stood back and returned to frowning at him. As thrilled as she was to see her long-lost childhood idol, his story sounded unlikely.

"Oh, really? You're going to be an old, old woman in two years, are you, *Sebastien*?" asked Alice, coming up behind him and tugging at a black curl which sprung back against his shoulder. "I guess this is a step in the right direction, then. Hormone therapy next?"

The cheeky grin left Pete's face and concern replaced it. "Alice, sis, how are you feeling? Are you sure you should be here? Do you want to sit down?" He looked around for a chair.

Alice shook her head and waved him away. "Nice of you to show up for my birthday, but you missed the pity boat by a couple of months. I'm fine now, really. My doctor thinks everything is going well, they got most of the cancer when they operated and the whizz-bang new medication seems to be taking care of the rest. I'm just tired and queasy, but I can live with that."

"Good," said Pete, distracted. "Yes, that's good."

"So, what brings you to our neck of the woods today, little brother? Crimes against croissants? Fraudulent French sticks?" She kept her tone light, but his presence worried her. Maybe it was the way he kept staring at her as though she was about to vanish.

"Nothing so outrageous, I assure you, Madame."

"Speeches soon," she said. "Then cake. Are you staying long?" She didn't say: *It might be nice if you at least stopped for a cup of tea and an explanation of where you've been for, oh, the past decade or so.* But it wasn't the time or the place to make a scene.

"I'll stay for cake," said Pete. "And Monica, where is your bundle of joy? I figured the little guy would still be attached to you."

"He's just over three months—closer to four months, now. A friend is looking after him back at the Birthing Home. I have plenty of photos, though, if you want to see." Monica raised her hand to her ear and let it hover while she waited for Pete to nod in approval.

"I'll leave you kids to it, then," said Alice, touching them both lightly on the shoulder. "I'll see if I can round people up for the formalities so we can all disappear and have a nap."

Alice stood at the front of the room and took shallow breaths. She tried to focus on the naval ship's lights on the bay. If she stared at the mirror just above Pete's head, right at the back of the room, she could watch the ship make its way to Crib Point. Her legs began to give way under her. She straightened and smiled as applause erupted around her. The Honourable Barbara Mathers was smiling and nodding at her, relinquishing the microphone to Oliver and stepping off the podium. Oliver glanced at Alice and cocked his head slightly, frowning.

She shook her head and tried to smile. He nodded and addressed the crowd.

"I'd like to thank everyone so much for coming tonight to help us celebrate my lovely soulmate's fortieth birthday. I'll be brief—you didn't come here to listen to me go on. I just wanted to say I'm so grateful for the twenty-five years Alice and I have already spent together. I'm thrilled at the medical advances that have beaten the cancer and allowed us to be together for, hopefully, another twenty-five years." He raised his glass. "To Alice."

Glasses around the room were raised and his sentiment echoed in a collective murmur. A woman dressed in black entered from a door at the back of the room, wheeling in an enormous cake awash with flame.

Oliver stepped back from the microphone and squeezed Alice's hand.

"Nearly there," he whispered.

The crowd burst into a polite rendition of 'Happy Birthday.' Alice gripped her glass and felt the temperature of the room seemingly rise with the hot air emanating from her guests' mouths. She saw spots start to appear randomly around the room and a high-pitched whistling interfered with the tune. Her face prickled and tightened, then seemed to lose all feeling. She slowly sank to the floor as her legs collapsed under her. Tired of fighting, she closed her eyes and gave in to the vertigo which washed over her, taking her floating away from the crowd, away from the nausea.

She was just... so... tired.

Then flashes.

Oliver's anxious face.

Monica holding her hand.

Pete whispering in her ear, "You're okay. You're going to be fine. Trust me."

A bed rolling up into a van. A mask placed over her face. Fingers brushing back her hair.

Bright lights. Mechanical blips. Needles. Drips.

Quiet.

Drifting.

Sleep.

CHAPTER 16

ALICE OPENED HER eyes. Dr Barnardos stood at the end of her bed, talking in low tones to Oliver. Oliver was frowning and shaking his head. Dr Barnardos crossed his arms and shook his head back.

Alice coughed. Both men turned to look at her.

"Morning," she said, brightly.

Oliver came to sit next to her. "How're you feeling?" He stared at her intently as though he'd be able to diagnose her ills by her response.

"Quite refreshed actually. What happened?"

"I've just been trying to find that out from Dr Barnardos. You collapsed at the party. I guess you didn't like my speech."

Oliver's attempt at a joke fell flat, overshadowed by his obvious irritation with the doctor.

"I wanted to wait until you were awake, Alice, so I could talk to you both," said Dr Barnardos.

"You've slept for fifteen hours straight, you know. It's mid-afternoon." Oliver said it as though she'd been slacking off, as though she'd missed a previously arranged engagement.

Frowning at the appearance of this sharp version of her usually warm and caring husband, Alice sat up on the bed and crossed her legs.

"Okay then, I'm awake now. What happened?"

Dr Barnardos walked the length of the bed, away from Oliver, and sat on a chair to Alice's left. He shuffled the chair around and fiddled with some papers, earning an impatient sigh from Oliver.

"Well," he started, then faltered.

Alice smiled at him encouragingly. Oliver glared. Dr Barnardos clasped his slender fingers together, took a deep breath, cleared his throat and began.

"The good news is, it's not the cancer. Tests show it's still in full remission. However, the hormone therapy that was used in combination with viral therapy prior to surgery appears to have potentially interacted with other drugs already in your system and seems to have perhaps rendered the other drugs temporarily inactive, causing certain reproductive functions to, ah, start functioning again."

"What? What does that mean? What's wrong with her?" Oliver burst out.

Alice placed her hand over his. "It's my contraceptive implant, isn't it?" she asked. Dr Barnardos nodded. "The hormone therapy for the cancer made it stop working?" He nodded again. "And now I'm pregnant?"

"Yes," he said quietly. "About eleven weeks, as far as we can tell. We'll do an ultrasound to confirm."

Alice gently moved her hand over her lower abdomen. The new curves she'd been noticing made more sense now. She idly wondered how soon her belly would pop out this time. During her second pregnancy it had happened soon after the twelve-week mark, almost overnight. If she was eleven weeks along now, it wouldn't be long before she started to show the distinctly rounded belly of a newly expectant mother.

"But she's forty years old," said Oliver.

"In the past, women have managed to conceive as late as fifty years old," said Dr Barnardos. "In fact, just a few decades ago the average age for a first-time mother was over thirty with many children conceived by women over the age of thirty-five. Growing numbers opted for medical intervention to deliberately conceive well into their forties. Of course, with this came many health problems for both the mother and the baby, which is why these days we..." He stopped his excited history lesson abruptly as he took in Oliver's stricken face.

"But I'm infertile. They said I couldn't, that I shouldn't..."

"Well, clearly getting on in years has made you more virile, my friend. Perhaps it's hanging about with children all day that's done it to you," chortled Dr Barnardos, misinterpreting Oliver's concerns and trying to lighten the mood.

"I'm terribly sorry, Alice," said the doctor, patting her hand to catch her attention. She'd been staring at Oliver for several minutes now and continued to do so as she withdrew her hand from the doctor's touch. He sighed and leaned back into his chair. "This has made it doubly difficult for you to recover from the surgery and the... unexpected result will be fed back to the research team immediately. I don't think this is a variable we considered. Our experience of cancer patients has clearly not included those as, ah, active as you two," he said. He cleared his throat, as though he were trying to swallow his own joke.

Alice willed Oliver to look at her. He turned from the window to face her with a worried frown. She cocked her head to the side and tweaked the corners of her mouth upwards, locking her eyes onto his and refusing to let go. She stroked the base of his thumb with hers and squeezed his fingers with her other hand. He raised his eyebrows. She smiled. He smiled too, then nodded.

"Will she need to go to a Birthing Home or can she stay at our apartment?" asked Oliver.

"Oh no, there's no need to relocate to a Birthing Home for a simple procedure. We'll book you in for tomorrow or the next day and you can go home a few hours afterwards. You'll experience some bleeding and a little discomfort for a day or so, but you should be feeling right as rain in no time. I expect the tiredness and nausea will dissipate within a week or so after some hormonal fluctuations." Dr Barnardos stood to leave, looking as satisfied as if he had solved global poverty.

Oliver also stood, his fists clenched. "She's not... we're not..."

Alice put her hand firmly over his. "We just need some time. It's a huge shock, I'm sure you can imagine," Alice explained calmly to the alarmed doctor.

He nodded, regarded Oliver warily, then picked up his folder and left the room, closing the door behind him.

"A procedure? You're not— We can't—" started Oliver.

"Of course not," said Alice. "But he's not the right person to argue about it with."

Oliver sat down heavily and stared at the wall. Alice took his hand again.

"We're having a baby," she whispered.

He turned to look at her, stunned and blinking quickly, tears starting to form.

"We're having a baby," he said, letting the tears roll down his cheeks in relief. He leaned over the bed, grabbed Alice around the waist and hugged her to him tightly. "Oh God, we're having a baby. You and me. Our baby. Finally."

Alice let him rest his head against her shoulder as her mind scrolled through their immediate options. The light in the room changed as the door slowly swung open again. Alice stared at the figure of her little brother, all grown up and filling the doorframe, hands clasped loosely at his hips.

"Okay if I come in?" he asked.

Alice nodded and he stepped across the threshold, pushing the door behind him until it closed. He locked it from the inside.

"We're having a baby," Alice told him, smiling.

He didn't return her smile. "I know. That's why I'm here."

"But... we only just found out. You can't know." Alice shook her head, a feeling of unease filling her chest.

"I found out when the lab uploaded your blood test results on Friday." Pete flashed her a small grin then. "I like to make sure I keep a close eye on my big sister's health and wellbeing. I came as quickly as I could."

"Well, that figures. It'd be too much to hope that you'd just dropped by to wish me a happy birthday, hey?" Alice's heart raced as she tried to keep things light.

Oliver raised an eyebrow. "Nice to see you again. Care to tell us what you've been up to all these years?"

Pete narrowed his eyes and chewed his lip thoughtfully. He glanced over his shoulder, out of the tiny window in the door and into the corridor.

"I can't stay long," he said. "I'm not supposed to be here."

"So, talk fast," said Oliver.

Pete frowned. "Alice, your pregnancy has come at a bad time."

"Yes, it's about twenty years too late," she remarked irritably.

"Charlotte White's suicide has sparked pockets of unrest in a number of Birthing Homes," he continued, ignoring her comment. "There have been reports of greater than usual resistance by some mothers to relinquishing their babies to appropriate Homes and there are certain... factions within the government who want to take immediate and forceful action to put a stop to these rebellions. Right now, we're managing to use our resources to persuade them to wait."

"We? Who's we?" asked Oliver.

Alice raised her hand and shook her head. "But we kept that out of the media. We had a deal."

Pete cocked his head and regarded her curiously. "There are ways to find—and transmit—information outside of the mainstream media, Alice. The news has been making its way through the teenaged population for some time now. As far as we can tell, it originated from a series of leaflets distributed near schools and a few Birthing Homes. The best theory we have is that the Conservative Party is using it as leverage to cause grassroots disruption." He paused and smiled wryly. "I guess they're finally taking note of the lessons learned from the rise of the Equality Party."

Oliver sighed. "There's that 'we' again. Who's 'we'?"

"Paper leaflets?" said Alice, confused. "What, just pieces of paper? No wonder it hasn't been picked up in any of our usual reports."

"Yes, paper leaflets," said Pete, grinning properly now. "Pretty ingenious, I thought. They've kept them well hidden—we've only managed to retrieve a handful."

Alice nodded and released a short, nervous laugh.

"First the backlash against the G.D.S., and now this. The political climate is very tense at the moment. Your pregnancy... they won't presume innocence, do you understand?" Pete knelt down beside Alice's bed and took her hand.

"I understand," Alice replied quietly. "Pete, I didn't do this deliberately."

"I know that. But I'm not the one you need to convince."

Alice nodded, trying to swallow the knot in her throat.

"I've added my number to your contacts. I'll do whatever I can to help you, just call me when you've decided what you want to do." Pete squeezed her hand and stood up. To Oliver he said, "I'm a monitor, part of an underground network keeping an eye on the Mater and Pater system. We were set up by the scientists who worked on the precursor to the G.D.S., to make sure it achieves its original purpose and no more. I can't tell you more than that right now."

"Oh, come on, are you serious?" said Oliver, half laughing. He looked at Alice. "Is he serious? Someone started a network of spies just to keep watch on how we raise our kids?"

Pete frowned at Oliver. "The Mater and Pater system was never just about raising kids, Ollie. It's a social system conceived and controlled by politicians whose primary goals are to retain power and amass wealth. The Equality Party may have been founded by idealists, but the government is run by politicians. You'd do well to remember that."

Oliver looked at Alice and opened his mouth to speak again. Alice shook her head.

"It's good to see you, Pete. It's a lot for us to take in, that's all. I'll call you if I need your help."

"Okay." He hesitated. "Stay safe, yeah? Don't do anything stupid."

"Not me. I'm the poster girl for planning and forethought." Alice smiled bravely. "You stay safe, too."

Pete nodded and left.

Alice turned to Oliver and took both of his hands in hers.

"We need to leave," she whispered. "Now."

Oliver sprang into action. He opened drawers to pull out the clothing he'd brought her that morning, assuming it would be an extended stay. He laid an outfit on the bed, shoes on the floor, and packed the rest into a small suitcase on wheels.

Alice pressed the surgical tape and cotton wool against the back of her hand and gritted her teeth as she slid the drip needle out. The alarm sounded as liquid dripped out of the end of the hollow tip.

"Turn it off at the wall!" she hissed to Oliver, who jumped up and flicked the switch on the wall next to the bedside table. They both froze as they waited to see if a nurse would come running. Minutes passed and the ward door remained closed. Alice swung her feet over the bed and leaned forward so Oliver could untie the back of her hospital gown. He helped her out of her gown and into her clothes. She slid her feet into her shoes and looked around the room, checking for anything they'd left behind.

"Ready?" she asked.

"Let's get out of here." He grinned and opened the ward door to check the hallway. It was empty. With a flick of his head to Alice, he slipped outside and walked calmly away, trusting her to follow.

CHAPTER 17

THEIR QUIET ELECTRIC car whooshed its way slowly up Nicholson Street in the descending twilight. Alice retrieved her earpiece from the overnight bag, attached it and scrolled through her messages. There were three missed calls and a message from Monica: *I want to be at the hospital, but I have to stay with Oscar. Will come when I can. Oliver says you're ok, I'll get news from him. Just wanted to say hi. Take care of you. Mon x.*

Alice messaged back: *Am ok. Out of hospital but tired. Will call tomorrow.*

She switched the display off and gazed out the window at an older woman walking her small, fluffy apartment-friendly dog. Owner and canine were wrapped in matching coats against the late autumn chill. What would her life be like as an older woman walking a toddler? Would they have matching coats too? Maters parented toddlers until they were in their fifties, but they had legions of help, full nights of sleep and state funding. Also, a lifetime of experience in raising children.

Compared to that, what did Alice have to offer this baby?

"Penny for your thoughts," said Oliver.

Alice looked at him, not sure where to start. She paused, then shook her head and shrugged.

Oliver smiled. "Let's not think, then. Let's just revel in our surprise parenthood tonight and deal with reality tomorrow."

"Not tomorrow," said Alice. "Tonight. I need to be at work tomorrow."

Oliver raised his eyebrows. She returned to watching the woman with her dog as they turned a corner and started to shrink into the distance.

"Feel free to revel until we get home," she said, placing her hand lightly on his thigh and leaning back into her seat.

"Hush, little baby, don't say a word. Daddy's gonna buy you a mocking bird," sang Oliver, belting out the words as though at a rock concert.

Alice laughed and closed her eyes. She now knew from experience that this horrible tiredness and nausea would soon pass, maybe even in a week or two if the doctor's estimate was correct. A lot would happen during that week or two, though, and she needed a plan.

Oliver swung the hospital bag full of Alice's clothing onto the sofa as Alice pushed the apartment door closed and placed her palm against the flat panel above the door handle. She deliberately took her time, listening to soft clicks as the internal bolts responded to her touch and slid across. Oliver's eyes bore into the back of her head, waiting. Finally, Alice turned to face him. He grinned, a silly bared-teeth kind of grin, and shrugged his shoulders like a small child. Alice frowned and put her hands on her hips, trying not to smile. The corners of her mouth twitched.

"Can we at least have a drink to celebrate before we get into the doom and gloom?" Oliver suggested.

"Green tea for me."

Alice sat down on the sofa and tucked her legs sideways underneath her.

"Ha. No bubbly for you for a while, hey?" he said, shaking his head. He was still smiling.

Alice softened her expression and shook her head. She searched his face for any sign that he was willing to deal with the reality of their situation.

"I'll get that cuppa, then. A beer for me, maybe," said Oliver, disappearing into the kitchen.

Alice grabbed the small screen lying on the coffee table and flicked the commercial shows on for a dose of normality. As she watched two sisters—wannabe chefs—argue over who'd put too much cream in a pasta sauce, the scene at the hospital seemed distant and surreal. She put a hand tentatively over her abdomen and pulled it back, feeling silly. As she did so she bumped her right breast and winced. The past couple of weeks the pain of her abdominal wound had subsided and she'd been able to sleep on her stomach again. Soon afterwards the tenderness in her newly swollen breasts had pushed her back to side slumber.

Alice gently touched her nipples and shivered as they burned and sent stabbing pains through the flesh. Had she known? Deep down, had she known the doctor was wrong when he told her it was the after-effects of the hormone therapy? How could a life have been growing inside of her for months without her knowing? Without her doctors knowing?

"It must be a tough little peanut," said Oliver, placing her mug of tea on the coffee table and sliding in beside her. He held his beer aloft and gazed at Alice's stomach. "Here's to you, little peanut," he said, swigging from the bottle.

Alice caught his eye, took his beer bottle and put it on the table next to her untouched tea. She held his gaze and took his right hand in both of hers and placed it on her stomach. They sat like that for a few minutes, staring at their hands together covering their baby.

"He's going to need to be a tough little peanut," Alice observed quietly. "Or she."

"Well, *she's* already survived cancer treatment and major surgery," said Oliver, sitting back and grinning. He sized up her stomach and frowned. "I guess I can see how the surgeons could have missed it. The stomach is fairly high, the uterus would have still been well below the pubic bone at that point."

Alice smiled and cupped her hand around Oliver's cheek. "Enough with the biology lesson." She leaned over and kissed him gently on the lips, then pressed her cheek against his.

Oliver wrapped his arms around her and pulled her over on top of him.

"Ouch!" complained Alice as she fell onto him, crushing her chest. She disentangled herself from him pushing awkwardly and painfully into his thigh as she did. "Jeez, careful, Ollie. Lady with a baby here. And sore boobs to boot."

He grinned sheepishly.

Alice sat up, adjusted her clothing and sighed heavily. "We need to talk about this."

"I know."

Alice paused, not knowing where to begin.

"Is there a process?" asked Oliver.

"Sure. It's called abortion."

Oliver's face darkened. "Surely there's a process of appeal, I mean? It's not like this is our fault. We haven't broken any rules."

Alice turned back to the screen and watched as the blonde sister turned red in the face and threw a plastic container of cream at the wall. She stormed out of the kitchen and the brunette sister watched in staged indignation as thick, white rivers oozed down the vintage wallpaper.

Alice stared at their own walls, a fresh, soft mint to complement the plush stone-coloured carpet. A long way from the child-friendly low-pile rugs of the Mater and Pater suburbs.

"Ollie, it's not about anything we've done. It's about what's best for society, what's best for the baby. The risks of giving birth to this baby are huge. I'm older, my health is unstable, the foetus has been exposed to god-only-knows-what drugs, alcohol and other foreign substances. I haven't been taking the proper pre-or-early pregnancy vitamins, so spina bifida is a risk. And on top of it all, there's the birthing end of the business. I've already had two caesareans. There's a possibility my uterus could rupture, killing both me and the baby."

As she spoke, she started to wonder whether she had done the wrong thing, leaving the hospital. When she'd walked out, her only thought had been to protect her baby. A soon-to-be warm, soft, snuggly bundle in her arms. Just like baby Oscar. She'd wanted to run, far away. With a pang of guilt, she remembered Monica's thinly veiled plea for help to plan her own escape. Which she'd chosen to ignore.

"Then again, there's a possibility that the baby will be just fine. And so will you," said Oliver.

Alice shook her head. "Even if you leave aside the medical issues, there are the political issues. They won't allow me to have a baby, not in this climate. *Illegal baby born to Executive Director in the Department of Genetics and Reproduction.*" She laughed wryly, sweeping her hands above her head as though imagining a banner with the words written across it. "Can you imagine it? The press would have a field day. The government would never let it happen."

Her nausea started to rise again, her chest clenched and her breathing came short and shallow.

"We can't *do* this, Ollie. I was wrong. It's pointless, it won't work," she said suddenly, her tone dull, as though announcing the end to a lengthy discussion about fitting in a hatha yoga class after work and before dinner.

Oliver knew that tone. He grabbed her wrist and pulled her arm towards him roughly.

"Don't," he warned. "Don't you dare dismiss our baby's life like that."

Alice shook him free and shuffled to the other end of the sofa.

"I'm not dismissing anything, Ollie. I'm simply being a realist. You might want to try it out some time."

She curled her feet up underneath her and turned the volume up on the show. Brunette sister and Blonde sister were crying and hugging. Oliver knelt down in front of her and tried to take her hands. She shook him off and refused to meet his gaze. Oliver grabbed the screen from her, stabbed at it to turn the projection off and threw it at the ground.

"Look at me, Alice."

She turned her head to face him, but the pain in his eyes was too much to assimilate. She closed her eyes and shook her head.

"This is not about politics, it's not about questioning your allegiance to the Equality Party or even doubting that you have the best interests of society at heart," he said. "This is the life of our son. Or our baby daughter. This is non-negotiable. I won't let you approach this like some publicity crisis or policy problem to be worked through."

His jibe at her day job brought her back to life. She opened her eyes and stared him down furiously.

"This is not a problem to solve at all, Oliver. This is a problem that can never *have* a solution which is acceptable to all parties," she said flatly. "Enough with your fucking idealism already."

She pushed him away, rose from the sofa and stalked towards their bedroom door. She paused briefly mid-course to take one last stab.

"Why would I want to spend all my days changing shitty nappies and wiping up snot like you, anyway?"

She walked through the door and slammed it behind her.

"Jesus, you can be a bitch when you want to be, Alice Mooney," he yelled through the door.

She heard the screen slam against the outside of the door, bouncing off and breaking into several pieces. Minutes later the front door of the apartment opened and slammed shut. In the silence of their bedroom, Alice curled up on their luxuriously soft bed, her cheek against the 2000-thread Egyptian cotton, and started to moan, keening loudly for the tiny baby that could never be.

An electronic jingle blasted Alice's ear. In the dawn light she slapped at her bedside table to turn the alarm off. She shut her eyes again, trying to contain the post-sobbing headache that pulsed through her forehead. One quick glance had been enough to tell her the other half of the marital bed was empty. She listened for kitchen sounds. Kettle boiling, bread being slotted into the toaster, the clink of cutlery being unloaded from the dishwasher.

Nothing.

Still fully dressed from the day before, Alice padded quietly out into the lounge room, half expecting to find Oliver asleep on the sofa.

Empty.

Alice poked her belly, just above her pubic bone, and felt the resistance, like a small armoured bubble, her womb poking up and over. She smoothed her hand over the curved mound which had formed, announcing a secret she could no longer hide. Third pregnancies. Clearly, they popped out even earlier than second ones. Alice didn't know anyone who'd had a third pregnancy. Two was the maximum. Successful or not, that was all you were allowed. It was natural selection, they said. The planet was overpopulated, after all, and resources grew ever scarcer.

She paused, shutting down the part of her brain that dealt with useless emotions such as pain and regret, and steeled herself for the day ahead.

After a glass of water and a few crackers—a nod to the morning sickness—she washed, dressed and left the apartment.

CHAPTER 18

ALICE HELD HER palm against the office building's elevator security box and pressed the button for level twelve. She looked down and realised that if she stood up straight and curved her back a little, her belly was obvious to anyone who was looking for it. As she stepped out on level twelve, she wondered if the news of her pregnancy had leaked yet. She wasn't putting much faith in doctor-patient confidentiality for something this scandalous.

"Alice."

"Olivia."

Alice nodded at her surprised assistant as she paced past her desk and into her own office. She sat at her desk and stared at the screen as icons whirred and arranged themselves, using the time to compose her thoughts.

Maybe if she just pretended everything was normal, it would be. Maybe the baby would just stop growing and *poof!* she could step back to yesterday when things were simple and her husband, daughter and grandson were one big happy family. Yesterday—before there were impossible decisions to be made.

"Alice."

"Chu." Alice looked up as he hobbled into her office and sat down, staring at her intensely.

"No cane?"

"It's healing. A few more weeks with the moon-boot and I should be right."

Alice nodded and tapped at her screen, starting up her e-mail program and checking the intranet notice boards for bulletins.

"Surprised to see you in today," said Chu.

"It's Tuesday."

"I seem to remember you being carted off in an ambulance from your own birthday party less than forty-eight hours ago. You don't think you should take a bit of time off? To get things sorted?"

Alice frowned and looked up. "I've broken no laws, Chu. This is not your concern."

"You're pregnant, yes?"

"Oh, for goodness' sake, is nothing sacred around here?"

Chu shrugged. "As far as I can trace it, the honourable Barbara Mathers requested a health status update from your doctor, who obliged, of course. She told the *dis*honourable Graeme Smythe and he's spent the morning gleefully letting it slip to anyone who'll listen. Which, when it's gossip as juicy as this, is pretty much everyone."

"Fine. Thanks for the warning."

"I'm sure it'll be all over the media before dinnertime. But back to the immediate problem of your actual pregnancy."

Alice rolled her eyes and gave an exaggerated royal wave.

"Speak," she said.

"Unauthorised. You're forty years old and this is your third pregnancy. I'd say that's at least three contraventions of the Reproduction Act, including population containment, illegal natural conception, and failure to adequately safeguard against genetic diseases. I'd say that makes it well and truly my business."

"You're assuming intent to procreate. There was no intent. You should be talking to the research team who screwed up my cancer treatment and illegally interfered with a state-issued contraceptive device," she responded calmly, meeting Chu's eyes.

His expression remained deadpan. Alice smiled inwardly, knowing she'd put a major chink in his argument.

"And the onus on you to deal with the unscheduled pregnancy responsibly?"

"There is none," she replied.

"But surely you're required to be seen to be complying with government policy?"

"There is no government policy dealing with unintended natural, subsequent pregnancies. Only unsanctioned intercourse prior to entry into a Birthing Home. Existing policy and legislation relies heavily on the infallibility of the contraceptive devices. For the past couple of decades that's been a reasonable assumption."

Chu raised an eyebrow and grinned.

"Did I pass?" asked Alice, smiling wryly.

Chu nodded and rocked back and forth in his chair.

"You'll do."

Alice went back to checking her e-mails. There were several requests for media interviews following her dramatic exit from her birthday party. A communications plan draft from Mary for the new G.D.S. campaign. Invoices requiring approval. It all seemed a little irrelevant. Chu sat watching her, tapping his fingertips together.

"So, what *are* you going to do now?" he asked.

"Get through the day," said Alice.

Chu nodded and stood. "Well, let me know if you need anything. Spew bucket, pickles, ice-cream. You know, anything. I was a deft hand at back rubs during my National Service." He stretched his arms and cracked his knuckles.

"Thanks."

Chu left, shutting the door behind him. Alice turned back to her computer and opened up Mary's communications plan. A notification appeared, a calendar request for a meeting with Barbara Mathers and Graeme Smythe at nine-thirty. Ten minutes. The office rumour mill had wasted no time in heralding her arrival.

She tapped her earpiece and checked for personal messages. Just one, from Oliver.

I'm sorry I left last night. I was wrong. I'll be home after my shift tonight... please tell me we can work this out. This is our baby, Alice, yours and mine. We've waited 20 years for this chance. I love you. xx.

Alice wrote back: *OK, we'll talk. See you tonight.* After a slight hesitation, she added: *xx.*

She placed the phone gently on the desk and tried to concentrate on the communications plan, reading three pages without seeing a single word. Her bladder distracted her. She checked the time and stared at her closed door. Four minutes. Just enough time for a toilet run in between level twelve and thirteen. She locked the computer screen, picked up her phone and opened her office door, steeling herself for the stares.

For once, Alice had Barbara's full attention. She had barely taken her eyes off Alice's abdomen since she'd walked through her office door. Graeme sat uncomfortably between the two women like an unwilling and unwanted mediator.

"Your doctor seems to think it's an accident," said Barbara finally.

Alice nodded.

"And yet you left the hospital in secret, refusing to deal with the matter immediately."

Alice met her eyes briefly then looked out of the window at the grey clouds. It had been raining since the night before and, here on level thirteen, the mists seemed to creep right up to the glass, fogging up the inside. Droplets slid down to the sill like tears. Alice drew a slight breath and turned back to the minister, waiting for her to get to her point.

Barbara rapped her fingers on the desk, stretched and cracked her neck.

"You've just turned forty, you have a daughter, a grandson and a demanding career which you seem dedicated to. Your partner is a Pater so you have access to small children to exercise any excess maternal instinct you may have. You've been undergoing cancer treatment for the past three months, so deliberately getting pregnant would be the last thing on your mind. Leaving an institution against professional advice is uncharacteristic of you. Your behaviour prior to this incident suggests you're a rational, law-abiding woman." Barbara stopped her clinical assessment abruptly and looked expectantly at Graeme.

"We don't believe you've done this deliberately, Alice," he said gently. The unfamiliar kindness sat strangely in his tone. It made Alice's skin crawl. "But we are baffled as to why you haven't dealt with it immediately."

Alice wasn't sure what to tell him. She wasn't entirely certain, herself, why she hadn't 'dealt with it immediately.' Something in her had just snapped when the doctor spoke of a new life—inside her—created against all odds with the man she had always loved, sometimes against all reason. When the doctor started talking about *medical procedures* she had felt the urge to just run. Run fast, hard and far.

In the cold light of day, it seemed childish. She had no way to provide for a baby, the risks of disease or deformity were extremely high and, let's face it, she was old. Her own daughter had a baby. It was obscene for her to be a pregnant grandmother.

"I needed some time to think things through. This has all come as quite a shock, as I'm sure you can imagine," she finally replied.

The sound of Barbara's grinding teeth filled the otherwise silent room.

"What 'things' exactly? I'm unclear what you could possibly have to think through. If you're actually *thinking* you would see that there is only one sensible option here. What you mean is you needed to process your *emotions*." She spat out the word with a scowl on her face.

Alice felt something like butterflies in her lower belly, like a soft wing tickling the very top of her pelvis. She gasped slightly and resisted the urge to bring her hand to her stomach. She bit on the inside of both of her lips and straightened her back.

"Is it the position of the department that I am required to terminate the pregnancy?" she asked.

Barbara glared at Graeme.

Graeme frowned and shifted in his seat. "Now, Alice, we're here to talk about what's best for you, what's best for the, ah, pregnancy and what's best for society as a whole." The attempt at kindness melted into sarcasm in his limited vocal repertoire.

"It's my decision, then?" asked Alice, glancing from Graeme to Barbara and back again.

Barbara looked away and stabbed at her screen, which lay on the desk in front of her.

"Well, we imagine you'll come to the *right* decision, of course," said Graeme.

"But there's nothing in law that covers this situation. I am not to be compelled either way?"

"No."

"You realise, of course, that all the other laws still apply?" said Barbara in a hard voice. "If you're indulging in some little romance about raising this baby with your lover in the countryside with blooming wattles and spring lamb, you'd better wake up and smell the Birthing Home."

"He's not my lover, he's my husband," said Alice quietly, turning the ring on her finger for emphasis. "So, you would be requiring me to leave my position and enter a Birthing Home. And after that?"

Barbara pursed her lips.

"I need all the information if I'm to make a *rational* decision about my current situation," Alice pointed out, trying to keep the sarcasm out of her voice but failing a little.

Barbara waved her hand at Graeme and went back to stabbing at her phone. Graeme cleared his throat and consulted his notes.

"If you decide to continue with the pregnancy, we consider it to be better for the emotional health of society if you do it privately. You would be required to leave Melbourne and travel to a place where you are not likely to be seen by the general public. After birthing the child and nursing it to the age of six months, the child would be transferred, anonymously, to a Home within visiting distance of your current residence. You would then return to work here and be permitted to visit the child each Sunday in the capacity of an Aunty, as to an orphaned child." His offer delivered, Graeme folded his hands in his lap and waited.

Barbara started to talk but Alice wasn't listening. Another butterfly kiss in her abdomen, then a quick wriggle, like a fish caught in a net. She stopped breathing, waiting for another movement.

"Well?" said Barbara irritably.

"I'm sorry?" Alice blinked.

"I think the offer is generous considering the circumstances, don't you?"

"I think you have no other choice, given the current legislation," said Alice.

"The legislation is scheduled for urgent review," interjected Graeme.

"But it won't act retrospectively. It's not relevant to my case." Alice stood. "I'll consider my circumstances and inform you of my decision as soon as possible."

"And remember, you're not to discuss this matter with any person who is not already aware of the situation. That includes the media," said Graeme as he escorted her to the office door.

"Of course," said Alice, reflecting that this was not a difficult agreement, given that most of the staff seemed to know already, which meant the media wouldn't be far behind.

"So. Some party, huh?" Mary dropped herself down on a chair in front of Alice's desk and cradled her large takeaway coffee cup.

"Yeah, some party," agreed Alice, looking up from her tablet and wondering if the whole department was planning to parade through her office one by one and throw obtuse opening lines at her.

"Looking up maternity wear?"

"Reading your fascinating communications plan about how we're going to convince the good people of Australia that the G.D.S. is the best thing they've ever seen."

Mary's shoulders started to heave as the belly laugh travelled up and exploded out of her mouth, shaking her coffee and sending hot, brown droplets shooting out over her lap.

"Ooooh, that's priceless," she hooted, holding onto her side. "The accidental-natural-conception lady selling lab-only conception."

Alice raised her eyebrows and passed Mary a box of tissues.

"You done?"

Mary chuckled, cleared her throat, giggled, sighed, then sat back and wiped her eyes.

"Yeah, I think so." She gave one last snort and then put on her serious face. "So. What are you going to do?"

"I'm thinking through my options."

"You have options?" Mary sipped her coffee, waiting for Alice to elaborate. Alice swiped at her tablet and twitched her nose. "I'm assuming the iron lady has already put in her ten cents?"

"The Honourable Barbara Mathers was very accommodating," said Alice, flaring her nostrils.

"Mm-hmm. What *is* the law about unintentional impregnations of forty-year-old women who were on state-sanctioned contraception?"

"There isn't one."

"Ha. The Honourable Barbara Mathers must be spewing."

Alice grinned. "Ms Mathers was somewhat perturbed by the notion of an unplanned pregnancy that appeared to be out of her jurisdiction, yes."

"Awesome. Have you spoken to lover-boy about it yet?"

Alice took a deep breath and reached for her earpiece. She swiped it with her index finger. No further messages.

"He's already thought through our options. He doesn't like them."

"Couldn't they just let him raise the baby? He's a Pater, he knows kid stuff."

Mary's own children lived an eight-hour drive away, in Adelaide. She'd moved to Melbourne for work three years ago and rarely spoke of them, travelling back to visit them maybe twice a year. As far as she was concerned, the system of birthing children then handing them over was a stroke of genius. She didn't really understand why anyone would want to raise their own kids if they could avoid it. Unlike Barbara Mathers, however, Mary was willing to allow people their own preferences.

"That option wasn't raised, no."

"You won't just terminate?"

Alice fiddled with her earpiece, swiping through pictures of Oscar sleeping, Oscar squinting, Oscar on his tummy struggling to hold up his heavy head and looking inexplicably surprised.

"Ollie doesn't want to."

"And you?"

A slight jiggle in her uterus, a feather-like stroke, like a finger reaching out to her. *Hey, I'm here. I'm real.* Alice brought her hand to her stomach and stopped breathing. Not eleven weeks pregnant then, thought Alice, surely at least thirteen or even fourteen weeks if she was feeling movement. Dr Barnardos had been wrong.

"I don't... it's complicated. There are risks. And practical hurdles."

Mary placed her coffee on the desk, leaned forward and covered Alice's hand with her own.

"I wasn't asking what the practical arrangements were. I was asking what you want. Figure that out and then go from there."

Alice stared at Mary's hand. At thirty years of age her skin was still smooth and soft. Short nails, no rings. Alice's own hands were starting to show signs of wear. Not quite wrinkles, but texture, as though the skin had shrunk and tightened around the natural contours of the underlay. She withdrew her hands and stared at them, inspecting the two brown spots which had appeared on the back of her left hand last summer. Too old. She was too old to be pregnant.

Flutters in her stomach, more insistent.

Tears splashed onto Alice's hand, distorting and magnifying the age spots. She blinked and let the tears fall faster.

"I want my baby," Alice whispered.

Mary nodded. She sat back and picked up her coffee again.

"Okay. So, we start from there."

Alice nodded and pulled out a tissue from the box on her desk. She wiped her eyes, took a deep breath and sat up straight, still unable to meet Mary's gaze, but nodded again, more firmly this time.

"You should work from home today. That communications plan is long, weighty and needs work. Such an important document requires your full attention," said Mary haughtily, rising from her chair and sticking her nose dramatically in the air.

Alice smiled and slipped her tablet into her handbag. The thought of anything Mary had drafted being less than perfect was laughable.

"You're absolutely right. Important and urgent. Certainly not something I can give my full attention to here in the office."

"Good girl. I'll see you tomorrow, then."

CHAPTER 19

ALICE'S HEELS CLICKED against the concrete, echoing through the otherwise silent basement car park. Alice slid into the driver's seat of her car and slammed the door quickly behind her, enveloping herself in the safe stillness of familiarity. In contrast to almost everything else in her life, her vehicle was a tip. She breathed in the smell of discarded burger wrappers, weeks old. Fossilised used tissues hid under the seats, and a dried-up apple core sat in the centre console in a sticky pool of melted ice cream. A single, stalwart yellow plastic leaf hung from the rear-view mirror. Once upon a time it had spread its fresh, lemony fragrance throughout the car, masking the scent of cheerful decay. Bereft of its former powers of freshness, it now acted as a reminder to Alice that she really should clean the car out at some point.

Nobody ever used this car except for her. Trips out with Ollie were in his car, which was professionally cleaned once a week, thanks to the Home budget. Another perk of Paterdom. He transported kids in that car, it had to be clean.

"*Where would you like to go today, Alice?*" the car politely enquired.

"Nowhere yet," replied Alice, cursing the law which required all cars to be self-driving. It had reduced road fatalities by ninety-three percent, she knew, but she still missed driving herself. Now, she leaned against the headrest and closed her eyes, wondering if anyone would notice if she just had a quick nap. She'd just started to drift off when her earpiece buzzed. Reluctantly, she tapped it and checked the display. Monica.

"Hello?"

"Mum? Are you okay? I know you were going to call me, but I was worried and I wanted to check on you, and I won't keep you long but I just wanted to make sure..." Monica's babbled stream of words petered out.

Alice froze, not sure where to start.

"Mum? Are you still there?"

"Yes. Yes, I'm still here. I'm okay."

"Is it... are you still in the hospital? Do they think the... has it come back? Did the treatment not work?" Monica paused as Alice's mind ticked over, trying to form the words she needed to say. "Mum, please, just tell me. I can handle it."

Alice laughed, a tinny, bitter sound. "I'm pregnant." There was silence at the end of the line. "I'm going to have a baby," she clarified.

"But... but you're old!"

"Thanks."

"Oh, god, sorry, I didn't mean—"

"Yes, you did." Alice laughed, properly this time.

"But you're forty."

"Yes."

"And on contraceptives. And you've had cancer treatment. And surgery."

"Yes, yes and yes."

"But how? What? I don't understand."

"You're not the only one."

"Wow. What are you going to do? Who knows? Have you spoken to Oliver? Your work? Will you be in trouble? How far along are you?"

"Um, I don't know. Everyone at work plus Oliver plus the doctor knows. They're trying to contain it. I'm not technically in trouble but they're not happy. I don't know how far along I am. The doctor estimates I'm about eleven weeks, but I'm guessing at least fourteen weeks." Alice paused, trying to decide how much to tell Monica, trying to decide if she was ready for this to be real or not. "I felt the baby move today. Just little flutters," she said quietly.

"Wow."

"Yes."

There was an extended silence as they both processed this information.

"Monica?"

"Mmm?"

"You can't tell anyone about this."

"I know."

"I'll come and see you as soon as I can. I have to figure a few things out first. It's complicated. Okay? Are you okay?"

"I think so. Of course. You go. I'll be fine. Oscar is fine."

"Okay. Bye then."

"Bye, Mum. Take care of you. And the little one."

Alice ended the call and stilled herself to see if the baby would move again, to convince her that it wasn't all a dream. It didn't move; maybe it was sleeping. Alice wished she could sleep too, but she needed to work things out with Oliver first. Tonight was too far away.

"Drive. To Oliver's Birthing Home," she commanded the car.

"*Certainly, Alice. I will take you to Oliver's Birthing Home. Estimated travel time: thirty-seven minutes.*"

The car pulled out of the car park, headed towards the freeway.

CHAPTER 20

A SMALL BOY SAT against the window behind the curtain, hiding himself and his collection of miniature cars from the world. He chose a green one from the pile in his lap and placed it carefully on the window sill, leaning forward and twisting his head to view it from all angles. He adjusted it several times to make sure it sat exactly flush alongside the purple car, which in turn lined up with the blue and the red and the orange cars next in line.

Alice watched from the curb, sitting in her car, transfixed by the small boy's movements. She wondered if he had any idea that he was sitting in full view of passers-by on the footpath or road.

The trials of adulthood made childhood appear simple. A series of seemingly pointless activities to pass the time until you grew up and had to somehow function in the world. To a child, though, their world is complicated, frustrating, frightening and exhilarating, often in equal measure and sometimes all at once.

The boy at the window twisted sideways suddenly, as though responding to a cue just out of the frame. He lifted his knees and the remaining cars streamed down from his lap and bounced onto the window sill, scattering the carefully arranged line-up of vehicles. The boy stared at them for a moment, blinking in surprise. The corners of his mouth turned down and a blush crept out from his ears and across his cheeks. He clenched his fists and opened his mouth in a distressed rage, jumping up and kicking the cars, the curtain and the window. An adult figure appeared behind him almost immediately to drag his tantrum away from the potential danger of broken glass.

"*You have arrived at your destination,*" the car reminded her helpfully.

"Yes, I know," she muttered, and dragged herself out of the car to face her husband.

"Hey." Oliver looked mildly frazzled as he opened the door. "Ellie, leave Tom alone. He needs some space right now," he called over his shoulder.

The little girl ignored him and continued to poke her brother in the toe with a puzzle piece while he scrunched himself up on the sofa, shoulders heaving.

"Ooooooow!" screamed Ellie as Tom retaliated by kicking her in the head, sending her flying backwards onto her bottom.

Oliver left the door open as he ran to pick up Ellie and comfort her, while telling her off for annoying her brother.

"Maybe I should go," said Alice, standing awkwardly in the doorway.

Oliver looked tired and irritated, as though the jovial part of his self had been removed overnight. He sat on the sofa next to Tom and clamped his arms around Ellie to prevent her from charging again. He spoke softly in her ear. She thrashed around and shrieked a couple of times but gradually settled on his lap, glaring at Tom and periodically jerking her body to test her restraints.

"No, stay," said Oliver quietly, without looking up.

"I could... We could... talk tonight. It doesn't have to be now. I'm sorry, I didn't think..."

"Stay."

Alice nodded and shuffled a few steps into the room, feeling like an intruder. Both children registered her presence at once and poked their heads up like meerkats testing for danger or excitement.

"Aya! Aya, Aya, Aya!" yelled Ellie, making one last, successful, attempt to break free from Oliver's lap and bounding over to Alice, smashing into her knees and wrapping her arms around her legs.

"Oof!" Alice braced herself at the last minute, narrowly avoiding tumbling backwards.

"Hi, Alice," Tom mumbled, who, after briefly looking her up and down, had clearly judged her unworthy of either fear or interest and went back to sulking, spinning the wheels of a toy car that he had salvaged from the earlier wreckage.

The whole scene felt so normal that Alice was at a loss as to where to start with Oliver.

Oliver rubbed his face and twitched his nose. "Cuppa?"

"Yes. Green tea, please."

Oliver smiled. "Sure. Still feeling nauseous?"

Alice took a few more steps towards him, dragging a giggling Ellie along on her leg.

"A little. Not so much now. I still can't face coffee, though."

Oliver disappeared into the kitchen and Alice followed him, swooshing Ellie along faster as they moved from carpet to glossy, slippery tiles. Somewhere between the microwave and the refrigerator Ellie fell off and lay sprawled on her back and laughed gleefully—a deep, satisfying chortle.

Ah, the life of a toddler, thought Alice, smiling.

"Up, up, Aya! Cuddles!"

Alice picked up the little girl and slung her over her shoulder so that her legs kicked the air and her little fists pummelled Alice's back while she squealed with delight. Alice turned sharply to her left, then to her right, sending golden curls flying behind her back.

"Where did Ellie go, Pater? She was here a minute ago. Where could she be?"

Oliver smiled weakly but didn't join in the game. "You're not really supposed to be lifting weights in your condition..."

"I here, Aya, I here!" yelled Ellie.

Alice pulled Ellie back over her shoulder and held her up, regarding her with feigned astonishment.

"Why, so you are! That's a relief!"

"Now I do cuddles!" declared Ellie, throwing her body forward and wrapping her arms around Alice's neck, her slobbery mouth and snotty nose snuggling into Alice's collarbone.

Alice looked down and sighed at the dark, wet marks Ellie had left on her top. At least she wasn't planning to go anywhere else today.

"I spoke to my boss," she started.

Oliver dipped the tea bag up and down in the boiling water, pulling it back over the lip of the mug to squeeze most of the water out, and plopped it in the sink to cool. He picked up Alice's tea mug and his own coffee and turned. Alice stepped back towards the bench, allowing him to pass, which he did without touching or acknowledging her. The Alice-and-Ellie conglomerate followed him into the lounge room and sat at the table in front of the tea.

"They know, then?" asked Oliver, crossing his legs and blowing on his coffee.

"Yes, of course."

"You went to work this morning?"

"Yes."

Oliver shook his head and stood slightly to peer over the back of the sofa. Tom hadn't moved. Oliver sat back down again and watched Ellie as she sat on Alice's lap and played with her earrings.

"You've scheduled a procedure, then?"

Alice ignored him and gently batted Ellie's tiny fingers away. She pulled at Alice's necklace instead, trying to bite the square, blue beads.

"I think I felt the baby move this morning," she said quietly, running a hand over Ellie's soft, white hair. "I'm, um..."

"What?" Oliver stared at her intently, waiting and encouraging. Barely hoping.

"I'm scared." Her voice caught on the second word and the tears started to flow again. Twice in one day. It must be the hormones, thought Alice irritably.

"Rooooooooar!!" yelled Ellie suddenly.

Both adults jumped. The toddler seemed satisfied and grinned, waving her clawed hands at Oliver and baring her teeth.

"I scary too! I a big scary monster!"

Alice laughed and wiped at her face. Oliver put his mug down, walked around the table and held his hands out to Ellie.

"Come here, big, scary monster," he said, swinging her up and onto his hip. "Do you know what we do to big, scary monsters around here?"

"We tickle them!" yelled Tom, jumping up from the sofa and charging at his little sister.

Oliver swung Ellie up at the last minute. Tom swerved to try to catch her, misjudged and crashed into Oliver front-on at waist height, sinking a clenched fist into him as he went down. Oliver, winded and caught off-balance, fell backwards. Alice watched in horror as Ellie's impossibly tiny head with the bouncing curls flew through the air, smacked into the kitchen counter and fell to the floor, crumpled and unmoving.

Tom started crying and clutched his arm where it had connected with a wooden chair.

"Ellie," croaked Oliver. "Ellie! Ellie!" He scrambled up from the floor, meeting Alice at the small girl's side a split second later.

"Don't move her," said Alice, as much to herself as anything, as she held out a hand to touch the silent body.

"Of course I wasn't going to move her, what do you think I am, an idiot? I know what I'm doing, get away from her!" he yelled, physically blocking Alice.

"I'll call an ambulance," said Alice, tapping her earpiece and barking, "Call. Ambulance here." She heard the emergency services operator come on the line. She turned away and cupped a hand around her ear to try to drown out Tom's wailing. "Is she breathing?" she asked Oliver, who was holding two fingers to a little, limp wrist. He glanced at Alice and nodded. "Yes, breathing. Okay, thanks. No, we won't move her." She ended the call, picked up Tom and went to open the front door as instructed by the operator.

Oliver sat and held Ellie's hand.

"She's not moving! Why isn't she moving? Ellie!" Tom's voice wobbled as his hysteria rose, his head twisting around in Alice's arms as he tried to see his sister.

Sitting heavily on an armchair, Alice rocked Tom and hushed him, telling him over and over that everything would be fine. His breath came in ragged gasps and Alice felt a warm liquid start to seep over her top and into her lap.

"I did pee in my pants!" cried Tom, mortified.

"It's okay, sweetheart, it's okay. We'll get a towel. Ollie, towels?"

"Hall cupboard."

Alice hunched over and carried the soggy little boy awkwardly to the bathroom, leaving him briefly while she tracked back to grab three towels.

"Okay, let's get you stripped off and into a shower," she said, running the hot water while she peeled his smelly layers off and dumped them on the floor.

He calmed down as the warm water cascaded down his back and over his face. Alice closed the shower door and left him to turn in circles, face upturned into the jet stream, while she yanked her own wet clothes off and sponged herself down with a flannel. Wrapped in a towel, she ran quickly to the study where she knew Oliver kept his spare clothes.

By the time they were both clean, dry and dressed in fresh clothes, the ambulance had arrived and the paramedics were preparing to lift Ellie onto a trolley. Alice and Tom stood and watched from the periphery, Alice's hand resting lightly on Tom's damp hair.

Oliver hovered around the paramedics, trying to stay as close to Ellie as possible without getting in their way. Once she was strapped onto the gurney Oliver held her hand and touched her pale, still face, cupping a tiny cheek in his enormous palm and stroking it with his thumb. He bent down, whispering something in her ear, and kissed her on the forehead.

A paramedic put his hand on Oliver's arm and nodded to him. Oliver stepped back to allow the gurney to roll out of the house. He turned and seemed mildly surprised to see Alice and Tom standing there, a silent couple, blinking off to the side.

"I'll go with her in the ambulance," he said, clearing his throat halfway through the phrase.

Alice nodded. "I'll call Margery. I'll stay with Tom until she gets here."

Oliver's gaze travelled from Alice down to Tom and back again. He frowned.

"We'll be fine," said Alice.

Oliver opened his mouth and closed it again. He nodded, glanced briefly at Tom and strode out the front door, clipping the door frame on the way in his disoriented state.

CHAPTER 21

COLOURS FLICKERED ALL around Alice in the grey light. Her legs were warm where she had covered them in a blanket but her upper body grew colder by the minute and her hands were icy. Rather than get up to turn the lights and heating on, she pulled the blanket further up her body, tucking it awkwardly behind her shoulders and shoving her freezing fingers between her warm thighs.

The screen was muted but she watched intently as a tall, confident presenter with a lovely green paisley jacket showed a tearful woman around her newly decorated house. If the subtitles were to be believed, the woman, a domestic servant named Jill who had the face of a capuchin monkey and a strange-looking hat to match, had fallen on hard times after her employer had died, leaving her bereft of her life's purpose, a roof over her head, and a weekly pay packet. The tiny one-bedroom flat in the middle of nowhere was all she could afford with her new part-time job as a packer at the local warehouse. But now it had a lavender suede sofa and freshly painted walls, so all was right with the world.

Alice wondered if a lavender suede sofa could improve her life, too. Perhaps she could scatter drops of lavender essence all over it and pretend she was lying down in a field of lavender. She closed her eyes briefly and pictured it: rays of soft sunlight, swathes of purple flowers swaying above her as she lay on her side and studied a caterpillar crawling on a leaf.

In her dream, Oliver lay at her back, his hand lazily slung over where her waist used to be, rubbing her protruding belly. He watched the caterpillar too, while small butterflies chased each other among the tall grass.

In her dream, a big nasty yellow wasp stung her in the thigh. The pain burned as it circled and came back to sting her again. And again. And again.

Alice cried out and woke to find her earpiece buzzing away beneath her right thigh where she had wedged it. She pulled it out, clipped it on and peered groggily at the projection. Ollie. She held her finger up to answer the call but was a moment too late. His name disappeared, replaced by a red arrow. Missed call. She closed her eyes again and waited for the second buzz.

The message came: *Ellie awake but confused. Staying overnight with her. Tests tomorrow.*

A small, thrashing flutter in her abdomen reminded her she wasn't alone. She rubbed her belly and spoke softly in the darkness.

"It's okay, little one. Everything's okay. We'll sort this whole mess out tomorrow. Tonight, we're going to mute the outside world and watch trashy television. It's been a big few days."

Holding down the button on her earpiece, she waited until the small green light dimmed. Instantly she panicked, wondering whether she should have left it on. What if Pete was using it to track her and keep her safe?

No, she told herself sternly. *You are taking a break. You are going to be totally reckless and just relax tonight.*

Standing and stretching, she paced up the stairs and into her bedroom, pulled the duvet off the bed and trailed it behind her back down to the living room. Padding through to kitchen she grabbed a large pack of cheese-flavoured corn chips from the bench and a bottle of orange juice from the fridge. Hugging both to her chest, she headed back to the sofa and bounced back down, wrapping herself up in the duvet.

"Well, these are certainly not Birthing Home-approved," she muttered, tearing the pack open and crunching several in her mouth at once. With her free hand she picked up her tablet and turned the sound up on the wall screen, flicking through channels until she settled on an aliens-versus-human sci-fi movie.

"Cathartic violence and a total break from reality, that's what we need tonight, bubba."

Her abdomen fluttered again in approval.

CHAPTER 22

"SSH-SSH-SSH. SSH-SSH-SSH." MONICA hushed rhythmically as she bounced an unhappy Oscar in her arms and paced her bedroom. He grizzled with his eyes closed and batted at his head, lashing out in exhaustion. Monica shifted him in her arms, holding him upright against her shoulder, his cheek nestled into her neck. He pushed at her breast with his arms, jerking his head backwards and screaming. She nearly dropped him.

"Please, bubba, please. Mummy needs to sleep. Please. I'm just so tired," she whispered, the tears running freely down her face now. The bedroom door opened and she looked up sharply, trying to wipe her tears with the crook of her arm without losing her grip on Oscar.

"I'm sorry. I knocked but you probably didn't hear me above this little guy," said Hunter quietly. He held out his arms for Oscar.

Monica handed him over gratefully and sank down on the bed. Oscar looked surprised and blinked rapidly, surveying the room from the new height of Hunter's shoulder. He grizzled and fussed. Hunter put his cheek against Oscar's and started to hum a two-note, off-key tune over and over. He swayed gently and rubbed the infant's back. Oscar blinked more slowly and relaxed his head down into Hunter's neck. Eventually his eyes blinked closed and stayed shut. Hunter continued to hum quietly but stopped swaying.

"He hates me," whispered Monica, tears dripping off her chin.

Hunter shook his head. "Of course he doesn't hate you, Mon, he just needed a change of scenery. That's just babies for you. They're gorgeous bundles of irrationality." He slowly lowered himself towards the edge of the bed, but Oscar started to fuss. "I might just stay standing for now," he whispered.

"He hates me, and I just want to... I don't know. I just want it to stop. I want to go. I just need some sleep," she sobbed.

"Lie down, Mon, close your eyes and get some rest. Everything will seem better after some sleep." Monica obediently lay her head on her pillow and pulled the covers up over her. She closed her eyes and fell into a dreamless sleep.

A reddish light streamed under the blinds when she next woke. Hunter sat in the comfortable breastfeeding chair next to Monica's bed, head back, eyes closed. Oscar lay on his chest, snoring softly.

Monica smiled, closed her eyes and drifted off again.

"Hey." A warm hand on the back of her head. "Mon." She opened her eyes and looked straight into Hunter's smiling face. "I think your little one's getting hungry. That's one thing I can't help you with, I'm sorry."

"Oh, thanks." She sat up and held out her arms for Oscar, who escalated from fussing to wailing as he got closer to her and smelled the milk. Oscar attached immediately, gulping deeply and regularly.

"What time is it?" she asked Hunter, who had sat down in the comfortable chair again and was watching Oscar with a small smile. He pulled his phone from his pocket and checked it.

"Seven-fifteen, give or take."

"Wow, five hours in a row. No wonder I feel vaguely human," she said, then tentatively touched the breast Oscar wasn't attached to. "Ow! And full."

Hunter laughed. "Don't worry, your body will adjust once he starts sleeping in longer blocks at night."

"God, I hope so. I'm really over the two-hourly feeding."

They both sat quietly and watched Oscar feed, listening to the sounds of the house waking up for the day. Cutlery clinked in the kitchen, footsteps fell down the hallway, a low rumble of indistinguishable voices made its way under the door from time to time.

"Is it just tiredness, then?"

"Is what...?" asked Monica warily.

"You were pretty upset last night. Is it just tiredness?"

Monica paused and considered ignoring his question entirely. She hadn't quite processed her thoughts about her mother's shocking news and wasn't ready to share them with anyone else. She kept her eyes fixed on Oscar.

"You don't have to talk about it. It's just that, I heard, well, some news. Maybe just gossip. You know what those online rags can be like."

"They publish some pretty crazy stuff sometimes," she agreed, looking up briefly, nervously.

"So, you haven't spoken to your mum recently?"

Monica looked at Hunter, critically evaluating him. He was smart, caring and insightful. He seemed to have the best interests of the children at heart. If the news about her mother's pregnancy was being reported online anyway, surely it was okay to talk to him about it?

"Last night. I spoke to her last night," she said.

Hunter nodded. "It's true, then? Why she collapsed at the party? It's not the cancer?"

Monica shook her head, feeling the tears burn at the back of her eyes again. Her breath caught and she concentrated on slowing her breathing. In and out. In and out.

"You must be so relieved," he said.

She looked up and was surprised to find him smiling kindly at her.

"Yes," she realised. "Yes, I am. I'm very relieved. Of course, I am." She laughed, a nervous staccato sound. "God, yes, when you say it like that, it's so simple. I'm relieved. It's not cancer. It's... it's a baby."

"Not death, then. Just new life. It's funny how that can seem just as traumatic sometimes."

"Hmm."

Oscar pulled his head backwards. Monica sat him up on her lap and rubbed his back. He emitted a loud, long burp.

Monica laughed. "Well, that was one from the boots, wasn't it, little one?"

"Will she continue the pregnancy?" asked Hunter.

"I don't know. I don't think she's decided. It's, um, complicated."

"I'll bet. I've never heard of anything like this happening before. Do they even have rules about it?"

"I don't know." Monica refastened one cup and unhooked the other, swivelling Oscar around and laying him down to feed at her other breast.

"There would be so many risks," said Hunter. "She's had surgery and anti-cancer medication, not to mention alcohol, the lack of a proper pre-pregnancy diet and then there's her age." He listed them off one by one, seemingly talking to himself as much as to Monica.

"I wonder if they'd make her move to a Birthing Home? She'd have to leave her job, surely. It wouldn't be good for the baby," said Monica. "I wonder if they'd let her move in here? That'd be weird. But cool."

"Women used to work through pregnancy all the time, you know."

"Seriously? How could you do it? I was lucky to make it up off the sofa to the dinner table half the time by about twenty-eight weeks."

"Yes, but you had a whopper of a baby. Most people don't have ten pound babies as their first."

"True."

"But you can read stories of our grandmothers working in high-powered jobs right up until they went into labour. Then they'd be back on the job when the baby was six weeks old. It would go into a care facility with ten other babies for up to twelve hours a day."

"Wow, how awful! And I thought it was hard to be separated from Oscar at six *months*. Six weeks would be heart-breaking."

"It would be. And you don't have to clean and cook and look after toddlers as well."

"I can't imagine having to do anything else in the first few months of this little guy's life." Monica looked down at Oscar and cupped her hand over his soft, downy hair.

He twisted slightly and looked up at her, locking eyes and continuing to gulp milk down faster than she could credit. Such electric blue eyes. She could almost believe he had sprung from her D.N.A. alone. Where was his father? He hadn't made contact at all, though he would have been notified of Oscar's conception and then safe delivery. How could he not want to know?

She touched his perfect nose lightly, resisting the urge to stroke his soft, full cheeks. The midwives had warned her against invoking his rooting reflex while feeding as it would cause him to turn his head and come off the breast. She wanted to try it, just once, to see if it was true, but feared messing it all up. The midwives knew what they were doing. Their information came from decades of scientific research.

"I'm not sure I can even give him up at six months," Monica said quietly, not daring to look up at Hunter. She thought she felt his disapproval burn into the top of her head, but when she looked up, he was smiling sadly. "I know I'm not supposed to think like that," she ventured. "But I can't help it."

Hunter nodded. "You'd be a bit of a monster if you didn't feel like that. It's perfectly natural."

"Thank you." Monica felt the tears well up behind her eyes again and her breath caught. "I don't know what to do."

Hunter moved to the bed and put his arm around her and the baby. Oscar tried to raise his head to look at this new person, while taking the nipple with him.

"Ow!" Monica put her hand to her breast and pushed Oscar's head back down. He came off and grizzled. "Sh-sh-sssh, it's okay, bubba, you keep feeding." She stroked his head and offered her nipple. He gazed at her warily and blinked before opening his mouth and latching back on.

"He's a smart little one," said Hunter.

Monica laughed. "How can you tell? He doesn't do much apart from eat, sleep and defecate."

"He's alert and curious—it's an early sign of intelligence. This little chap is going to take the world by storm."

"Yeah, well. First he'd better learn to sleep properly."

Hunter laughed. "He will. That's another sign, you know, lack of sleep. A sign of intelligence, I mean."

"Fabulous."

They both fell silent again, watching Oscar feed. Before Oscar was born Monica couldn't understand why anyone would want to go down the Mater and Pater career track. Spending all day, every day, cleaning up after children, wiping their bums, listening to their whining and helping them with homework. But since Oscar had come into her world she found she could quite happily while away entire hours just watching him. Pulling faces at him, smiling at him to see if he would try to smile back. Laughing at his perplexed newborn frown and revelling in his strange, guttural noises. Only a few more months and she would have to hand him over to someone else.

"What if I studied to be a Mater? Do you think they'd let me be a Mater in Oscar's Home when I graduate?" she asked Hunter, as excited as if she was the first person ever to suggest it.

"Mon."

Monica tore her eyes away from Oscar to glance up at Hunter briefly. She didn't see the approval she hoped for so she looked away again, basking in her fantasy of running, cap in hand and academic gown trailing behind her, to be with her son, who by then would be a toddler, perhaps, maybe a pre-schooler at most, surely?

Hunter put his hand over hers, both of them lightly resting on Oscar's warm, terry-towelled back.

"Mon, no. Don't go down that road. You'll drive yourself mad. You can't be Oscar's Mater. Why would you want to be, anyway? You're already his mum and that's very special too."

Monica slid her hand out from under Hunter's, shifting her support to Oscar's diaper-padded bottom.

"I can't give him up," she whispered desperately. "I just can't."

Hunter stood up and kissed the top of her head.

"You're tired," he said. "It's hard to think straight when you're tired. I'll let you finish up here. Come and get breakfast when you're ready and then maybe you can get some more sleep."

Monica nodded, keeping her eyes glued to her baby. Hunter paused, then sighed heavily and left the room, closing the door quietly behind him. Monica waited until she heard the click of the door closing fully. She took a deep breath and let her tears fall freely. Oscar continued to watch her silently as he drank.

CHAPTER 23

LICE KNOCKED ON a looming, mahogany door. Dozens of chubby baby cupids were carved into the wood, grinning menacingly at her as they aimed their arrows at her heart. The door creaked open, revealing a gaping black hole with a tall, thin woman standing, centered in the dark. She was grey. Grey skin, grey cape, grey dress cascading straight down to the black floor. In her arms she held a tiny grey bundle.

"Yes?" said the grey woman, in a soft, squeaky voice.

Alice, unable to speak, nodded towards the grey bundle in her arms and held out her own arms.

The grey woman cocked her head and regarded Alice curiously.

"Oh, you want your baby back? But, Alice, you forgot to feed him."

A bony grey hand floated through the black cavern and pulled back the grey blanket to reveal a tiny, decaying body. The baby's cheeks, once plump and rosy, had sprung holes and patches of green mould, shiny white jaws showing through and gleaming in the dark.

Alice screamed. A long, gut-wrenching scream, starting in her belly and crescendoing into a high-pitched strand of pure noise. When she ran out of breath, she opened her lungs, refilled, and started to scream again.

The woman in grey stood, expressionless, holding out the lifeless child to her.

"Alice, Alice, sweetheart, wake up."

Alice woke to find Oliver kneeling next to her, his face a picture of worry in the warm glow of the lamplight. Alice's heart raced and her breath came in ragged puffs. She raised a shaking hand to tuck her wayward hair behind her ears. Her cheek felt wet as her hand brushed past.

"Ollie," she whispered, broken.

"Sssh," he said, holding her to his chest and stroking her hair. "It's just a dream, my love, just a dream."

"It was awful."

"It's okay now."

"No. It's not. It's not okay."

"Do you want to tell me about it?"

Alice shook her head. The picture of the rotting infant burned into her brain. Sharing it would shift the horror from the murky dream world to reality. She held her breath, waiting for the panic to pass, listening to the steady beat of Oliver's heart and feeling its comforting vibrations against her cheek. She put her hand up against his chest, feeling it throb against her palm. After a few minutes her own pulse started to slow and fall in line with her husband's.

"How is Ellie?" asked Alice, willing her memory of Ellie's sunny smile to overlay the darker pictures in her mind.

"She's okay," said Oliver. "She'll be fine." More firmly, reassuring himself.

"Is she still in hospital?"

"No. The scans were clear today so she's back at Home with Margery tonight. Still having to keep a close eye on her, so there's an Aunty or Uncle there at all times for the other kids. I'll go back first thing in the morning to take my turn with her and give Margery a break."

"And Tom? Is he okay?"

Oliver smiled and cupped Alice's face. "He's five. He bounces back pretty quickly from most things as long as everything looks mostly back to normal. He's been fine since Ellie came home. We'll keep an eye on him, though."

"And you? Are you okay?"

The smile disappeared and Oliver's brow creased.

"I'm glad Ellie's okay," he said carefully.

Alice nodded. "There'll be repercussions?"

"There'll be an investigation. I've spoken to officers already and my advocate is confident they understand it was an accident."

Alice sat up and patted the cushion next to her on the sofa.

"I haven't been called about it yet," she said. "They mustn't think you're too dangerous."

"No. They'll review the CCTV footage. Or they might have already, I don't know. I suspect it'll end up being just a warning and probably some retraining about safe handling of small children. Nothing more than that. There's been no word about me not being able to be with Ellie, so they obviously don't consider me a danger."

It was Alice's turn to press Oliver's head against her chest. She kissed his wavy hair, smiling at its oiliness. Clearly Oliver hadn't paused for a shower in the past couple of days. The baby fluttered in her belly, making Alice catch her breath and sigh in relief. The dream was simply a nightmare, not an omen. She moved Oliver's hand to her stomach.

"You won't be able to feel it yet, but..." she paused, barely daring to give voice to her implied decision.

Oliver looked up at her in surprise and held his hand gently where she had placed it.

"It's moving?"

"Yes."

"We're keeping it?"

"Oh, yes," she whispered fiercely. "Yes, we are."

CHAPTER 24

ALICE WAITED WHILE Mary stabbed at her tablet, muttering to herself and huffing occasionally. She flicked a suspended silver ball on Mary's desk, sending it crashing into the next ball and starting the chain reaction of motion that would soon come back to her. She held her finger, poised, watching and waiting as the forward motion ran its course and started back. The last ball came back to touch her finger and she pushed gently. Faster and faster it went, mesmerising and soothing her.

"Aaaargh!" said Mary.

Alice jumped and looked up, her eyes momentarily unfocussed.

"Problem?"

"Oh, just Juanita. She wants a *closed* relationship."

Juanita was Mary's live-in girlfriend who had moved in under the guise of homelessness due to an abruptly terminated lease. Termites or something, Alice thought. It wasn't that Mary had other romantic interests she wanted to pursue, just that she didn't feel it was necessary to commit to anyone.

"Most people would consider that a good thing," said Alice.

"It'll give her ideas if I agree."

"Ideas?"

"She'll think she can buy my clothes and choose my food. Stuff like that. Who knows where it'll end?"

"A caring, supportive and mutually beneficial partnership perhaps?"

Mary glared at her.

Alice smiled sweetly. "Anyway, enough of your lovers' tiffs and back to actual problems. What's this about Charlotte White's gardener-lover?"

"What do you care about the gardener? Why are you even here? Haven't you got enough on your plate?"

Alice raised her eyebrows in reply. Mary sighed and turned to her computer screen, tapping on the keyboard.

"Okay, so he's been reported missing. Didn't show up to work, not at his house. Nothing suspicious, could have just checked out and gone on an extended holiday for all we know. It showed up on our reports because he's a person of interest. I just thought you should know."

Alice nodded. "How's the G.D.S. market research going?"

"Not bad. As we expected. We got a bunch of average Joes in a room late last week and asked them what they thought of it. Also did an online survey. Issues we need to address include loss of autonomy, fear of Franken-babies, fear of the unknown, basically. People don't understand the scientific process. They don't see the benefits. All they see is third party control."

"An educative campaign about the benefits? Isn't that what we did when the G.D.S. launched?"

"Yes, we did. But I don't think we emphasised the problems enough. The need for a solution wasn't there."

"So, we need to place a few news items of things going wrong before the G.D.S. came in."

"Yes, I agree. I've been onto the National Medical Records Archive, asking them to unearth a few files we can drip feed to the media over the next few weeks. Is it okay if we arrange media access to one of the Homes for the Genetically Damaged?"

Alice nodded. "See if you can find one or two mothers of new babies who have benefited from the G.D.S. in the past six months. Someone who still has their healthy baby with them. Preferably with a genetic disease in the family that manifests physically. It needs to look good on camera. Hopefully we can get shots side by side of healthy baby with mother and disabled pre-G.D.S. child."

Mary nodded, scribbling on her tablet with her stylus.

"And, Mary, see if you can find out more about the actual scientific process they use for the G.D.S."

Mary stopped and looked up, frowning. "You know that's patented, right? It's top secret or something."

"I know. See what you can do."

Mary nodded. "We'll need at least broad brush-stroke details along with an attractive scientist and a shiny, white laboratory to give the impression of accountability and openness anyway. I'll visit in person. See what I can see."

"Thanks. No need to tell the world. Just background information for you and me."

"Gotcha. Anything else?"

"No. Just keep me updated, yes?"

"Sure."

"And go easy on Juanita. She's a keeper."

Mary pulled a face. "Yeah, yeah. Now go and do some pregnancy yoga or something, baby mumma. Get out of my hair."

Alice smiled and headed back to her own office, giving the silver balls one last push as she stood.

Walking through the office felt like walking a restrained gauntlet. Eyes stared, caught her own, she smiled, they echoed the smile but not the sentiment, and looked away. Repeat.

Alice closed the door to her office gratefully and leaned against it for a moment. She reached to her right and started to twist the long, white pole that would close the blinds and give her some privacy against the curious, the uncomfortable, and the potentially malicious.

At her desk, she tapped the large touch screen set on a slight angle in front of her and waited for it to wake up. She flicked through her inbox. Dozens of F.Y.I. e-mails, staff including her in conversations about work in her department in case she wanted to intervene. Normally she would skim them all, but today she was happy to remain in ignorance. She was about to shut it down when a media release circular caught her eye.

Charlotte White former lover missing.

Alice wrinkled her nose. Charlotte White was supposed to be out of the media altogether. She tapped the e-mail to forward it to Mary and sent it with a simple "?" at the start of the body text. The reply was immediate: *"On it."*

Alice continued to scroll, her thumb caressing the screen as she worked her way through everything from strategic plans to lost property notices. An e-mail from the ministerial inbox reminded her that working on a solution for her unexpected 'problem' was a priority and that a report was expected as soon as possible. She sighed and pressed the red cross next to it. Delete.

The subject line 'Ripped jeans are back' from cooldude57@gmail.com made her smile. She tapped it open:

Hey, sis, call me when you can. I have news.

Alice tapped her earpiece, selected an entry in her contacts labelled CD and waited. It rang out and went to voicemail.

"Your fashion faux pas are disturbing, little bro. Call *me* when you can."

CHAPTER 25

"NO, IT CAN'T be."

"*It is. Your baby has an incurable genetic disease. Denying it won't help. You need to sort out what you'll do now. How will you support your baby? What will you tell the father?*"

"*I don't know! Gary left me penniless and alone! Oh, Rowena, what am I going to do?*"

The overacting of late-afternoon period television dramas made Alice laugh. Or, not quite laugh, but guffaw slightly at least. She sipped from her mineral water, glancing down at the handwritten note lying next to her on the sofa. Ellie was still suffering headaches and had been asking for Oliver. Of course, he had gone immediately and would stay overnight with the little girl.

She checked her earpiece for updates. A missed call from an unknown number but no messages. She left it on silent and put it down on the coffee table. The crying baby soundtrack on the television seemed to grow louder. Alice frowned and startled at a sudden crash at the apartment door. She stared at the door, waiting for something to happen.

"Mum!" The shout reverberated through the timber, accompanied by muffled crying, a mixture of both infant and adult tears.

Alice jumped up from the sofa and walked quickly, her hands shaking slightly as she slid the bolts across and unlatched the door.

"Monica, what are you doing here?" Alarmed, she ushered her daughter and grandson into the apartment, checked the landing and shut the door, quickly re-locking it.

"I'm sorry, I'm so sorry."

Alice took in Monica's unbrushed hair, the black circles under her eyes, the pram, stuffed backpack and screaming baby.

"Sweetheart, what have you done?"

"I'm sorry, I just couldn't," she sobbed.

"How did you even get here?"

"I... I just left. I took the train. Then I walked. I can't go back. I just can't. They can't have him. He's my... he's my son. He's my little boy."

Oscar let out a long, sharp wail, followed by short, staccato bleats of distress. Alice lifted him out of the pram and held him up to her shoulder, staring at Monica while she shushed the baby and rubbed his back. She shushed more and more furiously, trying to compose herself and kick her brain back into gear.

"Sit, um, sit down, Monica," she said, giving herself some time to swallow her own distress and find the words she needed to make everything right.

"Did you tell anyone you were leaving?"

"No."

"So, nobody knows where you are?"

"No."

"Okay. Okay, we've got a little bit of time then."

"Please don't make me go back, Mum," she whispered.

Alice paced with Oscar, rubbing his back and hushing him, her cheek nestled against his soft head. The wailing became less insistent, his breathing less ragged.

"Does he need to be fed?"

"No, I fed him an hour ago. Just before we left."

Alice nodded. Monica sobbed quietly now, not meeting Alice's eyes.

"I shouldn't have come, I'm sorry. I don't want to get you into trouble. But I'm not going back."

Alice twisted her head backwards to try to see Oscar's tiny face without disturbing him. He had fallen silent and his breathing had evened out and deepened. Still rubbing his back, she altered her path and sat down next to Monica. She stared at her, frowning, worried.

How could she explain to her daughter that this was futile? That this was not the way to effect change? That one person could never hope to make a difference against an established machine and there was no point in trying. If she didn't return to the Birthing Home she would be labelled a bad mother for going against scientific research, selfishly trying to keep her child with her instead of allowing the state to give him the very best start in life. The best food, the best care, the best education, the best socialisation.

How could she explain to Monica that her son would not thank her if she withdrew him from society? That as he grew, he would grow to resent her, she who had taken from him every opportunity for success. She'd had no specialist training, she had no material support, nothing to offer him except love—that ever intangible, oft-quoted but eternally messed up and useless emotion.

Alice watched Monica's face. Giving birth and nursing a tiny, helpless infant had brought her feisty, independent daughter completely undone. Her priorities had shifted, her sense of self had blurred. Her sleep-deprived, emotional brain could not process and accept rational reasons for why she should offer her flesh and blood up to someone else to give him a better life. Her primal instinct could not comprehend anything but the desperate need to hold onto her baby.

Memories of similar emotions, long past, made Alice want to join Monica in her tears. Experience had taught her that the tears, too, would pass. Instinct would be broken and the rational side of her brain would stomp all over any lingering emotion. The survival instinct would prevail. Survival for her, for her son, in a society that no longer held the bond between parent and child to be sacred.

Alice clenched her jaw and swallowed. "You're tired. Get some sleep and we'll figure it out in the morning, okay? It's late."

Monica tucked her legs up under her and crossed her arms, closing in on herself.

"I'm tired, Mum. I am so tired. But having a sleep is not going to make this all better. Nothing will be different in the morning."

"Yes, it will be. I'll get to make your breakfast for the first time ever," said Alice quietly, willing her to understand everything she wanted to say but couldn't.

Monica looked up and met her gaze, then rubbed at her wet eyes, sniffing.

Alice tried again. "I make a mean pancake stack."

Monica laughed, then coughed, then sniffed again.

"Okay. I'll sleep in the guest room," she said, nodding to herself as though this could quite possibly solve all their immediate problems. "Where will Oscar sleep?" she asked suddenly, her panic rising visibly. "Oh god, I didn't think of that. There's no crib. He can't sleep in the pram all night, it's not safe. And he can't sleep in my bed, I might roll on him and suffocate him!"

"He'll be fine. He can sleep in the middle of my bed surrounded by pillows. I'll sleep on the recliner chair. I'll bring him to you if he cries out."

Monica nodded slowly, peering up the stairs into the dark cavern that was Oliver and Alice's room.

"He'll be fine," said Alice, quietly but firmly.

"Okay."

They both sat, waiting for nothing, staring at Oscar as he slept.

"Go," said Alice.

Monica stood, peering at Oscar one last time, as though it might be the last, before she turned away to pick up her backpack and head to the guest room.

"Mum."

"Mmm?"

"Thanks."

"Sleep well, sweetheart. We'll work it out."

An hour later, Alice had returned to her original place on the sofa, watching crappy soap operas. She smiled as the sound of her daughter snoring drifted down the stairs. A family trait, especially during and after pregnancy.

Every ten minutes or so she went to check on her grandson, who was also fast asleep. She had lied when she said she'd sleep on the recliner. Her pillow and duvet were already set up on the floor alongside her bed to keep a closer eye on the vulnerable infant.

Alice sipped her tea and breathed deeply, revelling in the feeling of her own baby doing backstroke in her belly. This one was definitely a night owl. Not a peep during the day and then back-to-back football and tango sessions in the evening. On the sofa next to her, her earpiece started to vibrate. Alice picked it up and attached it to her ear: 'Monica Home.' She considered ignoring it, but decided that could make a bad situation even worse.

"Hello?"

"Is this Ms. Mooney?" a crisp, irritated voice asked.

"Yes, it is. I presume you're looking for Monica?"

"You know where she is, then?"

"Yes. She's here."

The voice paused. "You realise she has committed an offence, of course, Ms. Mooney? She has absconded with a ward of the state. This is very serious. I suggest you return her and the child immediately."

Alice pursed her lips and narrowed her eyes.

"Yes, this is extremely serious," she shot back. "As a Birthing Home midwife, you should be ashamed of yourself. My daughter arrived at my apartment this evening in a distraught, exhausted condition with a distressed infant. As we both well know, it is *your* responsibility to ensure that new mothers are, at all times, supported physically, mentally and emotionally to ensure infants are given the best start in life possible. How on earth can you possibly have allowed the situation to become this dire?"

"Ms. Mooney, our Birthing Home provides the highest quality of care to all our new mothers and infants. If your daughter is unable to manage, even with this level of support, then I suggest—"

"*My daughter* is an extremely intelligent young woman from a long line of excellent quality D.N.A. material on both sides of her family tree. If she is having difficulties caring for *her son* then I suggest you take a serious look at your so-called *quality care*. And I suggest you do this before I take the matter of your gross negligence any further. I will expect a full report of the review of your systems within the next week."

"Well."

"Well?"

"I suppose it won't hurt for her to be returned in the morning. I presume you have made adequate accommodations for the child?"

"You presume correctly," said Alice coldly. "I will return Monica to your Birthing Home tomorrow, at my convenience. I expect that you will take extra special care of her while she and her son recover from this traumatic experience."

"Yes, ma'am. Of course, we will."

"Good." Alice ended the call and smiled smugly to herself. Sometimes it paid to have a good grounding in bluff.

CHAPTER 26

A SHRILL WAIL WOKE Alice up. She forced one eye open and waited, tensed for action. When no further sound erupted from the bed next to her, she propped herself up on one elbow and cautiously peered over the edge of the bed at the little bundle sandwiched between two sunshine-yellow pillows. Oscar was still. Alice lay down again and prayed he'd had a brief nightmare and fallen asleep again. What did babies dream about anyway? Milk running dry? A particularly painful poop?

"Uck!" he exclaimed suddenly.

Alice's head shot back up, just in time to see two tiny hands wave aimlessly in the air above the pillows.

"Ge. Gah!"

So. Not asleep, then. She sighed and forced herself up onto her knees, leaned over the bed and pulled Oscar towards her by his feet.

"Hey, little man, you really don't get this whole 'sleep' thing, do you?"

Oscar regarded her with great surprise as she rolled him onto his side and tilted her head so her face was level with his.

"Ge," he replied. "Ooo, mmm."

"Sleeeeeep, little man. It's that thing that's meant to happen at night time."

"Aah-ah-ah-ah!" said Oscar, waving his arms at Alice and hitting her on the nose.

"It's just as well you're cute."

Oscar beamed and hit Alice in the face again as she picked him up.

"Mummy's still asleep so we're going to be veeeeery quiet and go for a walk," Alice whispered. Oscar stared into her face and listened intently. "You fed less than two hours ago so you should be fine for a while."

Alice dressed quickly, pulling on track pants and a long cardigan, shoving her hair into an elastic band and her feet into runners. She sent a quick message from her earpiece to the office, explaining she was unwell and could be contacted in emergencies only.

Alice carried Oscar down the stairs to the living area and, with one hand, fiddled with the folded pram's buttons and levers, swore profusely, and eventually got the pram assembled and the bassinette attachment into a slightly reclined position after kicking the base twice.

"You'd think they could have figured out how to make these things user-friendly by now, wouldn't you, Oscar?"

"Ger."

"Ger, indeed," she said, swinging him over her arm and sniffing his bottom before placing him gently into the pram and clipping his safety belt. "You'll be fine for another half hour."

Oscar provided a running commentary of soft baby noises as she scribbled a note for Monica and left it on the bench.

As Alice pulled the apartment door shut quietly after her and pushed the lift button, she closed her eyes and wished she was back in her warm, quiet bed. The reality of the exhaustion of looking after a newborn had faded in her memory.

She pushed baby Oscar into the lift and pressed the button for the ground floor. How would she cope with the same rigours at forty after having her own baby, she wondered? Without someone to prepare her meals and pay the bills, do the shopping, washing and cleaning? The enormity of what she'd agreed to take on with Oliver started to sink in.

Alice nodded to the doorman who opened the door to the apartment building for her. She thought he contained his surprise at seeing a pram outside of the suburbs well.

"Everything all right, ma'am?" he asked.

"Yes, thank you. Just taking my grandson for a morning stroll." She smiled and nodded at him as though it was the most natural thing in the world.

He hesitated briefly, then nodded back and closed the door behind her.

"Well, you are going to be the talk of the hired help for weeks to come, my dear boy," Alice said to Oscar. He completely ignored her, so busy was he surveying their surroundings as they whooshed by his pram.

Alice breathed in the cold, crisp air and paused briefly at the corner, debating whether to take the safe, uninhabited route of the early morning university grounds, or head into the closest cafe strip and grab a coffee. For the first time in weeks, her stomach didn't lurch at the thought of the smell.

"From memory, I can have up to two coffees per day safely during pregnancy. Does that sound right to you, kiddo?"

Oscar looked at her, cocked his head, frowned and blinked.

"Sure, Nanna, whatever you say," she muttered for him out of the side of her mouth, ventriloquist-fashion. "You know, I'd really appreciate it if you'd join in the conversation. You're making me look bad. Talking to oneself is the first sign of madness, you know."

"Da-da-da," said Oscar.

"Yes, you're right. Who cares what anyone thinks? My pregnancy will be all over the mainstream news pretty soon anyway. I may as well get as many proper coffees as I can before people start telling me how to run my body." She made it only a few more steps before her earpiece vibrated.

"Hey, big sis."

"Hey, little bro."

"You're keeping the baby, then?"

"Yes." Alice paused. "You really do keep a close eye on things, don't you?"

"Alice, I can get you out of there. If that's what you want."

A solution to everything. Alice badly wanted to say yes, okay, how soon, tell me where to go. She closed her eyes and gripped the pram handle tightly, picturing an apartment in Sweden with her own mother—who would, of course, be miraculously cured of her own chronic malady—sun streaming through the window and her with long, glossy hair, holding her smiling infant aloft while her mother laughed next to her.

She shook her head and opened her eyes, seeing Oscar staring at her curiously. *His* mother was asleep back at Alice's apartment. She pictured Oscar taken from his mother and given to another Oliver, a different Margery. Loving and caring and kind and professional. But not Monica.

"I can't."

"Sis, you can't stay."

"I can't leave without them. I can't leave Oliver and Monica and Oscar here and just vanish."

A deep sigh sounded down the line. A lengthy pause.

"I'll see what I can do. You'll be ready within a week?"

"Two weeks."

"Two weeks is too long. One week—even that may be too long."

"Okay."

Another pause.

"Stay safe, yeah?"

"Always."

The line went dead. The bubble of normality burst; Alice no longer felt like having coffee. She turned the pram around and headed back. Her earpiece buzzed again. She checked the projection—unknown number—and ignored it.

Oscar lay on the cream plush pile rug in front of the wall screen, chatting to the presenter who was giving an update on the stock market, and waving his arms at her. Alice stood in the kitchen lining up eggs, bacon, tomato sauce, barbecue sauce, sweet chili sauce, a loaf of bread, several condiments and a bowl of aerating pancake batter. She frowned at the frying pan as she rubbed at a black mark on the stainless steel.

She wanted everything to be perfect for when Monica woke up. She wanted to cook her daughter her favourite breakfast. Except that she had no idea what that was. Alice had never cooked breakfast for Monica. Not once. Not ever. The thought of all those missed mornings made her want to cry, vomit and scream all at once. As if that wasn't enough, the morning sickness was starting to kick in again because she'd made the mistake of not eating before going for a walk.

She was absolutely on edge by the time Monica emerged from the guest room.

Alice took a deep breath, swallowed and ground her teeth. She tried to smile while digging her fingernails into her palms. It didn't go well.

"Good morning, sweetheart. Did you get some sleep?"

Monica eyed her mother cautiously, frowning.

"Are you okay?"

"Yes," said Alice, forcing herself to relax a little. "I'm fine. Just feeling a little nauseous, that's all."

Monica nodded. "And you seem okay, too, little one," she crooned to Oscar as she knelt down next to him. "Has your I.Q. dropped a few points from staring at a screen?"

"Mmm. Mmm. Ger," said Oscar, lifting his chin towards Monica and waving his arms and legs.

Monica picked him up as he started to cry. Cradled in her arms he stopped crying and started snuffling, nuzzling into her breast. When he didn't find what he was looking for immediately, he started to fuss again.

"Hungry, hey?" asked Monica, sitting down to feed her baby.

"He's been as good as gold. We went for a bit of a walk."

"That would've earned you a few stares," said Monica, smiling.

She seemed much calmer today, Alice thought, after some sleep. Or was it the different location?

"Just from the doorman. I'm sure he's called all the news networks by now."

"Front page news! Baby spotted outside of the 'burbs! And it's not even Sunday!" Monica laughed wryly.

"I got a call last night from your Birthing Home. I assured them you were in good hands and I'd bring you back today."

Monica nodded but didn't meet Alice's gaze. "I know it's for the best. I just got... I don't know. It was just too much."

Alice went back to rearranging the condiments and turned the fry pan on.

"So, what would you like for breakfast?" she started brightly. "I can do pancakes with ricotta, banana and honey. Or eggs and bacon on toast. I'm told my omelettes are particularly light and fluffy."

"Um, I'm not really hungry. Maybe just some buttered toast and a cup of tea?"

Alice's face fell. She switched the pan off and turned away, flicking the kettle on and popping two slices of toast down.

"Sure, coming right up."

Alice arranged the buttered toast and two cups of tea on a wooden tray and carried it over to the sofa. She placed the plate of toast next to Monica on the sofa where she could reach it with her free hand. Cupping her hands around her mug of peppermint tea, she tucked her feet up and sat next to mother and baby, saying nothing, staring at the screen.

Oscar fed, burped and fell asleep in Monica's arms. She picked up her lukewarm cup of tea and sipped at it, careful to avoid bumping Oscar or spilling any on him.

"Um, so... So, what time do we have to be back at the Birthing Home?"

"I told them we'd be there when it suits me." Alice looked at Monica and smiled. Monica smiled back. A small win. "Sometime today. There's no rush. Are you okay... with going back?"

There was so much packaged up into that one question that Alice didn't know how to put it into words. Are you actually as calm as you're behaving? Are you going to break down when we get there? Will you become hysterical and harm yourself or your baby in the middle of the night? Or run away again? Will you fight them in a couple of months when you have to drop Oscar off with his new Mater and Pater? Will you be able to stand going to your Sunday access visits without causing a scene and having your visiting rights revoked? Will you cry every time you pump the excess breast milk and swallow the tablets to help it dry up faster? Will you get used to it after a while? Will it become normal?

"Yes."

Monica's tone was decisive but Alice looked down and saw her daughter's hand tremble slightly. She looked away.

Monica continued, "I mean, no. I mean, I... I don't have a choice. So, yes."

Alice sipped her tea and kept her eyes on the wall screen. She spoke quietly and chose her words carefully.

"What if you did have a choice but it meant leaving everything else behind?"

"I'd leave. Of course, I'd leave."

The desperation and hope in Monica's eyes nearly broke Alice's heart as she turned towards her mother.

"There might be a way." Alice glanced sideways at her daughter. "But I want you to think carefully before you give me a final answer. You need to understand what it is you're giving up."

Monica nodded expectantly.

Alice sighed and rubbed her forehead. "You would need to leave Australia, taking only Oscar. There would be no guarantee you would ever be able to finish your studies, or have a career, or a partner, or a comfortable and stable life. You would be supported initially, but then you would have to make your own way in another country, doing jobs that may be far beneath what you're capable of."

"Yes. I'd do it. We'd figure it out." Monica became more animated as she spoke. "You and I could take turns looking after each other's babies and going out to work. You could get work easily, I could do secretarial work, or cleaning, or something. We'd be fine. We could do that. When? How soon?"

Alice nodded slowly, swept a single finger over Oscar's soft cheek and turned back to the screen.

"Maybe a week or so, but nothing's certain yet. Don't say anything more. Don't pack a bag. Just be ready to go when the time is right." She looked back at Monica. Monica nodded. "Okay, finish your toast and tea, then, and we'll make the most of this extra day. Maybe we'll pop Oscar in his pram for a sleep and we'll go out for coffee."

"Sounds great." Monica beamed.

"I just need to check on a few things for work first. It'll give you and Oscar time to get dressed and ready."

In her home office, Alice waited for the screen to come to life. She tapped in her password and started scrolling through her e-mails, looking for anything urgent. She opened one from the minister, summoning her to a meeting a few days from now, requiring a decision. It used phrases like 'regrettable leave without pay' and 'forced our hands.' Alice closed her eyes and rubbed one side of her face, feeling suddenly exhausted. She deleted the e-mail and saved the meeting invite into her calendar. She continued to scroll. Nothing urgent; one from Mary to let her know the gardener still hadn't shown up but that she'd planted a rumour that he'd run off with a new sweetheart, to take the heat off the Charlotte White angle.

She tapped on a sound file in her inbox—the missed call, from this morning, and a garbled, distressed voicemail.

"Ms. Mooney, this is Dean Johnston. I'm Charlotte White's, um... You interviewed me at your office, remember? There are... there are things you need to know. I... um. You can't call me back. Maybe... I'll send you an e-mail. It will be published today. I thought you should know first."

Alice frowned and tapped on an e-mail from 4985033888@gmail.com with the title 'This will go live soon, am giving you access now.' The body contained nothing but a website address. She clicked on it.

THE SHOCKING TRUTH ABOUT AUSTRALIAN GOVERNMENT G.D.S. EXPERIMENT

Australians have been sold a lie by their own government. Not satisfied with their current policy of routinely ripping babies from the arms of their mothers, they have taken the social experiment into the darkest laboratories. Their so-called G.D.S. (Genetic Diversification System) is being used to create a race of superhumans, devoid of empathy and susceptible to control by the Stalinesque government of the day. When will they stop pretending it's a democracy and admit they've brainwashed the Australian population into accepting their own downfall? How can a society call itself a proper society when it's just a pack of drones blindly following a heartless leader?

"Call Mary," Alice commanded her screen.

"You coming in, then?" asked Mary, without preamble. "It came up on our online monitoring reports."

"Yes, I'll be there in an hour."

"You don't need to, you know. It's just some crackpot, publishing nutso conspiracy theories on some European freedom fighter blog. Mainstream media will never pick it up."

"No, it's more than that. Arrange a meeting with the minister, will you?"

Alice ended the call and strode back into the living room, picked up her bag and headed for the door.

"Mum?"

Alice stopped, her palm raised to unlock the door. She shut her eyes briefly, took a breath and turned around.

"I'm so sorry, Monica. I have to go into work for an hour or so."

"But we were going to spend the day together. We were going to get coffee..." she trailed off.

"We will. We still will. But right now, I have to go. This is important, Mon."

Monica watched as her mother opened the door, nodded to her once, and then was gone.

"More important than us, you mean." Monica bit the inside of her cheek. Her eyes burned.

CHAPTER 27

"MAINSTREAM MEDIA WON'T pick it up, hey?" Alice burst into Mary's office seventeen minutes later, waving her tablet triumphantly.

"Pfft, slow news day. It'll die down by tonight."

Alice slumped onto one of the visitors' chairs and put her elbows on her knees, propping her head on her palms and massaging her temples.

"You okay?"

"Headache. I'll be fine."

"Ibuprofen?"

"Pregnant. Can't."

Alice closed her eyes and wished she could keep them that way. Her shoulders ached from trying to sleep on the floor, her head ached from lack of sleep, and her stomach churned with a combination of guilt and a niggling sense of fear.

She opened her eyes and gazed at Mary levelly. "What if it's not just a crackpot theory?"

"Seriously? Come on, have you read the original post? Even the mainstream rags that are reporting on it are giving it a few inches of space and headlines like 'Wild Allegations About the G.D.S. Appear To Be Unfounded.'"

"I've barely had to do anything. Just field a couple of enquiries saying 'no, there's no basis to the allegations; no, we don't know who's behind them; no, we're not creating superhumans—otherwise all babies would be born sleeping through the night and feeding properly.' Which they're not, just to be clear."

"No, they're definitely not," Alice agreed.

"Are you sure you're okay to be here?" Mary came around from behind her desk and sat next to Alice. "Jokes aside, you really don't need to be. You've got enough to worry about, figuring out what you're going to do with yourself. The Equality Party doesn't care enough about you to warrant this sort of dedication to the job."

"I didn't get much sleep last night. I was looking after Oscar."

Mary raised an eyebrow.

Alice crossed her arms. "Monica came by in tears, saying she couldn't bear to give him up. I let her stay the night."

"Shit, Alice. You're in enough trouble already. Have you let her Birthing Home know? You must have, or there'd be a full-scale search by now. What did you tell them? Is she back there now?"

"No, she's still at my apartment. I came here first. I'll take her back this afternoon."

"I hope you told her to get over herself. Seriously, who does she think she is? And who does she think is going to support her? What, you're going to let her live in your apartment or something?" Mary paused long enough to take a sip of her coffee, then launched straight back in. "I never thought you'd end up with one of the irrational ones, Alice. I mean, we all find it hard to go back to our daily lives after having babies, but we all do it. It's not like you never see them again. She'll see him every week. Every—single—week!"

"You finished?"

"Sure. I mean, sorry. I know she's your daughter and all, but I just think… Jesus, she's lost her mind or something."

"No, Mary. She hasn't lost her mind; she's shifted her focus. To Oscar."

"One baby? One fucking baby? Alice, if she stays on track and goes back to her medical research, she can help thousands of babies. Let me talk to her. I'll talk some sense back into her." Mary spat the words out while leaning back in her seat and rolling her eyes so far back into her head, Alice was quite sure she must have swallowed them.

Alice shut her eyes for a moment and remembered a soft, silky nose, a chubby, cleft chin and the thoroughly intoxicating feeling of being drawn into the depths of her own baby's eyes.

You're mine, said the eyes. *You're me, and I am you. Wherever you go, I will follow you; wherever you leave me I will feel you, until the day we die.* She shivered slightly and drew air deeply and deliberately into her lungs.

"Bearing a child didn't change your focus?" she asked Mary.

"Hell, no. I knew nothing about raising kids and I didn't want to learn. I know a shitload about how to get into people's heads and convince them to act in their own best interests. So that's what I went back to doing."

Mary leaned forward and picked up the file she'd brought in, pushing it towards Alice, who stopped it with her finger and stared at the blank beige casing, frowning.

"And *you* are bloody good at making sure I've got a clear path to get the job done. That's what you do, Alice. You make things happen."

Mary stopped and sat back again, clicking her short nails against each other on her right hand. She watched Alice, her brow creased with worry.

"Don't do it, Ali," she said softly, realisation deflating her.

Alice kept her eyes down and opened the folder, scanning without reading.

"Shit, Al. I know you want to help her, but she's a kid. She doesn't understand what she's asking. She'll get over it." Mary crossed her legs, picked up her coffee from the side table and cradled it in her palms. "We all do. Eventually."

Alice looked at Mary curiously. "Would it be easier to get over the loss of a child or the loss of a career, do you think?"

Mary stood. "It's not a choice. If she stays, she gets to have both. She's lucky, Alice. Remind her of that—lucky. Our grandmothers didn't get a choice. They had to do both, at the same time, with fuck-all help."

"Watch your language, will you?"

"Oh, for fuck's sake," Mary muttered into her coffee lid. "Just read the brief and sign it, will you?" She strode towards the door but stopped, her fingers on the door handle, and sighed. "And if you need any help getting her and the kid out... you know where I am."

Alice smiled. "Thank you."

Mary shook her head and left, swinging the door shut behind her.

"See you in half an hour at the meeting," Alice called after her.

Thirty minutes later, Alice walked into Barbara's office with feigned confidence, as though it was just any other meeting on any other day. Barbara sat at her imposing leather desk, flanked by two senior legal staff and her ever-present ministerial minion, Graeme Smythe, the department secretary. She ignored Alice and Mary as they sat on the two plain chairs set out for them, as far away from the desk as the confines of the room allowed. Alice was tempted to offer to move them outside the door and simply shout her questions from an adjacent cubicle.

Instead, she sat.

Graeme cleared his throat, as though to silence the non-existent chatter. Barbara continued to tap at her tablet with her long talons. The legal staff sat to attention, important-looking black leather compendiums perched on their crossed legs.

"So, Ms. Mooney, have you reached a decision regarding your, ah, *unexpected* condition?" asked Graeme.

"You mean the baby?" Mary asked, chewing on her thumb.

Graeme glared at her. One of the lawyers started writing in his black leather compendium.

Mary shrugged. "Well, you know. Alice is pretty tired today. I'm sure she *expected* to be well rested. She's also managed to beat cancer, which was pretty *un*expected. Given you've invited the legal pit bulls, I figured it was just good manners to clarify things for them."

Alice sucked in both her lips and bit down hard to stop herself from laughing.

"Why are *you* here?" asked Barbara, looking up at Mary. "My meeting is with Alice. Not you."

"Good practice to have a support person present at meetings like this. Call H.R. They'll explain it all," said Mary.

Alice inclined her head towards Mary and raised an eyebrow.

"Fine, I'll shut up now," she muttered, leaning back.

Graeme cleared his throat again. Mary rolled her eyes.

"So, Ms. Mooney—" he started.

Barbara held her palm aloft, calling for silence. "Alice. Let's cut to the chase, shall we? Are you planning to continue the pregnancy?"

"Yes. I'm continuing the pregnancy."

Both lawyers stopped writing and looked up. Barbara tapped her pen five times and wrinkled her nose.

"Alice, you're an intelligent woman. I know this because we had your I.Q. tested before you started here. You're from an excellent bloodline. I know this because I've been intimately acquainted with your genesis for a long time now. I was an assistant on the breeding pilot program which was responsible for your genetic design and conception. I briefed your mother on the risks and benefits involved in signing up herself, and her offspring, to the program. She's an intelligent woman, too—she agreed to sign up. The fact that she changed her mind after the death of your firstborn just shows how dangerous—and enduring—post-partum emotions can be." Barbara paused and cocked her head to the right. "She nearly derailed the whole program. Did you know that?"

Alice shook her head and clenched her teeth. "My mother was very unwell. If she was so *irrational,* as you say, she would not have been capable of making a *rational* decision about her participation in the program. Persons who are not of sound mind cannot sign themselves up for anything. The contract would be null and void." Alice paused and smiled wryly. "That is, if we're really talking about what's *legal* here." Her head swam. What program?

Barbara pushed her tablet to one side and laid the stylus neatly on top of it. "Your mother was asked to choose between the wellbeing of her country and you. She eventually left the country—and *you*—and moved to Stockholm. Like I said, an intelligent woman. Are you sure you don't want to reconsider your decision to continue your pregnancy?"

"No, I don't. Thank you." Alice refused to rise to the bait.

"It's just that we do so value the work you've done for the department, and you could do so much good for the G.D.S. You have a unique combination of empathy with the common person and a canny ability to use your analytical mind to figure out exactly what is required to bring them along with you. For the greater good of society, of course. We would so hate to lose that."

"I'm pregnant, not dying. Anymore."

"Yes, but you must understand that we can't possibly allow a pregnant forty-year-old to continue in the role of a senior public official."

"You intend to terminate my employment?"

"Oh, goodness, no, we couldn't do that. Could we, Leon?" Barbara addressed the senior lawyer closest to her, who looked up from his leather compendium.

"No, but suspension with pay for the period of gestation would be possible. To prevent public unrest."

"You see, Alice? We are not unreasonable. We would pay you at your current salary level to sit around and be a human incubator." Barbara picked up a paper clip and rotated it between her fingers. "Just not here. You'd need to find somewhere less visible to... gestate."

Alice felt Mary's light touch on her arm and realised she was grinding her teeth audibly.

"And what of the health of my child? Given this is a natural conception, can I expect any... significant *genetic* differences... compared to my first two children?"

"Well, Alice, you are well past your prime, aren't you?" Barbara smiled sweetly. "And what with the poor genetic match you make with your husband combined with whatever cocktail they injected into your body during your cancer therapy... well, I guess you'll just have to wait and see, won't you?"

Alice looked at the black leather compendiums, trying to decipher the notes the lawyers had made. She noticed they had stopped writing a few minutes ago and sat, watching Barbara nervously.

"I'll need to take some time to consider my options, based on the new information you've provided today."

"The new, strictly confidential, information you've been provided with today," said the most senior lawyer.

Alice gave him a withering look. "Yes. I'll need a week. Then I will give you my final answer."

"That sounds fair. Your suspension will commence immediately, of course. The official line will be that the experimental cancer therapy failed and you require additional rest and possible treatment. It will be no surprise if you need to attend hospital for a... procedure... after that. Or if... anything should happen to you."

"Is that a threat?" Mary burst out, as though she had physically broken free from self-imposed restraints.

"Oh, Mary, of course not!" Barbara laughed. The lawyers looked alarmed and started writing again. "I'm just laying out the statistical probabilities relating to miscarriage and potentially serious and life-threatening maternal complications for a pregnancy such as Ms. Mooney's."

Barbara smiled at Alice. Alice smiled back. She rose and held out her hand to Barbara, who took it limply in her own. Neither woman shook.

"I'll collect my things and be out of the office within the hour. I'll inform you of my decision within one week from now. Thank you for your due consideration of my *unexpected* condition," said Alice quietly and evenly.

She turned and walked out of the office. Mary followed her.

Alice got into her car and set the manual override. She needed to feel in control. The tyres squealed as she yanked the wheel roughly around the underground car park bollards. Around the ramp and up. Around the ramp and up. Too many curves, making her dizzy, disoriented, nauseous. She braked suddenly as she misjudged the final bollard. Reversed, turned, drove forward and scanned her pass at the gate. She sat while she waited for it to rise, nudging forward inch by inch.

"Come on!" she hissed at the door.

She could see the outdoors, could almost smell it through the air conditioning vents. The front of the car rolled forward and emerged from the car park gradually. Once the door was clear of the car roof she slammed her foot on the accelerator.

Pulling out of the side street she narrowly missed a tram and slid on the smooth rails in the middle of the road as she headed right, back towards her apartment. At a red traffic light, she tapped her earpiece.

"Call Pete," she commanded.

He answered immediately. "Hey, sis."

"I need the medical records from my first birth," she said. "Not Monica. The baby b-before," she stammered. "The one who... who died."

There was silence, then a sigh, on the line.

"Why?"

"Can you get them?" she asked, a slight crack in her voice.

"If the records still exist, yes. I can get them."

"I need them. Please." Her voice softened, eyes fixed on the traffic light ahead. "I need to know why it happened. I need to know... if it'll happen again."

"Stillbirths happen for all sorts of reasons, Alice."

"I need to know," she said again.

"Alice, there are things that you don't know... that you might be better off not knowing. Are you sure you want to go down this path?"

"What do you know, Pete? And why don't I know it, too? This is my baby we're talking about," she pleaded.

"It was safer that way. You stayed in Australia, you're vulnerable. And it served no purpose at the time." Silence, waiting. "Alice?"

"Just tell me. Now."

Pete sighed. "I think you need to speak to the professor."

"Which professor, Pete?" Alice ground her teeth in frustration.

"Professor James Stansted. He's at the University of Melbourne. He was on the original G.D.S. development project. Now he spends his days drinking dry and dry at Jimmy Watson's. He can tell you everything you want to know."

"So, what, I just show up at Jimmy Watson's and wait?" She was furious, frightened and—somehow—vaguely hopeful. Her jaw ached with anticipation.

"Just Google him, Alice, his contact details are on the university's website."

Alice ended the call and pulled the car over. She picked up her tablet and tapped in the professor's name. His university contact page came up immediately. Professor of psychiatry. No classes, no current research projects, no phone number. No wonder he had time to burn. Maybe her brother had the wrong person. Surely, she needed to speak to someone in genetics or medicine? She tapped on the e-mail link and started typing.

Subject: Questions about my genetic profile

Dear Professor Stansted,

My name is Alice Mooney. I have questions about the stillbirth of my first child and whether it relates to my genetic profile. I have been ad-

vised that you may be able to assist me in my enquiries. I would be grateful if you could meet with me as soon as possible.

She read over the words and wrinkled her nose. Before hitting send she added:

I hear the dry and dry at Jimmy Watson's is particularly refreshing at this time of year.

CHAPTER 28

ALICE PULLED UP in front of her apartment building and called Monica to come down. It was time to go back to the Birthing Home. As she waited in the car, she opened the door to let the fresh air in and swung her legs out onto the curb. Head bent forward, she closed her eyes and breathed.

An older woman walked briskly out of the building's entrance. She wore black pants and a bright green t-shirt—clearly an evening relief worker for pre-schoolers heading out to the suburbs for the night shift. As she approached Alice she slowed, looked her up and down and frowned. The woman glanced over her shoulder and squinted.

"She's coming," she told Alice. "I rode the elevator with her, hard to get enough space for the pram. What a precious baby!"

Alice paused, raising a hand self-consciously to smooth her hair, then nodded, unsure what to say.

The woman looked pointedly at Alice's stomach and nodded.

"So, it's true?" she asked.

Alice nodded again.

"I wish you all the best, my dear. You do what needs to be done, what's right for you and your little one. Some of us are old enough to remember another time, you know."

"Thank you," said Alice.

"It wasn't all bad."

Alice nodded, uncomfortable, and looked towards the apartment block, willing Monica to appear. Her mental telepathy paid off as she heard the fussing of a baby and saw Monica walking slowly, pushing the pram with one hand and reaching into the bassinette with the other.

The older woman followed her line of sight, then nodded to Alice and continued on her way.

"You okay?" Monica asked Alice as the pram rolled up next to her.

"I'll be fine."

"Straight back to the Birthing Home, then?"

Alice nodded. "I'm..."

Monica held up her palm and shook her head. "Don't. I know you're sorry. Let's just go."

Alice looked at the pram, then at the car and frowned. "I don't have a baby capsule."

"Oh."

They stood and stared at each other for a few moments.

"I read somewhere that when cars were first invented they used to let kids play in the back seat while the car was moving. No seat belts at all," said Monica.

Alice raised her eyebrows. "That so?"

Monica nodded and reached into the pram to pick up Oscar. "And the babies often slept in the footwell of the passenger seat."

Alice stood back silently and opened the car door for Monica and Oscar. Monica settled into the passenger seat and wrapped her arms protectively around Oscar, snuggled in his soft nest of blankets.

"Car, go to Birthing Home of Monica," commanded Alice.

Car travel clearly agreed with Oscar, who had stirred slightly when they took off, but stretched his little arms, fists in the air, and fell asleep again almost instantly with the vibrations of the engine. The car progressed slowly through the city streets and onto the freeway for the long journey back to the suburbs. The only sounds were soft baby snores. Alice glanced across at her daughter occasionally but was unable to catch Monica's eye. When she wasn't peering down at her infant son, she was staring out of the window, expressionless.

Alice tried to imagine what Monica was going through. She thought she understood, but what her daughter had done—taking her baby out of the Birthing Home, thumbing her nose to the laws—was something she had never thought to do herself. It had just never occurred to her.

Alice pulled up at the curb a few houses down from Monica's Birthing Home.

"We're here," she said a few minutes after stopping the car, when Monica hadn't moved.

"I know." Monica stared out of the window and clasped her hands together until her knuckles turned white. "Maybe we could wait until Oscar wakes up?"

Alice bit her lips, wishing she could agree. "Someone might see us driving with Oscar. They wouldn't approve."

"Parents used to routinely take their kids for car trips to get them to sleep. Even in the middle of the night," said Monica quietly.

"That sounds dangerous." Alice tried to picture stumbling about in the middle of the night, sleep deprived, with a screaming baby, and thinking getting into a manual motor vehicle was the best solution. Sleep deprivation really did do strange things to people.

"Read that somewhere, too, did you?"

Monica nodded. "Just a book one of the girls gave me. It's sort of a collection of all the weird things parents used to do before the Mater and Pater system came in. There are some pretty funny ones, actually."

"Such as?"

"Leaving your baby unsupervised in a pram at the bottom of the garden for a couple of hours a day. Like some sort of bean plant."

Alice smiled. "I wonder if they ever sprouted?"

Monica snorted, then laughed. "Bean sprout babies!"

"With curly tendril legs and pods for toes!"

Oscar startled and woke, whimpering slightly. Alice watched Monica reach down and pick him up, tipping him slowly up so he had time to brace his heavy head.

"I don't want to go back," said Monica, nuzzling her nose into Oscar's ear and inhaling his milky scent.

"I know."

"Promise you'll come back for me and Oscar?"

"I promise."

Monica looked up and stared into her mother's eyes, flicking her gaze from one to the other, trying to focus and weigh the truth of her words. Her mother always left. She had always come, every Sunday after breakfast, without fail. But she always left again, before the Sunday spaghetti bolognese was served. Alice promised to come back, that was something Monica could trust; it was what would happen when she did come back that she was wary of.

"I should go," she said, shifting Oscar upright onto her shoulder.

"Car: open trunk," said Alice. She swung her feet out of the car and moved quickly to pull the pram out and shake it open, ready for its passenger. Monica placed Oscar into the bassinette and tucked the blankets in around him. He peered at her and smiled, a huge grin.

Monica's face softened as she smiled back and brushed his cheek with her thumb.

"Come on, bubba, let's get you inside and fed, hey?' She looped the pram's safety bracelet around her wrist, grasped the bar and kicked the brake up to allow the wheels to roll. Without turning back, she headed off quickly down the footpath. Alice watched her for a moment and fought the urge to go after her, put her daughter and grandson back in the car and just drive as fast and as far as they could go.

"Get a grip, Mooney," she said to herself under her breath. "Places to go, people to see, plans to make." She shut her eyes, took a deep breath to underscore her pep talk, got in the car and slammed the door.

CHAPTER 29

THE TIRED, LINED face which greeted her at Oliver's Home did not belong to the person Alice was expecting to see.

"Oh, Margery, hi," she said, a little too abruptly. "I'm sorry, I didn't mean..."

Margery smiled kindly, opened the door wide and stepped back. "Come in, Alice. He's not here but sit and have a cuppa with me anyway. I'd love some company."

Alice stepped across the threshold and looked around the unusually quiet and empty house.

"Where is everyone?"

"The elder two are at school, Ollie's taken Ellie to a check-up with the neurologist down at the Monash Children's Hospital and Tom is in his room, building a Lego spaceship. I think he's trying to escape the chaos," she chuckled conspiratorially. "Are you off the caffeine? Do you want some peppermint tea, maybe?" Margery and Alice both looked down at her stomach, which Alice immediately covered with her hands. "Not much chance of hiding that little one any longer, is there?" Margery smiled and disappeared into the kitchen.

Alice sat down and sank into the sofa. She could almost taste the peppermint tea rolling around her mouth and was suddenly very thirsty and very tired. She closed her eyes and listened to the sounds of Margery moving around the kitchen. Drawers opened and closed, cutlery chinked and the kettle provided a boiling bass to it all. Alice spread her aching hands out on the sofa on either side of her and rolled her shoulders. Everything hurt; the tension of the past few days was taking its toll.

Margery brought two steaming cups of tea into the room and placed one on the table in front of Alice. She sat down on the sofa opposite and cupped her hands around her own drink.

"Day off?" she asked, as though Alice popped in for social calls all the time; as though a senior public servant just took days off willy-nilly whenever the whim struck.

"I've been placed on leave," said Alice, leaning forward to pick up her cup and settling back again to blow on it. "To think about my future."

"I see." Margery waited.

Alice sat and blew some more. Tentatively, she took a sip and burned her lips. Margery continued to wait.

"Do you know when Ollie will be back?" asked Alice.

"No."

Alice wrinkled her nose and peered into her peppermint tea. She knew this tactic, had used it herself a thousand times. Keep the silence going to get the subject talking. She imagined it was a useful way to extract information from kids as well—using the natural human compulsion to fill up the silence to get at the truth. Alice knew what Margery was doing, and yet...

"I have to consider what's best for the child," she started.

Margery nodded but said nothing, looking down into her own tea.

"Of course, it's not had exactly the best start in life already. I have to consider the possibility that..." Alice cleared her throat and trailed off, unable to end her official line. The advice she would have given someone else in her situation. Who knows what condition this baby

would be in? Was it the best thing for a child to be born severely disabled? What sort of future was that to give a child?

"I was one of the first to try to raise children in the Home system,
you know," said Margery thoughtfully, as though she had forgotten
this titbit until that very moment. "Before there even was a proper
Home system."

"Oh?"

"Mmm." Margery blew on her tea and took a sip. "Oh, that's lovely,
that is. Good quality peppermint tea, straight from the backyard."
She took another sip, then leaned back and put her cup on the small
table next to her. "I'd been an au pair in Paris, you see. This was back
in early 2001, before the twin towers and all that. Before the world
went mad. I came back to Melbourne to finish my studies." She
sighed heavily and faced Alice. "That's when I met your mother."

"My mother?"

"July 2001, Identity in Modern Europe, that was the class we took
together."

Alice leaned forward. "You knew my mother?"

Margery ignored her, lost in memory. "She was heavily pregnant
with Pete by that stage and they needed an extra hand a couple of
days a week at the communal home she and her friends had set up.
And I needed to work to pay for my tuition. A social experiment, she
said, to prove that there was a better way to do things. 'A communal
way of living that released women from the shackles of reproduction,
lifted men above the restraints of capitalism, and protected vulnerable children.' That's what they spoke about. It sounded like pie in
the sky to me, even back then. But I was glad someone was trying, at
least. And glad for the job."

"That doesn't sound much like the Equality Party."

"Oh, it wasn't. To start with it was a small radical feminist group—all bohemian idealists. It wasn't until they joined with the trade unions and disenfranchised men's groups that they gathered momentum and formed the Equality Party. I was long gone by then. It was all a bit... *radical* for me, I suppose."

"But you said you worked at the Home, that my mother got you a job. Why don't I remember you?"

Margery smiled. "Don't you? I've often wondered, all these years working alongside Ollie, whether you saw something familiar in me. But I suppose you were only five or six when I left. Memories fade so quickly when you're a small child."

"You never said anything."

"I promised your mother I wouldn't. She was desperate for news of you after she left. When Ollie was assigned to my Home... well, Monique thought that if you knew I was friends with her, you'd hold it against me."

"So, you've been, what, spying on me all these years? Sending reports to Sweden?"

Margery rocked back and forth gently and laughed. "Oh, Alice." She shook her head. "Look around you, my dear. I believe we call it surveillance these days, not spying." She waved at a fixed camera in the corner and sipped at her tea. "No. I wasn't spying on you. I've been keeping an eye on you, just as any concerned family friend would. That's all."

Alice nodded slightly.

Margery peered at Alice over the rim of her cup. "She loves you, you know. Very much. And misses you... *very* much."

Alice shook her head. "I don't want to...'

Margery held up a hand. "It's okay, I just thought you should know. You have more pressing issues to think about right now."

"We're going through with the pregnancy but I... I can't give up another baby. But I can't raise it either, I wouldn't have a clue what I was doing."

"Ollie would. And he would teach you."

"But what about your kids? And I've got Monica to think about, and baby Oscar."

Alice felt the fear rise up from her stomach and clench her throat. She shut her eyes and breathed. There were too many problems, too many variables, not enough time.

"Our decisions are never easy once we step off the path that was built for us, Alice. That doesn't mean we shouldn't go and explore. It just means you have to figure out which decisions are the most important. Once you've made the important decisions, the rest will fall into place."

"But I need to do what's best, for the sake of the child," said Alice, falling back on the mantra that had been drilled into her all her life.

"Why?"

Alice frowned. "What do you mean, 'Why'? Because children must be protected and nurtured and given the best possible start in life."

Margery stared intently into her cup. "Think on this. At some point in our history it became normal to assume that women will part with their young children, that they will cry and mourn and, sometimes, suffer irreversible psychological damage because of the separation. We have come to accept that this must be done because it is best for the child. Yet, these women were once children, too. When did we stop considering what's best for the mothers?"

Alice stared at Margery, bewildered.

"The Home system was started by people with the best of intentions. But it has gone too far now, Alice. It's time somebody stepped in." Margery raised her eyebrows at Alice. "I'll let Oliver know you dropped by." She rose and brushed past Alice to unlock the door.

Alice took the hint and followed her.

"Now, why don't I walk you to your car?" Margery ushered Alice through the door and stepped through after her. "Ah, that's lovely, that is. Fresh air and space, nowhere to mount a microphone. Nothing quite like it."

Margery put her hands on her hips and breathed deeply. She continued in a low voice and spoke quickly.

"Sweden is a good place to raise a child, Alice. They've managed to strike a reasonable balance. Children are supported by the state but they stay with their families. It's better that way. Not perfect, never perfect. But better." She nodded as though this was the final word on the matter. "If I don't see you again, give my regards to your mother. She's an incredible lady who gave up a lot for what she thought was a good cause."

"I should go." Alice was suddenly uncomfortable. She didn't want to hear this. Monique had abandoned her. That was the narrative around which she had built her independence. She got into her car and programmed the long drive back into the city, her head spinning.

In the silence of her cold apartment, Alice stared at the string of numbers she had typed into her screen. Her finger hovered over the delete button. It was a voice call she had thought about making many, many times in the past two decades. She'd rehearsed how it would go, being alternately angry and understanding; allowing her mother to be regretful or stubborn and cruel. She could never quite make the imagined conversation go well enough to convince her to make the call for real. She'd always changed her mind at the final moment. But now, the possibility of a mother who hadn't completely abandoned her, who had made sure she was still watching over her, tipped the balance.

Alice swallowed and hit the call button. It rang twice before connecting to silence.

"Mum?" she said, tentatively, wondering if the connection had failed.

A muffled crash at the other end of the line, then muttering. "Alice?" Softly, with hesitation.

"How are you?"

"Alice. Oh god, it's really you." Whispered, followed by a sob.

Alice bit her lips together and swallowed again. "Pete says you're doing well," she lied.

"I'm managing..." Monique's voice seemed to fade. "...to get out and about sometimes."

"That's good."

"It's been a long time, Alice."

"Mum, why did you leave me?"

A pause. White noise.

"I tried to stay. I did. But your baby, Alice. Your poor baby. It was my fault, all my fault. I broke. And I couldn't put myself back together."

Tears burned down Alice's face. Hot tears of rage.

"But I needed you after... and you left. You left." Clenched teeth.

"I'm sorry. I'm so sorry." Her voice sounded suddenly so far away.

"Why couldn't you have tried harder? You should have tried harder."

Alice's face was hot now, her head pounded. Her jaw throbbed from where her teeth gnashed against twenty-year-old wounds.

"My daughter has a baby son now, Mum." Silence. "They're going to take him away." She clenched and unclenched her fist, waiting.

"I saw a caterpillar yesterday," came the reply. "He said it will be dinner time at quarter past three today. I find that odd, don't you? Dinner time is normally four o'clock. Every day at four o'clock."

"Mum? Mum, I don't know what to do," she whispered.

"Will it be quarter past three soon, do you think? My clock has stopped. I can't find it."

Alice closed her eyes and ended the call.

CHAPTER 30

MONICA MOVED AROUND her room at the Birthing Home, muttering to herself and responding to Oscar's attempts at baby conversation from time to time.

"Sure, you'll come back again. Probably to tell me you've changed your mind and won't help me," she scoffed, pulling a tangled mess of baby onesies and blankets out of a drawer and tossing them onto the bed. She picked up a pale green singlet, shook it out, carefully folded it in half, then half again, and placed it neatly back in the drawer.

"Gah," interjected Oscar, kicking his legs at her from the floor.

"Gah, indeed, bubba boy. I mean really, where does she get off telling me to wait? Wait around for her, go back to the Birthing Home and pretend like nothing's happened. I've made my decision, I'm not a child anymore, I don't need her help."

She picked up another green onesie and folded it, then a yellow and two white ones.

"I could just up and leave here any time, you know, Oscar. I don't need to wait for her. I'm sure I'd find somewhere for us. There has to be a way, I could look it up online or something, on the dark web."

And finally, she folded the blankets, finishing up with a white wrap with little pictures of blue flowers and pink teddies. She shoved it roughly into the drawer on top of the others, toppling over the small tower of onesies as she did so.

"Mmmmm-ah!" said Oscar.

"Yep, you said it, kiddo," said Monica, placing her hands under his arms and lifting him up into the air.

He smiled and cooed at her, raised high above her head. Encouraged, she slowly jiggled him up and down. He giggled a little—at least, she thought he did—a brief outburst of gunfire-like sounds emitted from his tiny mouth. As she raised him up, she turned herself in a circle. He gave no warning as he opened his mouth again and a thin stream of white, smelly liquid spewed forth.

"Ah!" shrieked Monica, nearly dropping him. "Yuck! Yuck, yuck, yuck! Gross!" She put him down on the blanket and grabbed several of the wraps to try and wipe away the vomit that dripped down her hair, face and cleavage.

Oscar began to cry, though it was unclear if he was in distress or simply upset that the merry-go-round had stopped. Maddy burst through the bedroom door, baby Jenny on her hip.

"Are you okay?" she asked, then burst out laughing as she surveyed the scene. She picked up a spare wrap and knelt down to mop Oscar's mouth. "Did you spew on your Mummy, Oscar? Was she doing flying babies again?"

"You'd think I would learn, but no," said Monica.

Oscar stopped crying, blinked and stared into Maddy's eyes. "Ooh, g', ah," he said, frowning.

"Yes, I know, you couldn't help it, could you? Here, play with Jenny while we get Mummy cleaned up," said Maddy, sitting her five-month-old daughter down next to Oscar.

Jenny waved her arms excitedly at Oscar and slapped them both down on his tummy at once, promptly keeling over and falling on top of him. Oscar chuckled and patted her on the head.

Maddy used the same cloth to wipe the remaining liquid from Monica's hair while Monica stuffed her wrap inside her bra to mop up any drops that had trickled into there.

"Don't worry, we've nearly gotten ourselves through another whole day. Only half-an-hour 'til bedtime," said Maddy brightly.

"Not many more bedtimes to go for you now, are there?" Monica took the soiled wrap from Maddy, mashed it with her own and dropped both of them into the laundry basket.

"Well, aren't you just full of sunshine today. Your sleepover in the outside world really did you a whole lot of good, hey?" Maddy tried to smile but the corners of her mouth just wouldn't be pushed up. She sat down cross-legged on the floor and rescued Oscar from being pinned underneath Jenny.

Freed of her speed hump, Jenny pushed herself up on her hands and knees and started rocking back and forth. She moved her right knee forward but knocked over her right hand as she did so and keeled over to the side. Maddy laughed as Jenny lay there, looking a little stunned. "Hand *and* knee, little girl, you gotta move them both."

Jenny picked up the soft material book that lay near her and started chatting to the brightly coloured pictures of balls, cups and dogs, rolling slightly from side to side on her back.

"I wonder if she'll start to crawl before she moves on to her Mater and Pater?" said Maddy wistfully, reaching out to touch her daughter's bare, pudgy foot.

Monica sat beside her friend silently, not quite knowing what to say. She reached out her arms to take Oscar, suddenly not wanting to miss even a minute of contact with him. Maddy took a deep breath, huffed it out and sat up straight.

"She'll get to spend more time with her older brother when she moves in with them, that'll be great, and she already knows him because she sees him every Sunday, which is a bonus. It's always nice for kids to have other kids around to play with. And his Mater and Pater are really lovely. He loves them to bits. Did I tell you he's started walking?" She chattered on to fill the silence, though her voice nearly broke when she spoke of her son's love for her substitutes.

Monica laid her hand on Maddy's arm and watched Jenny play. Maddy bit her lip.

"It's for the best, you know. Research shows that, overall, kids fare much better in a setting with qualified parents than they used to in the old days when everyone just sort of powered through making the best of a bad situation. Better start to school, improved mental health, and all that..." she trailed off.

"What will you do when she goes?" asked Monica.

"Oh, I got a place studying engineering, didn't I tell you? Yes, electrical engineering at Monash University. I had it confirmed a few weeks ago," said Maddy, wiping at a wayward tear. "I'll be okay, you know, really I will."

Monica nodded, disbelieving.

"The tablets they give you to dry up your milk—no one talks about it—but I think it dries up more than your milk. It's a relief, really. It helps you get through the first few months."

"Oh," said Monica, thinking that explained a lot.

"And after that, you'll get pregnant again so you'll have plenty to keep you occupied, and you'll have your Sundays." Maddy had moved beyond trying to convince herself and had turned to reassuring Monica.

"And what about you? You won't be getting pregnant again."

Maddy placed her hands on her stomach and stared at the carpet. "No. But they have other tablets for those who have... hormonal fluctuation issues. They're longer term—some people just don't adapt well to their new life outside the Birthing Home. Something about an imbalance of hormones caused by not being physically close to their child. They think it's a physiological thing."

"Oh."

"Hey, I'm hungry. How about we go and see if Joe's got dinner ready yet?" Maddy scooped up Jenny and stood a little too quickly, catching herself on the end of the bed to balance herself while she held her daughter in a tight one-armed bear hug.

Monica smiled sadly and checked the clock on her bedside table.

"You go. I might wait a few more minutes and give Oscar a quick feed. I'm trying to avoid the midwives as much as possible after yesterday," she said, referring to her unscheduled absence from the Home.

She'd had a stern lecture from the head midwife on her return a few hours ago and had since kept to her room as much as possible, hoping to avoid another meeting before the night nurse arrived.

The regular night nurse was far less stringent in her enforcement of official ideology. She figured if the girls kept the babies alive and out of her way for the evening, it was a job well done. She could usually be found snoring on one of the recliners unless there was an emergency brewing.

Twenty minutes later, Monica was sitting on her bed, propped up by a vertical pillow at her back and dozing lightly while Oscar fed in his sleep at her breast. Fatigue had overcome hunger as the daylight faded and they had both nodded off.

She stirred at a noise, waking enough to realise she'd been woken, but not alert enough to identify what it was that had woken her. Frowning and stretching her stiff neck, Monica looked down at Oscar, who had also stirred, stretched and gone back to sleep-sucking. She gently pulled him off her nipple, watching it elongate and then snap back as he finally relinquished it, then re-hooked her bra cup and pulled her top down. Craning her ears, she heard a crashing noise in the kitchen, a raised voice and then a scream. The shrill sound of the fire alarm started up at the same time as the sickening smell of smoke reached her nostrils. She felt her panic rise.

Oscar woke and started to cry. Holding him in one arm, she rushed to the door and touched the handle to open it.

"Shit!"

She snatched her hand back as the hot metal burned into her fingers. Wisps of smoke started to lick their way under her bedroom door. For a moment she stood and stared, stunned. She looked at the ceiling, waiting for the sprinkler system to kick in and shower them all. The silver nozzle stayed alarmingly dry. In a muddy state of mind Monica gazed curiously at the smoke and backed away towards the bed. She heard sirens in the distance, becoming louder, and shook her head to clear it.

Dumping Oscar unceremoniously on the bed, she moved swiftly to the window and turned the winder vigorously until the window opened as wide as it could. She reached up and pulled the pins that held the flywire in place, pulled out the mesh rectangle and hurled it on the floor. Peering out, she could see flashing lights to her right, towards the street. A narrow strip of grass continued to her left and stretched into the darkness, on the way to a laneway. There were no sirens in the laneway. She looked back at the fire engines and made her decision. There would be no waiting around to be rescued from her tower by her mother, who might change her mind again at any moment and lock her back in. She would make a break for it now, while everyone else was distracted, and take her chances.

Thanking her own laziness, she grabbed the backpack still full of blankets, nappies and clothes and pushed it through the open window. She peered down after it and back to Oscar, who lay on the bed—red in the face from screaming. It wasn't a long drop by her estimate, but the opening was small.

Red flames had started to seep under the door and the edges were singed. She picked up the pillow and dropped it carefully out of the window so that it landed near the backpack. Next, she ripped the duvet off her bed and wound it around Oscar until only a nose, mouth and a few eyelashes appeared through a single gap. She held him out the window and kept her grip on the package for as far as her arms would reach, then dropped him in a straight line, onto the backpack and pillow. He fell no further than the length of a ruler.

Monica dropped straight after him and gathered him up quickly. Away from the shriek of the alarm, he stopped crying and started to fuss, his tiny mouth rooting around for the missing nipple. Monica put the backpack on her back, posted the pillow back into the now-burning room, and scooped up the soft, bulky bundle that held her son. She didn't intend to leave any clues for her pursuers.

From her position at the side of the house she could see the night sky lit up by the flashing lights of several fire engines on the street. She took one last look at the house, flames shooting out of the roof, and turned away from the street, into the darkness of the backyard and out towards the laneway. She took two steps and crashed into a dark figure. A bright light flashed in her face, blinding her.

"Monica," said the figure in a low growl.

She kicked out in panic and tried to scream. A hand was clamped across her mouth and she felt a sharp sting in her arm. Oscar was lifted from her arms as she crumpled to her knees.

CHAPTER 31

ALICE LAY AWAKE in the dark, picturing Monica back at the Birthing Home, distressed and alone. The guilt made her stomach hurt. Speaking to her mother, after years of silence, had only made things worse. It had brought her raging anger and pain to the surface, without relieving anything. Worst of all, she still couldn't decide what was best for her daughter—stay in Australia and keep her career, or leave and keep her baby.

She sucked in her cheeks and bit down hard, willing the physical pain to calm her. She rolled onto her side to ease the strange pressure on her abdomen and immediately regretted it. Alice remembered this was the annoying stage of pregnancy when lying on her back felt odd but lying on her side made it feel as though her stomach might just sort of slide off at any moment.

Placing her hand on Oliver's broad back, she took comfort from the rhythm of his steady breathing. The strange shift work hours that came with Paterdom meant that, for her, waking in the middle of the night to find he'd slipped in beside her sleeping body was not an unusual occurrence. Normally she'd snuggle up to him and fall back to sleep quickly, but tonight her brain had already started to tick over and anxiety had set in.

She pushed herself up in the bed, supporting her back with a pillow, and grabbed her tablet from the bedside table. Turning the Wi-Fi back on, she leaned against the pillow and closed her eyes, waiting for the new messages to roll in. She peered at her screen. Three minutes past five o'clock.

There was just one message, from Professor Stansted: *The dry and dry is particularly refreshing when consumed in the rear courtyard first thing in the morning. Jimmy Watson's opens at 9.00am. I look forward to your company at that time tomorrow, Ms. Mooney.*

At 9.07am Alice sat in the wine bar's cool leafy courtyard, sniffing the jug of brown liquid sitting on the table. It smelled so good and had only a hint of dry vermouth to flavour the dry ginger ale. It was barely alcoholic at all. Surely just one sip wouldn't hurt her unborn baby? It would certainly help her nerves.

She pushed it a few centimetres towards the empty seat across from her and went back to rotating her straw around the inside of her glass of sparkling mineral water. Oliver would be up and heading off to work already. She'd left a note, telling him she'd gone for a walk to clear her head. It wasn't a complete lie.

She tried not to huff with impatience, and instead clenched her toes into the rubber soles of her walking shoes and bit her tongue inside her mouth. The morning air was fresh and she found herself wishing she'd ordered a hot drink, but the smell of coffee still made her stomach churn a little and she was becoming thoroughly sick of peppermint tea. She lifted her straw out of the liquid and started randomly attacking and popping the fizzy bubbles that rose to the surface.

"Alice."

Alice startled and turned, seeing a tall, thick-waisted man with oily, unkempt hair and a sweat-stained business shirt and tie.

"Professor Stansted," she said, standing too quickly and sending her flimsy faux-wrought iron chair clattering to the ground.

He smiled and looked her over as he bent down to pick up the chair. He righted it and indicated the cushion with a flourish of his hand and a raised eyebrow. Alice sat, confused and unnerved by the discrepancy between his appearance and his manners. Silently, the professor skirted the table and lowered himself onto the vacant chair. He glanced briefly at the glass and jug, long enough to aim the liquid's downward trajectory into the smaller receptacle, then went back to staring at Alice. Alice watched the glass, fascinated. The thin stream of liquid ended just as the level in the glass reached a finger's width from the rim.

"Call me James," he said, sitting back in his seat and resting his hands across his pin-striped belly. "You are the spitting image of your mother, you know." He grinned then, like a schoolboy playing a prank.

"I wouldn't know, I haven't seen her since I was a teenager," Alice retorted.

"Prickly the same as her, too," he mused, cocking his head to the side and raising an eyebrow.

Alice waited for him to say something else, but he didn't.

"You knew my mother, then?" she asked, picking up her glass and taking a sip.

"Yes, I did. I knew your mother very well. But you didn't come here to talk about her."

"No."

"You're pregnant," he said, nodding towards her belly.

Alice looked down and realised she had rested her glass on her slight bump, making it even more pronounced.

"Yes," she said, replacing her drink on the table and pushing her chair forward slightly. Her stomach vanished below the lip of the table.

"How far along?"

"I don't know. Just over three months, I think."

"And you want me to look into my crystal ball and tell you if it's all going to be okay?" The professor leaned forward to pick up his glass, threw back his head and downed the contents. He raised the jug to refill it and grinned at her again. "Well? Am I wrong?"

"Of course not. I mean, no. I..." Alice stopped and bit down on her tongue so hard she tasted blood. She clenched and unclenched her fists below the table and tried to slow her breathing. "I just want some information about the potential genetic risks of carrying this child to term and I was led to understand that you could assist," she finished in her best high-level meeting voice.

The professor slapped his palms on his knees. "Oh, you really are just like your mother," he roared with laughter, pulling off his glasses and wiping his eyes with an enormous handkerchief he had pulled from his trousers.

"Can you help me, or not?" asked Alice, her voice clipped and strained.

"It's not often I get to chat with lovely young ladies like yourself, especially not on such a beautiful morning in these rarefied surroundings. Let's not rush things. That baby of yours isn't going anywhere in a hurry." He took a sip from his glass and flagged down a waiter who had started taking the chairs down from the tables and wiping them clean.

"Turkish bread and dips, please, young man. And make sure they're pregnancy-friendly. No raw egg. You look young enough to remember your National Service training, eh?"

The startled waiter looked from the professor to Alice, who frowned back at him.

"Certainly, sir." The waiter nodded at the professor, took one last look at Alice and scurried back inside the bar.

"How is your mother these days, then? Still enjoying Sweden?"

"I don't know, we don't really talk. I hear she's doing well," said Alice, not willing to share her recent conversation with this man.

"Ah, a bit of an upset there?"

"No, just a distant relationship, I guess you would say. Nothing unusual about it, really," said Alice carefully.

"No, I suppose not. And your brother? He's still flitting about making a nuisance of himself?"

Alice smiled despite herself. "Yes. Yes, he is." This man, whom she'd never met nor heard of, seemed to know her family intimately.

"He's always had a nose for trouble, that boy. The best thing your mother ever did was get him out of Australia. You've had the good sense to at least look like you're toeing the line on most things. Well, until now, that is," he said, smiling at her belly.

The young waiter reappeared carrying a large tray with olives, toasted Turkish bread, and three small pots filled with pink, green and beige pastes.

"Beetroot, avocado and hummus dips, sir. A healthy selection for expectant mothers," he announced, placing the tray on the table in front of Alice and bowing slightly.

"Bravo, good man," said the professor approvingly. "Now, if you wouldn't mind seeing we're left in peace for a half hour, I'd be most appreciative."

The waiter nodded, turned on his heel and vanished again through the door, closing it firmly behind him. The professor picked up the knife and a slice of toast and lathered the bread with pink paste. Then he sat back in his chair and crossed his legs.

"Okay Alice, what do you really want to know?" He took a large bite of the bread and chewed.

"I want to know if, in your professional opinion, it's safe for me to go ahead and have this baby."

"No. You don't," he replied, his mouth stuffed with food.

"I beg your pardon? Yes. I do. That's exactly what I want to know," Alice shot back at him.

The professor shook his head and swallowed. "No, my dear, you could get that information from your own department. Any minion could tell you that the risks of your baby being born with a congenital defect are increased because of your age, your cancer treatment, and your complete lack of pre-conception and early pregnancy care." He picked up his glass and drained it. "Try again," he said gruffly. "Don't waste my time."

Alice glared at him before picking up a nearly-black, elongated olive. She rotated it slowly and watched her fingertips glisten with olive oil. She placed it on the table, next to her glass, and wiped her finger on a napkin.

"I want to know why my son died," she said quietly.

"That's better," he said. He rapped his fingers on the cold marble and swiped at a wayward crumb. "Your mother..." he started, then stopped and wrinkled his nose. "No, I think we need to go back further than that." He leaned forward and peered at the closed door, then sat back again, uncrossed his legs and grasped his own hands. "When I was a wet-behind-the-ears grad research student I managed to get myself a postdoctoral fellowship on a cutting-edge project that aimed to reduce the skyrocketing rates of mental illness in our society."

"Combining what we already knew about mental illness—that it seemed to run in families; and what we knew about the new field of epigenetics—that not only were we born with particular genes, but they could be altered by particular circumstances, we set out to create a world of happy, well-adjusted individuals." He stopped, picked up his glass and drained the contents. "We meant well."

Alice picked up the jug and refilled his glass. She paused, then tipped some into her own glass and sniffed it.

"The rumours are true, then, about genetically engineered babies?" she ventured.

The professor raised a stern finger. He cleared his throat and took a sip of his full glass, then settled back into his chair.

Alice huffed quietly to herself and took a sip from her own glass.

"As the studies continued, we concluded that the only way we could prevent the onset of mental illness was by selecting uncorrupted genes and ensuring certain factors—emotional stability, appropriate affection, adequate living facilities and nutrition—were present in the subject's environment in their key developmental years. Of course, we concluded that it wasn't possible to stamp out mental illness altogether, but the incidence and severity could certainly be reduced.

"The political number crunchers who held the state purse strings were unimpressed by our conclusions. They wanted a guaranteed cure for mental illness, which we couldn't give them. The drain on the economy in terms of medical expenses and time lost at work was enormous. Certain members of the government were, however, very impressed with *some* of our findings.

"When we isolated the factors responsible for mental illness we also stumbled across the potential for using gene editing—alongside the epigenetic phenomena—to curtail extreme emotional responses.

They hoped that, under the guise of public health, they could breed out the bleeding-heart do-gooders who wanted to help everyone, no matter how 'deserving'. The bean counters saw their chance to build a population that would respond favourably to economically rational policies, without balking at the human cost of those disadvantaged by them."

"They wanted to build some sort of super human race?"

"In a way, yes. You see, they had this wonderfully sound theory called economic rationalism; a blueprint to a wealthy nation where everyone benefitted. Well, everyone except for the chronically ill, disabled, destitute... But it had a fundamental flaw. It assumed that human beings make decisions that are in their best interests. Sadly, that is a resoundingly false assumption.

"Nor did the theory account for poor parenting and sub-standard education and living environments. So, they figured they'd redesign imperfect humans to function properly within a perfect economic system—beginning, of course, with their genetic makeup.

"Of course, *we* didn't know of these... *other* plans. We were idealistic young geniuses who were going to arrest the skyrocketing rates of mental illness with a wave of our cross-disciplinary magic wand."

He stopped to wave his hand grandly through the air.

"Implementing the plan was where your mother and her communal child-raising experiment came in. It provided the perfect standardised environment in which to test the genetic factors.

"You already know that story. After the Equality Party's landslide victory, the system in which you were raised was extended into what we now know as the Mater and Pater system, essentially six-day, round-the-clock childcare.

"It was relatively simple to get the public on-side—initially, at least—with the 'best interest of the child' in mind. Shocking stories of childhood poverty, neglect, abuse and paedophilia, fuelled by the digital beast of the Internet.

"Of course, once we had the best interests of the children at heart and permanent, fail-safe contraception was developed, it wasn't a huge step to set up the Birthing Homes. Then came the ban that penalised anyone that attempted procreation outside of the system. After all, it would be selfish to doom a child to lifelong disability and illness."

"And the genetic element?" Alice prompted, impatient for him to finish stating the obvious.

The professor sat back in his chair and folded his arms across his stomach. "Long-term live experiments to refine the genetic process continued even as the system was being built around them. And that, my dear, is where you and your family come into the picture. Including, of course, your firstborn son."

"My son?" Alice froze, her heart contracting. "But he didn't survive."

The professor reached for an olive, popped it in his mouth and regarded her silently for several beats.

"No, he didn't. The scientists who worked on his genetic profile... miscalculated. Sadly, we didn't realise until the last minute. It was a work in progress, you must understand. But we couldn't allow him to be born." He took another sip and glanced at the door again. "Believe me, Alice, you wouldn't have wanted to meet him. He would have grown up to be... well, let's just say they went a little too far with trying to erase empathy from his genes."

"You murdered my son," whispered Alice, her hands shaking.

"He was part of an experiment which was terminated," he said flatly.

Alice barely heard his next words as she fought back tears of rage and grief.

"Your mother was an idealist and an advocate in the fight against mental illness, mostly for personal reasons to do with her own mother and grandmother, and what she feared was waiting for her. She volunteered herself—and her bloodline—as the first human test subjects."

"So as far as you're concerned, I'm basically a lab rat," Alice spat out, clenching her fists. "And my son was a disposable specimen."

"Oh, you're much more valuable than a lab rat, Alice," he said softly, with a smile in his eyes. "You're living proof of the sheer brilliance of the project. Your mother's inherited tendency to anxiety and depression have not manifested in your psychiatric makeup at all."

"'Tendency to anxiety?' She had a complete nervous breakdown."

He raised his eyebrows and continued. "You do, however, still have a slight excess of empathy."

Alice turned away from him and stared at the wall, willing her heart rate to steady itself. She couldn't afford to lose control now, she needed to know everything this monster could tell her. What she really wanted to do was grab his throat and squeeze until there were no words left. Anything to stop his story of horrors.

Finally, she took one last breath and faced him.

"And my daughter?"

The professor turned his glass in his hands. "Your daughter is perfect, Alice. Your daughter is the genesis for the entire foundation of the Genetic Diversification System. You should be proud."

Alice let out a primal roar, stood and hurled her own glass at the wall, where it splintered with a satisfying smash. She exhaled, picked up her handbag and regarded him with a stony expression.

"It may disappoint you to know that your perfect creation has begun to become thoroughly undone by the emotions of early motherhood."

"Yes, so I'd heard," said the professor, unperturbed by Alice's outburst.

"How widespread are these... experiments? How many subjects now, other than the original group?"

"Oh, it's no longer an experiment, my dear. It's national policy and practice. Why do you think the government banned natural conception at the same time they introduced the G.D.S.?"

Alice stared at him, searching his face and waiting for him to elaborate. He shook his head slightly and lifted his glass to his lips.

"Why are you telling me this now?" she asked.

"Because your brother asked me to. I signed on to a mission to improve peoples' lives through scientific intervention. The chief purpose of the G.D.S is to reduce expenditure and improve bank balances, not help people. I'm doing what I can to try to make this right, Alice. Part of that is giving you the information you need."

"I have to go now." Alice sensed he had no more of use to tell her and she didn't think she could hold herself together any longer. She stood to leave and almost fell through the door as the young waiter pulled it open from the other side.

"I'm really not the monster you think I am, my dear," said the professor quietly, raising his glass to her without smiling.

Alice nodded and pushed past the confused waiter, into the dark hallway of the restaurant.

CHAPTER 32

O
UT IN THE cool morning sun, Alice turned north up Lygon Street and walked quickly, her footsteps weaving as wildly as her thoughts, through the crowded footpath of coffee-seeking university students and staff.

She'd call Pete, she resolved. Get him to delay their leaving for another few weeks while she figured out what to do. She couldn't let the G.D.S. continue. She felt sick that she'd done so much already to impose it on an unwilling society. What would she tell Monica? She'd understand, surely. There was still more than a month to go until Oscar was due to be transferred to a Home. Monica could just sit tight in the meantime. She'd be fine.

Alice stopped at a major intersection. Waiting for the traffic lights to turn green, she flicked through the contacts in her earpiece and dialled the office.

"Mary, I need your help," she said.

"It's okay, I'm already on it," said Mary bluntly. "They're still sifting through the wreckage, but no bodies have been found. No sign of Monica and Oscar. Do you think she would have done a runner?"

Alice opened and shut her mouth. She wanted to vomit.

"Alice? You there? We'll find her, don't worry."

"What? What happened?" she managed.

Mary paused. "I assumed you'd heard."

"Heard what?"

"Isn't that why you're calling?"

"Mary!"

Mary sighed. "There was a fire at Monica's Birthing Home over-night. They're saying it was an electrical fault. Monica and Oscar appear to have escaped through a window, but they've vanished."

"Oh."

"I'm guessing she hasn't contacted you, then?"

"No."

"Did you have a fight? Any reason she wouldn't come to you?"

"No."

"That's not a good sign."

"No."

"Okay, well, keep in touch. I'll let you know if I hear anything."

"Okay."

Alice ended the call and crossed the road against a sea of pedestrians going in the opposite direction. She kept walking until she reached her apartment building, turned into the underground car park, found her car, opened the door, slumped into the driver's seat and closed her eyes. She had no idea where she planned to go, but she was sure she needed to go somewhere. Find Monica. Talk to Oliver.

"No, no, no. She's fine. I'm sure she's fine. What if she's not fine? I'm just so tired, bubba," she whispered to the bump, rubbing her hand in slow circles as her little one fluttered inside her. "It's not supposed to be like this."

For a moment she allowed herself to crave the safety and predictability of a Birthing Home. A nice warm bath, a back massage and long naps punctuated by tasty, healthy meals that appeared, almost magically, at regular intervals. No responsibilities, no decisions to be made, all the rules set out before her simply to be followed. Her mother and her friends had been right—work and babies just didn't mix.

This pregnancy was exhausting. Her body was two decades older, she held down a demanding job, and Oliver wasn't around to cater to her every whim. Now her daughter had disappeared with her grandson and she had no idea where they were or whether they were safe.

Alice wiped at tears which suddenly sprung from her eyes. Damned hormones. She swallowed and closed her eyes but that only made it worse. She felt the ghost of her mother's slender, cool hand brush away the rivers that ran down her cheeks. She heard memories of a soft voice murmuring incoherent words of comfort. Clenching her eyes tightly, she tried to make a picture of her mother's face appear. Fair hair, shoulder length curls. Long nose, soft voice. Blue eyes, like hers? No, grey like Pete's. Or was it green? Alice bit down on both lips until the pain became too much and she opened her eyes, focused on the concrete wall in front of her and took shuddering breaths.

She briefly considered just starting the car and driving as far as the fuel cell would take her. Her own mother had fought so hard, made so many personal sacrifices to make the lives of others better. Alice suddenly felt like she'd failed on all levels. Her work had been instrumental in warping the system Monique had built, and she couldn't even keep her own daughter safe.

Alice bent her neck towards her left shoulder and felt the stretch. Straightening her back, she rubbed the base of her neck where the tension ache started. It occurred to her that she was no longer a wide-eyed nineteen-year-old with no experience and no connections. She tapped her fingers lightly on the steering wheel and made a decision. This time it would be different. She wouldn't be crushed by the system again. If her mother could manage it, so could she.

Alice projected her earpiece screen and stared at it for a moment. She took a deep breath and commanded the system to call an unlisted number.

"Hey." Her brother's voice was soft and cautious.

"You knew about the trials, didn't you? About Mum's involvement?" she asked.

He paused. "Yes."

She clenched her fists. She wanted to tell him how many times she'd stood outside the hospital where her baby had died, hoping for answers, when all along he could have given them to her. How badly it broke her to eventually give up, accept that it was her fault—something she'd done wrong, a bad food she'd eaten; a pregnancy vitamin missed—and move on as best she could.

Instead, she said, "I see."

"Monica will be fine," said Pete, switching topics. An olive branch. There was a voice in the background, a low growl. "It's Alice," said Pete, his voice muffled. "Yes, I understand."

"Pete?" said Alice, wondering if the line was breaking up.

"I'm here."

"Who was that?"

"Just a... a friend. It's nothing."

Alice frowned, a feeling of disquiet settling in her stomach. "Have you heard anything? From other... monitors, maybe?" The word still felt strange on her tongue.

"No," said Pete. He cleared his throat. "No, I haven't heard anything."

Alice nodded. It would be okay, she told herself. Monica was strong, smart and quick-thinking. Besides, Mary knew her way around police intelligence and would easily track the investigation. The authorities would be throwing all their resources into finding

Monica and Oscar; they would make sure mother and son were found and returned safely. There was nothing for Alice to do apart from wait—and hope—and use her influence to intervene once Monica returned.

"I need your help with something else." Alice chewed her lip, waiting. Pete was silent. "I think I know how to fix this, but I'm going to need collateral, something to trade."

He hesitated. "What are you planning, Alice? I already told you I can get you and Monica out of the country, just give me some time."

"It's not enough, Pete. I need to do something, to clean up this mess. Our mess." She paused. "It's not a full plan yet. More of an idea, but I'm working on it." She briefly outlined the bare bones and what she needed from him.

He exhaled down the line. "I think I've got something you can use, but you're not going to like it."

"Pete, it's important."

"Okay. We've got a file on Smythe, from your department."

"Graeme Smythe?"

"Yeah. He's a piece of scum, Alice. He's worse than you think. The sex parties you've probably heard rumoured—they happened. But it involved minors."

Alice's stomach bottomed out. "Oh, Pete, not children."

"We managed to get the parties shut down and the perpetrators... taken care of quietly. But we couldn't touch him without endangering our network; we could only contain him and keep an eye on him. We made sure the rumours about the sex parties were put out to take the heat off the... other stuff. A few people were starting to ask questions. Believe me, Alice, I'd love to get my hands on him and make him pay for what he did, but the evidence has to stay buried."

Alice swallowed. "I won't make the images public. I just need them for... personal persuasion."

"Blackmail."

"Sure, if you like."

He paused and then continued softly. "Are you sure about this, sis? Smythe has powerful connections—"

"Yes. I'm sure. I'm absolutely sure. Any dirt that's thrown at Graeme will stick to the minister herself. And allegations of this nature—the public won't just ignore them. And once an investigation starts... this is the fuel to get the momentum going, Pete. The Equality Party has been in power for too long. They've lost sight of what equality really means." Alice could almost hear her brother's grim smile.

"You're your mother's daughter, Alice Mooney," he said at last. "Okay, then. Give me a day or two. The files are held by one of our other monitors in a safehouse, but it should be easy enough to get them to you. As hard as it is to look at, you'll have the evidence you need."

Alice ended the call and sat for a moment.

"Car, take me home." She leaned back against the headrest and shut her eyes.

CHAPTER 33

ALICE WOKE WITH a start and winced as she lifted her kinked neck off the car seat's headrest. There was a rap at the window and a familiar face grinned in at her. She opened the door slightly and waited for Oliver to move so she could push it wide enough to slip out.

"Couldn't bear to sleep in the bed without me for a moment longer, hey?" He stepped aside and held the door for her.

"Oh, I'm home. I must have fallen asleep. Sorry, I'm just really tired," she mumbled, grabbing his free hand and letting him pull her to her feet.

Oliver shut the door while Alice rubbed her shoulder and stretched her neck.

"What time is it?" she asked.

"About midday. I just got home."

"Mmm," she managed, wishing she could just close her eyes again.

"I've got good news." Oliver put his arm around her waist to steady her as they walked. "Ellie's got the all-clear from the neurologist. I stayed over at the Home last night just to make sure she was okay, but things should go back to normal now." They both glanced down at her protruding belly. "Well, normal-ish, anyway."

"Oh god, Monica," said Alice, her knees buckling under as she remembered.

Oliver braced his knees and tightened his grip around her. "What's wrong?"

"She's disappeared. There was a fire."

"What? Is she okay?"

"I don't know. I haven't heard."

Oliver pushed the lift button while Alice fished around in her handbag for her earpiece. She hooked it over her ear and projected the screen. No messages. Oliver took her handbag from her and steered her through the opening steel doors.

"There must be some news by now," said Alice, scrolling through her e-mails and news service alerts.

Birthing Home fire risks lives of three babies.

'Miracle': no lives lost in Birthing Home inferno.

Alice scanned the articles quickly. No mention of a vanishing mother and baby. She frowned.

Any news? she messaged Mary.

"Do you need to call someone? Go somewhere? What can I do?" asked Oliver, pushing the button for their floor.

"I don't know," whispered Alice. "I'm just so tired."

Pregnancy tiredness was not like normal tiredness you could just work through, she knew. The strain of the past few days was too much. She needed to rest. Her head felt light and she ached all over.

"Let's get you inside and into bed, then. Do you want me to call Mary to see if she's heard anything?"

Alice nodded and let herself be guided into their apartment and through to their bedroom. Oliver gently undressed her and helped her into warm pyjamas.

"I'll get you something to eat. What do you think you could man-age?"

"Toast. Just buttered toast, please. And maybe some chips. Do we have any chips? The crinkly ones," Alice muttered into the pillow, her eyes closed.

Oliver brushed his hand over her cheek. "I'll have a look."

Alice felt like she was free-falling through the bed. Weightless and spinning, down through the atmosphere. Her stomach lurched. She threw the covers back, rolled out of bed onto shaky legs and crawled to the adjoining bathroom. Pushing the toilet lid up, she just man-aged to peek her head over the top before vomiting a thin stream of brown liquid into the bowl. The lid crashed back down on her head and she moaned.

"Ollie!" she cried out, sobbing before the next wave of nausea hit. She felt his large hands sweep her hair up and secure it with one hand. With his free hand he passed her tissues to wipe her face. She took them and slumped back on her heels.

"Alice, sweetheart, you've been pushing yourself too hard."

Alice shook her head and shifted her bottom along the tiles. Her stomach heaved and she braced herself for another round of dry retching. Oliver held her hair back until she'd finished.

"Do you have any other symptoms? Other than nausea and dizzi-ness?"

Alice did a mental catalogue of her body parts. "No, I don't think so."

"Just pregnancy and exhaustion, then. Let's get you back into bed and see if some food, drink and rest will revive you."

Alice nodded. He spoke as though to a child. Soothing and reas-suring, striking a delicate balance between buying into the fear and allaying it. She accepted the warm, damp flannel Oliver handed her to clean herself with. When she'd finished, he squatted down and put one hand under her knees, the other around her back.

"Hands round my neck," he said. He stood and carried her slight frame back into the bedroom and deposited her onto their soft bed.

Alice ate the dry crackers he brought her—the buttered toast forgotten—and washed them down with sparkling mineral water, enjoying the saltiness and realising how thirsty she was. Oliver sat and watched her.

"I haven't been taking very good care of you, have I?" He smiled.

Alice managed a small smile back.

"I promise I'll try to be around more. I'm sorry. Sleep now. I'll find out what's going on with the search for Monica and Oscar. You're no use to anybody if you make yourself sick with worry and exhaustion. We need to look after *our* baby now, too."

Alice nodded. She closed her eyes and listened to Oliver's heavy footsteps as he padded out of the door and down the stairs to the kitchen.

When Alice woke again it was dark and the apartment was quiet apart from the tap-tapping of fingers on a computer screen. Tentatively, she placed a hand on her abdomen and gently pressed down with her fingers. No movement. She swallowed and pressed again. The pressure wobbled the small mound slightly. She felt a flutter and breathed in sharply and raggedly with relief.

"Hey, bubba, you okay in there?"

There was no further response. Satisfied, Alice slid out from under the covers, pulled her dressing gown on and headed carefully down the stairs to the living room.

Mary sat on the sofa with her back to Alice; legs crossed, earbuds in and neck bent, staring at her tablet screen and tapping away. Alice smiled, skirted the sofa and sat down lightly beside her. She waited. After a moment Mary looked up and yelled in fright, ripping the buds from her ears. Alice shot out an arm to catch the screen as it started to slide onto the floor.

"Hi!" she said brightly.

"Jesus, Mary and freaking Joseph, woman. You could frighten the life out of a bloody zombie," said Mary, clutching her screen protectively and glaring at Alice.

"Any news?"

"Not yet."

A picture reel started to flash in Alice's mind: Monica, dead in a gutter with Oscar crying helplessly; Monica, locked up in a secret jail without Oscar at all. She shuddered and shook her mind to clear it.

"Ollie's gone?" Alice asked, refocusing her attention.

"Yeah, he had to go to work. He called me to come and sit with you." Mary frowned. "So technically, I'm baby-lady-sitting."

"She thinks she's funny..." Alice said to her bump, shaking her head.

"Oh, hey, that Mater who works with Ollie dropped in while you were sleeping. She left a flash drive for you, said it had some photos on it you might need." Without looking up, Mary waved a small black plastic tube in Alice's general direction. Alice caught her arm and extracted the drive from Mary's hand. She turned it over, frowning.

"Margery gave you this?"

"Yeah, Margery, that's her. What is it?"

Alice ignored her question, dropping the plastic case into her pocket.

Mary looked her up and down. "You okay now?"

Alice nodded. "Feeling rested. And pregnant." She looked over her shoulder at the kitchen. "Also, hungry."

"Good." Mary indicated the fridge with a flick of her head. "Lover-boy left you a meal in there." Steadying her tablet and shifting her legs slightly, Mary went back to tapping.

"You're not a very good baby-lady-sitter, you know."

"Mmm," said Mary, without looking up.

"No Juanita? You're welcome to bring her around if you like, I'd love to meet her."

Mary stopped tapping. "She's not around anymore."

"Oh, I'm sorry."

"Don't be. She wanted me to come and meet her kids. Her *kids*. I don't like spending Sundays going to meet my own kids, let alone somebody else's. We're just not compatible." She shrugged. "It's okay. I'm not really a people person anyway."

"You don't say." Alice smiled wryly. Mary ignored her.

Alice wandered into the kitchen and spread some chocolate-hazelnut paste onto three slices of bread and took the plate back into the living room.

"So, they're looking for Monica and Oscar?" she asked.

Mary looked squarely at her, then back to her computer. "Of course, they are. They're just doing it quietly."

"What do they think happened? Has she done a runner?"

"She's got an infant and no vehicle. It's unlikely. There's a surveillance car parked out the front of your apartment block so it's fairly clear they know you're not involved personally."

"So, abduction then?" Alice felt her panic rising. "But who? Why?"

Mary put her tablet aside. "I don't know. I've been trying to find out. Nobody's taking credit for it, at least not publicly or through the channels I've got access to."

"What do we do now?" asked Alice, barely containing her irritation. She wasn't used to not having the answers.

"We wait. And order pizza," said Mary, eyeing Alice's plate and tapping her earpiece.

Alice nodded.

While Mary ordered enough food to feed a small army, Alice picked up her own tablet from the coffee table. She plucked the flash drive out of her pyjama pocket and plugged it into the screen. The images started to load and she opened them in a slideshow. Her stomach churned with each click. Young girls, naked, their horror and despair clearly burned into the pixels on the screen. In one, a familiar adult face—Graeme Smythe—clearly confirming his guilt.

Alice removed the flash drive and slipped it back into her pocket just as Mary finished placing their food order. She felt sick but she knew that with this evidence, she would bring the children's tormenter to justice and put a major dent in the credibility of the Equality Party. The images would also be the bargaining chip she needed to trade for her family's safety.

She thought of her promise to her brother, to ensure the images stayed out of the public arena. She sent him a silent apology. The stakes were too high to turn back now. She would make sure the repercussions wouldn't touch her. Her family would be safely out of Australia by the time the fallout began. And if she played her cards right, she'd be able to trigger the beginning of the end for the G.D.S.

"For the sake of the children," she whispered.

CHAPTER 34

MONICA WAS VAGUELY aware of being lifted into a car; a door closing; an engine starting; then nothing.

When she woke again it was dark. She opened her eyes, concentrating on forcing her blurred vision to make out discernible shapes. Her head throbbed and her mouth was dry.

"Hey, Mon, you awake?" A familiar face smiled at her in the rear-view mirror.

Monica moaned softly as the car jolted over a pothole in the road. She tried to lift her head, panic rising, trying to identify the face in the gentle glow emitted by the headlights in the dark. Her mind spun. Centrifugal forces pushed her back down into the car seat.

"It's me, Mon. Uncle Pete. It's okay, you're safe. Your baby is next to you in the capsule. The sedation will wear off very soon." He paused. Monica stared at him, struggling to keep her eyes open. "You got lucky—I was out doing a bit of recon. Wasn't expecting to have to rescue you from a blazing inferno. Put a bit of a hole in my plan, but nothing like a bit of an adrenaline rush, hey?" He grinned. "Sorry about the sedative, there wasn't time to explain."

Monica nodded as her thoughts sloshed around in her head, trying to focus. Uncle Pete, her piratey hero, her foggy brain told her. No, not a pirate. What, then? She blinked rapidly and frowned, trying to make sense of it all. Alice must have come through, this must be her way of getting her out. She breathed out and relaxed, giving up on rational thought and submitting to the sedative. Pete the pirate had come to rescue her. He wasn't going to take Oscar away from her. They would sail the seven seas together...

"You're safe now." A pale hand reached back and patted Monica's shoulder. "Close your eyes and get some rest."

She made sure her arm was securely around Oscar before allowing her head to drop backwards onto the headrest. She heard electronic bleeps and then her uncle's voice came through the car's sound system.

"Yep."

"I've got her," said Pete.

"I told you to stay away from there," said the voice at the end of the line, irritably.

"I saw smoke and flames so I went in."

The voice was silent for a moment. "She and the kid okay, then?"

"Yeah, they're fine. I'm bringing them to the safe house now."

"Just make sure you're not followed, okay?"

"I'll try," said Pete, just before Monica slipped from consciousness.

CHAPTER 35

OLIVER HAD LOST all feeling in his left leg. He shifted his awkward position on the floor of the younger kids' room and tried to extricate the index finger of his left hand from Ellie's tight grasp without waking her. He held his breath as she gave a startled gasp but relaxed as she slowly let out her breath, rolled onto her back and smacked her lips loudly. He smiled, wondering if she was dreaming about yoghurt, her favourite food group. Reaching out his hand, he gently brushed back the strands of hair that had fallen in her eyes. There were no visible signs of her head injury, and the headaches appeared to have subsided. There had been no complaints of pain in the past twenty-four hours. Still, he felt the guilt of an accident that he probably couldn't have avoided.

Oliver held his breath and shook his foot out, then raised himself to his knees and stood on it tentatively. He turned and tucked Tom's duvet back in where it had broken free from the wall and was threatening to slide right off the bed. He wondered if he could possibly feel any more protective of a child who was genetically his own. He would walk over hot coals for both Ellie and Tom. Each Sunday morning, they went out with their genetic mother; sometimes their genetic father. But each Sunday evening they came back and wrapped their arms around him or Margery; each Sunday evening they came *home*.

He padded down the hallway, past the closed doors of the two older kids, and into the lounge room where he flopped down on the sofa next to Margery and rubbed his hands through his thick hair.

"They're both out cold," he announced.

Margery leaned forward and pushed a mug of tea towards him. "I'll stay until they announce who's getting a rose," she said, without taking her eyes off the wall screen.

Oliver shook his head and chuckled. "You and these dating shows."

"It's not a *dating show*, Oliver. It's a careful selection of a life partner. These people are searching for a *soulmate*."

Oliver picked up his mug and leaned back into the chair with it. "Well, your shift is over. Feel free to stay as long as you like, but I'll get up if we're needed."

"Mmm," replied Margery.

The truth was, Margery had no real reason to leave. There was nobody waiting for her to come home since her husband had walked out on her more than a decade ago. She was effectively married to her job as Mater and spent many more hours at the Home than was required of her. Oliver worried about what would happen to her when it came time for her to retire. She would probably stay on as an on-call helper, but leaving the kids full-time would be hard for her.

Picking up a tablet that had been left lying on the sofa between them, Oliver checked the news services. Still no word about Monica and Oscar. The official cause given for the fire was an electrical fault; it had been confirmed and the blame game had begun. For a Birthing Home to be allowed to get into such a state of disrepair was unthinkable. Someone's head would roll.

"Bloody cost-cutting," he muttered.

"She'll be okay, you know," said Margery, peering over his shoulder.

"You mean Monica?"

Margery nodded and turned back to the screen. "Yes. And Alice. You don't need to worry yourself about them. They'll be fine. Might be best to start thinking about what will happen to you. Will you be fine?" She regarded him softly, with the concern of someone who had known him for many years.

"Yes. Of course, I'll be fine," he replied automatically.

"Now, come on, Ollie. This is me, you can talk to me. You've always wanted a baby of your own. One to live with you all the time, just like the olden days. Here's your chance, my boy. What are you going to do about it?" Margery picked up her tea and blew on it while she waited.

"I'm not sure there's much I *can* do. Alice doesn't seem to think there's any way they'll let us keep the baby. I'm not really sure she... that she wants to."

"Of course, she wants to. She's just scared, Ollie. And as for practicalities, there's always a way. Maybe not here in Australia, but in another country?"

"I've been thinking through all the options, Marge. I'm just not sure there's a good option in there. I can't think of an option where I get to keep Alice and our baby plus you and the kids, short of shipping you all out of the country together." He laughed half-heartedly.

"Well, you'll just have to pick the choice you can live in peace with."

"And what about you? What choice will you make, if I'm gone?"

Margery smiled and patted his knee. "I'll be here for the kids, don't you worry. Long enough for me to see we get good Mater and Pater replacements in. I've got everything I need here. I'm happy."

Oliver nodded. "Okay. I'll talk to Alice."

CHAPTER 36

“MMM, DAMN THEY do good pizza in Carlton. You can't get pizza like this down bayside.” Mary picked up two wayward olives from her otherwise empty plate.

“No, but they do some genuinely awesome seafood,” said Alice, remembering her last beach-front meal with Oliver and frowning at the memory of the non-pregnancy-friendly oysters she'd consumed. She shook her head slightly; there were plenty of other things to worry about that she could actually do something about without worrying about the ones she was powerless to change.

“Mary,” started Alice, putting her hand in her pocket and wrapping her fingers around the flash drive for courage. “There's something else I need your help with.”

“Help with?”

“That article—the online one about the supposed government conspiracy, you remember?”

“Crackpot conspiracists chasing you down the street again?” asked Mary wryly, her eyebrows raised.

“No, it's true. The conspiracy, I mean.”

“The Franken-babies?”

Alice waved her arm, batting away Mary's disbelief. “Okay, not quite nuts and bolts in the neck, but genetic engineering, yes.”

“Oh, please, we know they're doing that—it's public knowledge. Decreasing congenital disease and disability, improving population health, blah, blah." Mary threw back the remainder of her glass and stood up and stretched, then headed towards the kitchen.

"It started out like that, yes. A trial to reduce the incidence of mental illness through genetic engineering. But it progressed."

"Uh-huh. To nuts and bolts in the neck?" said Mary, holding the refrigerator door open with her elbow while she refilled her glass.

"Mary!"

"Okay, okay. No nuts and bolts. Continue, please."

Alice waited until Mary was settled on the sofa again and giving her full attention.

"My daughter, Monica, she's extremely intelligent but sometimes she can be a little... abrupt. She sometimes doesn't connect with the emotions of others particularly well," said Alice hesitantly.

"Sounds like a girl after my own heart, really. So much simpler to live without all that angst and crap. It's easier to see things more... clearly."

"Yes, you two have rather a lot in common." Alice looked at Mary curiously and wondered for the first time whether Mary's mother had been among the first test subjects. It would explain a lot. "It's not an accident, her personality. It's genetically engineered. As was mine."

"Well that makes sense," said Mary, swirling the liquid around in her glass.

"It does?"

"Well of course it fucking doesn't, that's the stupidest thing I've ever heard. Why the hell would they do that?" she exploded, leaning forward and slamming her wine glass down so hard on the coffee table that the stem snapped. "Oh, Jesus, now look what you and your bloody Franken-babies made me do."

Mary stomped off to the kitchen, taking the half-empty bowl of her glass with her. She returned a few minutes later, noticeably calmer and with a sturdy mug, topped up with alcohol.

Alice sat and waited, hands quietly in her lap.

"This is big, Alice, I need a bit of time. And maybe some more wine. Who the hell told you all this anyway, that nut-job gardener? Has he shown up again?"

"It wasn't him. It was a professor, from the university. He was on the research project that was the precursor for the G.D.S. He knew my mother."

"Shit, Alice, no wonder you sounded so panicked." Mary was lost in thought for a moment, processing the news. She moaned and rubbed her temple with her free hand. "No, I give up, I don't get it. You're going to have to lay it out for me."

Alice paused to search for the right words.

"A person with controlled emotional input is much more likely to vote for economically rational policies. You wouldn't need to be photographed kissing babies to make people think you're a nice person. And voters wouldn't care when you're accused of aborting damaged foetuses by the dozen..."

"Because a rational population would be quite happy for you to abort babies that aren't smart enough, or healthy enough, because that makes logical sense—because it's still ultimately for the sake of the children," finished Mary.

"Yes—just fewer, more perfect, children."

"Shit, Alice. Why did you have to tell me? I think I would have preferred to do an ostrich on this one and stick my head in the sand."

"You might not feel that way if it had been your baby who'd been considered not quite... up to standard," said Alice coldly.

"Not..." started Mary, the realisation obviously hitting her hard and fast.

"Yes. My son."

"Oh, Alice, I'm so sorry."

"The gene editing program has already been rolled out with the G.D.S., Mary. Barbara Mathers and her cronies waited until Monica turned eighteen—to make sure their prototype made it through puberty unaltered—and then implemented the gene editing process across the board."

Mary whistled. "That's a fairly long-term game, though. They'll need to wait another eighteen years for their investments to mature and gain the right to vote."

"A government with a long-term plan. Who'd have thought?" Alice laughed bitterly.

"Pity their prototype has gone rogue. Clearly they didn't factor pregnancy and maternal instinct into the epigenetic soup. Maybe they'll just give up."

Alice raised her eyebrows. "Maybe you'll invite Juanita back to pick up your dry cleaning and polish your shoes."

"Yeah all right, no need to get personal." Mary paused. "Actually, this makes a whole lot more sense now." She picked up her tablet, swiped a few times and handed it to Alice.

Alice started to read through almost impenetrable scientific jargon. "What am I looking at, Mary?"

"When I was at the labs the other day, doing research for the new G.D.S. comms campaign, I took a snap of some papers. One of the lab staff shoved them in a drawer as soon as I came in, so I figured they were important."

"And...?"

"If you scan down to the bottom of the first page, it talks about gene substitution and phasing out the median. It took me a while to figure it out and, when I did, I thought I must be wrong. But if what you've said is true, then this probably is, too."

"*What*, Mary?"

"They're planning to implant women with either smart genes or compliant, dumb genes. And not even their own embryos—just babies that have been selected to look like them so nobody gets suspicious."

Alice felt her nausea rise. "Why would you bother creating babies that aren't super-intelligent?"

"Someone's gotta clean the bathroom, don't they? Haven't managed to get robots to do the job yet."

"So, tell me, what do you think a rational me would do right about now?"

"Well, for starters you'd get yourself to the closest hospital to rid yourself of that unscheduled and probably damaged foetus," said Mary. "Then you'd leave your obviously irrational daughter to her own devices, rescue your grandson and have him tested for emotional abnormalities at your earliest convenience. And you'd let the government continue with their little experiment because really, we all like to have a clean bathroom."

"Mary!"

"Just telling it like it is."

"Fine, so let's assume that I'm not my rational self. I'm a thoroughly comprised, inferior early edition. What do I do now?"

Mary shrugged. "That depends. What do you want to achieve?"

"I want Ollie and me and our baby and Monica and Oscar to all live together as one big, happy family. Maybe with a pet dog and a white picket fence, too." Alice tore the crust off her half-eaten slice of pizza and nibbled on it.

"You don't ask for much, do you?" Mary watched her eat. "I think laying low for a while is a good option; getting out of town altogether is an even better one." She took another sip of her wine. "There's been some chatter on the dark web about the Birthing Home fire. It looks like the sprinkler system may have been deliberately turned off, remotely."

Instead of replying, Alice pulled the flash drive out of her pocket and placed it in Mary's palm.

"Pete thinks the government is worried Monica and I will try to keep our babies. The Equality Party can't afford to have their precious 'prototypes' turning defective. There's already unrest in some Birthing Homes over leaked information about Charlotte White's suicide note, saying she killed herself because she refused to produce babies only to have them taken away. Having Monica and I publicly refuse to toe the line could spark a full-scale rebellion." Alice nodded at the flash drive that Mary was turning over in her fingers. "I think I can use this to keep us safe, if I can find the right person to trade it with."

Mary plugged the drive into her computer and scrolled through the images. She raised her eyebrows. "Are these...? Shit, Alice, is that...?" She put the screen down. "I feel sick."

Alice nodded and replied in a steely voice. "I'm sorry." She pointed at the computer. "There's names, dates and places in there as well. But with the information you've got about gene editing, we won't need to release them publicly. We can use your information to push the tide of public opinion against the Equality Party. The images will just assure our safety."

Mary whistled and leaned back, her hands crossed behind her head. "Okay, so you're planning to find someone who you can hand these to, in exchange for helping you get what you want?"

"Yes. Pete has contacts to ensure a safe passage to Sweden, but he can't guarantee our safety here. And I can't just do nothing about the genetic manipulations now that I know about them. I'm not sure Pete has the appetite to help me with that. He's known for decades and done nothing," she said bitterly.

Mary raised an eyebrow. "You need someone with influence and power who has an interest in ending the G.D.S. How about, say, a senior politician whose daughter recently killed herself to protest the G.D.S.?"

Alice nodded slowly.

Mary continued: "A man who is also rumoured to have voted, behind closed doors, against supporting the G.D.S. but was forced to support it by a party majority."

Alice tore another piece off her pizza crust without eating it. "You're a genius. I need to speak to Charlotte White's father, Richard White."

"And, Alice, you need to release the images publicly. Forget about the gene editing. If you want to convince people, you need to hit them where it hurts—their heart, not their mind. People might get irritated about a possible future tampering with their genetic structure. But show them images of children—their own children, that they were forced to give up—actually being abused by a senior public servant appointed by the government? They'll be baying for blood in the streets. The Equality Party will be lucky if they last the week."

Alice bit both her lips and chewed on them. She sighed. "You're right, as usual. Okay, let's do it."

"One last thing. Taking on Graeme Smythe, who has Barbara Mathers on his side, over child abuse allegations is serious, Alice. He's not going to plead guilty to the death penalty without a fight. And he's bound to suspect you've had something to do with it."

Alice smiled. "Barbara Mathers will throw him to the wolves after he's arrested and charged. She'll be too busy running around, trying to contain the reputational damage it'll do to her government, including the G.D.S. He's been her right-wing man for years, she's allowed a *paedophile* to be in charge of a national program for babies. You can imagine what the public will make of that."

"You and I are part of that department, too, Alice. This could rub off on us." Mary frowned.

"I wasn't planning on going back anyway," said Alice quietly.

Mary shrugged. "I guess I could do with a change of department."

"Making sure Graeme can't trace it back to me, that's where you come in. I need you to get this information to the media and the police anonymously. The timing has to be carefully managed."

"I'll see what I can do," said Mary. She tapped on her screen and pulled the flash drive out. "Okay, I've got the files saved on here now. And... damn, you can't talk to Richard White tonight, he's still flying in from Canberra. He attended a parliamentary inquiry on..." She scanned the screen and shook her head. "Ugh, I don't know, something boring."

"There's no point in talking to Mr. White until I find Monica and Oscar. I can't keep them safe if I don't know where they are," said Alice. "I'll leave you to it, then. I need to see Ollie tonight." She held out her hand for the flash drive.

Mary deposited the drive into Alice's waiting palm. She held Alice's hand for a moment.

"Look after you and the little one, yeah?" said Mary softly, staring intently into Alice's eyes. "Ollie and Monica, they're both adults. Oscar is Monica's responsibility if she decides to run. Your baby has nobody but you now. You understand?"

"Yes," said Alice. "And Mary, thank you. For helping me connect the dots."

Mary let Alice's hand drop from hers and flicked her head towards the door. "All right, touchy-feely time is over. Now go save the world or something."

Alice grinned and left.

CHAPTER 37

THE GENTLE THRUM of the car engine stopped. Monica fought her way up through the fog in her mind.

Car. She was in a car. With Oscar.

She drifted deeper again.

A baby squawked. Her eyes snapped open. She pushed at the car door and tried to get out, but became tangled in her seatbelt. With clumsy hands she fumbled with the buckle and released herself. Following the sound of her baby she skirted around the back of the car, using the trunk as a crutch while she willed her legs to stop threatening to collapse. Near the passenger door on the other side, she found him on the ground, still safely in the capsule. She grabbed the handle and tried to pick him up but was stopped by a hand on her arm. The grip was firm and tight; it made her elbow throb and she felt the finger marks for several minutes afterwards.

"It's okay, you can keep your hand on him, but I'm going to help you carry him," said Pete through the gloom. "You're still a little groggy from the sedative and I don't want you dropping him."

Monica blinked rapidly and held on to the handle of Oscar's capsule. She frowned and looked across at Pete, who gripped the other side of the car seat handle. She nodded. Pete nodded back and started to walk slowly. Monica followed, lifting her feet higher than usual over the unfamiliar terrain to avoid tripping.

Pete suddenly changed direction and the capsule wobbled. Oscar started to fuss again.

"Nearly there, little one. Then Mummy can feed you and you can both get some sleep," said Pete softly.

Monica could see a pool of light ahead, illuminating four wooden steps leading up to a porch and a white door. She tried to adjust her eyes to see the rest of the house, but it was pitch black. No street lights, no moon, and even the stars seemed to have vanished.

At the top of the stairs Pete pressed his palm against the door frame. Monica heard a click as he pushed the door open and steered her inside, down a short hallway, and into a small bedroom that was mostly bed and nothing else. Monica focused on the pillow as she trudged over and dragged herself up onto it.

Pete set Oscar down next to the bed and turned to leave. Oscar snorted and snuffled and let out a sharp wail. Pete stopped at the door and smiled.

"You should be fine to still breastfeed him with the sedative you've had. It was only a mild dose, but it's had a huge effect on you because you're already so tired. There's a jug of water on your bedside table there and I'll be right next door if you need anything." He tapped the doorframe lightly and pulled the door shut behind him.

Monica picked up her wailing infant and placed him on the bed next to her, his angry face against her breast. He latched on and started sucking, never once opening his eyes. Moments later she was snuggled under the blankets, warm and drowsy.

Through the thin walls of the house, fragments of a conversation reached her ears as she sank into slumber, lapping at her mind like waves on the shore, eroding her sense of ease and morphing into nightmares of shouting and running and searching. But she was tired, so tired...

"She's safe for now..."

"She's not even supposed to be here. How do you know you weren't followed?"

"...let her mother know, she'll be worried."

"No... first thing she'd do is drive here. We can't take the risk she'll be followed. ... lay low for a day or two."

"They wouldn't..."

"Just don't, okay?"

CHAPTER 38

ALICE WAITED FOR the car to swing in line with the curb and the engine to switch off. It felt lonely out here in the dark and cold, slivers of light peeping out from behind curtains up and down the street. It was past bedtime for the little ones in Mitcham. Eight o'clock. The older kids would be still awake, doing their homework. The senior year students would have mixed anxieties as winter progressed, especially the girls. Were they more nervous about their final exams, or their impending pregnancies?

At least they had each other to talk to. Huddles in the lunch hour, fretting equally about graphing polynomial functions and acquiring stretch marks. The boys would be making jokes about looking forward to their sperm donations. Teasing the girls about which one might be bearing his child. The girls would retort with reminders that they'd be the ones waiting on them at all hours of the day and walking the halls with crying babies at night. After a few years they'd all be off to further study or apprenticeships, leaving their babies behind in the suburbs.

Alice wondered how many would stride off, unaffected, and how many would push back against the forced separation from their infants like her own daughter. Was it a sign of mental illness developing, this inability to separate life into neat emotional compartments? It had happened to her own mother, the anxieties from all facets of her life bleeding into each other until the dam walls she'd so carefully constructed started crashing down, all the worries joining together into a river of nightmares that swept her away.

Alice had been so angry with her for not trying harder, for not staying close to her after the stillbirth of her first child. In recent weeks, with her own neatly built emotional compartments fraying at the edges, she thought she understood her mother better than ever before.

She shook her head and opened the car door, grateful for the blast of cold night air to strengthen her own mental walls.

Oliver ushered her inside with a soft grin. "Hey, lover, this is a lovely surprise."

"Soulmate," Alice corrected.

Oliver laughed. "Margery's just headed off for the evening. You want a cuppa? I was just boiling the kettle."

"Sure," said Alice, the tense muscles in her jaw starting to relax as she surrendered to the cosy chaos of Oliver and Margery's Home. Fragments of chalk lay strewn among the beanbags below the chalkboard.

"Any news?" he called from the kitchen.

"Not yet."

"I'm sure they'll find them. They can't have gone far."

"No. I mean sure, yes, they'll find them," said Alice, irritated at his casual attitude.

A dozen books were scattered across the sofas where the kids had left them after their bedtime stories. Alice tidied them into a neat pile, relocated them onto the coffee table, and sat down. A head full of messy curls appeared at the end of the sofa. Alice's heart leapt briefly.

"Ellie. Hi. What are you doing out of bed?"

"Where's Pa?" demanded the little girl rubbing her eyes in the bright light.

Maternal Instinct

"He's making a cup of tea. In the kitchen."

"Oh," said Ellie, regarding Alice suspiciously. "Is he coming back?"

Alice smiled. "Yes, of course he is. Aren't you supposed to be asleep?"

Ellie wrinkled her nose. "I try to sleep but I can't. I close my eyes reeeeeally tight..." Ellie demonstrated, tensing her entire body and squeezing her eyes shut. "...but then they get all open-y." Her eyes popped wide open. She stuck her thumb and forefinger against her right eye and pulled her eyelids further apart until Alice could see the blood vessels surrounding her eyeball. "See?" she said triumphantly.

"Ellie, put those eyeballs back on your pillow, please," said Oliver, carrying two steaming mugs of green tea into the lounge room.

Ellie pouted and scooted back down the hallway.

"Hard day at work?" asked Alice, taking in Oliver's messy hair and tired eyes.

Oliver passed Alice a mug and rubbed at his eyes with his free hand. He yawned widely.

"Ah, I love this time of night." He lowered himself onto the sofa next to Alice, took a sip of his tea and lay his arm along the back of the seat cushion. "The older two are dressed for bed and banished to their rooms. Tom and Ellie are in bed, asleep."

Ellie popped her head around the door frame and giggled.

"Ellie is *in bed*. Asleeeeep," repeated Oliver, without turning his head.

Light footsteps pattered back down the hallway and a door slammed.

"That kid. I don't know where she gets her second wind from. Six-thirty at night and she's having a complete meltdown over bath time, demands to go to bed early because she's far too tired—her words, not mine—and over an hour later she's wide awake again and running up and down the hallway."

Alice smiled and, resting her hand lightly on her stomach, sipped her tea gingerly. She waited for Oliver to settle and turn the wall screen on, watched him flicking through channels on home design, healthful cooking and tropical beach getaways to Port Douglas.

Why now? thought Alice. Why did everything have to become so complicated just when she and Oliver had finally sorted themselves out? He had accepted Monica as part of their lives, Alice had only barely started to daydream about Sunday outings with the three of them and baby Oscar. Watching him grow, learning to walk, the cycle of life all over again. It could have been so easy. And then it wasn't.

Oliver sighed, stopping on the paradise channel.

"Man, to have a nice, warm holiday from cold, wintery Melbourne with my incubating soulmate. Now *that* sounds nice."

Alice seized the opportunity. "What if we could get even further away? Stay in a warm climate permanently?"

"Move up north to Port Douglas?" asked Oliver, frowning. "It's a bit touristy, I don't think they have Homes up there. Although Margery would love the warmer climate. It's worth asking, I'm sure the kids wouldn't mind. Their genetic parents aren't particularly involved and they could get discount flights on a Visiting Plan anyway and..." he trailed off, sipping his tea and imagining himself into the travel show.

"I met with Barbara, my minister, yesterday."

At first, she thought Oliver hadn't heard her. He didn't respond.

"We can't raise this baby here, in Australia," she said, moving Oliver's hand from the back of the sofa and onto her stomach. "They won't allow us to raise the baby together. They say it would set a precedent, look bad for the government."

Oliver's eyes followed his hand, looking slightly bewildered. Alice sighed inwardly, frustrated again at her husband's chronic inability to see reality through his rose-coloured glasses. And yet, it was also what she loved so much about him. He leaned forward and placed his mug on the table, freeing up both hands to cover Alice's expanding belly.

"I've been thinking," he started hesitantly. "You could go away for a while, tell everyone you're getting treatment for the cancer, that it's come back. When the baby's born it can come and live here with me and Margery. You'd be able to visit whenever you liked." He looked at Alice pleadingly.

Alice took both of his hands and moved them off her belly, shoving them a little too roughly to cover the grinding of her teeth.

"Ollie, be rational. Please?" She took a deep breath and tried to swallow her exasperation. "Too many people know about the pregnancy already. And you're not due for a new arrival here for at least three years."

Oliver stared at her stomach. She took his hand in both of hers and glanced up to where she knew the surveillance camera was mounted. She turned her back to it.

"Pete can help us," she whispered. "He's using his network to find a way to get us out of the country safely. We can go to Sweden, or somewhere warmer, if you want. We can raise our baby together."

"And Monica and Oscar?"

"They would come too."

"I can come too? Me too?" sang a child's voice as Ellie came running through the lounge and launched herself into Oliver's lap. "Where we go?" she enquired, sitting up, back straight, nuzzling her nose against Oliver's.

He softened and hugged her.

"To the moon, Ellie-bellie! We are going to the moon in a big space rocket and we're going to eat ice-cream and jelly snakes. But first you have to stay in bed and have a big, big sleep."

"I can sleep in rocket! It long way to moon," said Ellie, crossing her arms and digging her shoulder into Oliver's chest.

"Come on, baby girl. You go back to bed and go to sleep. Pa is very tired and needs some rest too, remember." Oliver pointed to the hallway, wiggling his eyebrows.

Ellie pouted, slithered off his lap and stalked towards the door. She stopped and peeked back at him through her curls.

"You not go moon without me, okay?"

Oliver shook his head and crossed his fingers over his heart. "I swear. We'll have matching spacesuits and everything."

Ellie nodded her approval and slipped through the door.

Oliver grinned and turned back to Alice, who was staring after the little girl. The grin slid off his face, replaced by concern. He put both of his hands over hers. Alice blinked once; a single tear escaped. Oliver opened his mouth to speak.

"Don't say it," she whispered, shaking her head.

"Alice, Ellie is as much a daughter to me as Monica is to you."

"No," she moaned. "She's not. You're just her carer, you're not her father. *This* is your child, in here." She pulled his hand against her stomach, willing him to feel their child move.

"Alice, I'm so sorry. You're asking me to abandon four of my children who depend on me, in favour of one child who doesn't even know me yet." He pushed his hand against her abdomen warmly and hugged her closely with his free arm. She sobbed into his shoulder. "I desperately want this baby, Alice. We can make it work here, we can find a way to make you and our baby safe."

Alice pulled back and wiped at her tears angrily. It wasn't fair. None of this fair.

"No, we can't, Ollie. If I stay, at best our baby will be taken away. At worst, it won't survive at all—the stakes are too high for the Equality Party, there's too much unrest already. I can't live through either of those scenarios again. I just can't take the risk, I'm sorry."

Oliver stroked her hair and gently tried to pull her to him. "This baby that we made, against all odds, it's ours. I want him—or her—to be born safely and to grow up in a loving and safe home, just like this one. I would love it if it could be *this* Home. I want to be a part of her—or his—life, every day. But Ellie is my baby, too, as are the other kids here. Ellie doesn't understand about genetic lines and political stakes. All she knows is that I'm always here for her. I look after her when she's sick, I laugh with her when she's happy, I put her to bed and sing songs to her. Because I'm her Pa. I can't abandon her. She has to come first."

Alice nodded, choking on her tears.

"I know," she croaked. "I'm sorry, I didn't think it through. I just thought—"

"Of your own children," said Oliver, cutting her off. "And that's as it should be." He smiled sadly. "I love you Alice Mooney, I love you so much. It kills me to say this, but I think you should go. If you truly believe that our baby's best chance at a good life is somewhere other than here, I'll trust you on that. Take Monica and Oscar with you and go."

"But I can't..." Her tears flowed freely now.

"Ssh." He held her head against his chest. "You'll learn how, Alice, I know you will. I have faith that you'll do a wonderful job of raising our child. You've learned from a master, right?"

Alice looked up at him and tried to smile at his half-hearted joke. She swung her feet up onto the sofa and slotted her head into his armpit. They stayed like that for a long time, silently watching a cooking show, then a gardening show.

Eventually she stood up to leave.

"I have to go back to the apartment. I can't stay the night here."

"No, of course not."

He stood and they both walked woodenly to the door.

Oliver held her closely and whispered in her ear. "I love you."

"I love you too, Ollie. I'll... see you soon."

"Yes," he said, choking slightly. "See you soon. Take care of you. Take care of our baby." He spread his hands over her belly one last time, allowing the warmth of his skin to sink through the material of her shirt.

Without meeting his eyes, Alice placed her own hand over his for a moment, then lifted it off her stomach and replaced it at his side. She turned and walked quickly out of the door without looking back, got into her car and drove into the starless night.

CHAPTER 39

ALICE KICKED AT the blankets and sheets which had become tangled around her while she slept. It was nights when Oliver was on sleepovers that she missed his ability to anchor the sheets most. He was a restful, reliable sleeper; she slept like an eggbeater. After a few attempts she gave up trying to straighten the duvet with her feet and threw the whole thing off the bed sideways.

She felt sick as soon as her feet hit the floor and reeled back against the bed. It was hard to isolate the source of the nausea. The guilt of depriving Oliver of his flesh-and-blood child lay heavy on her. It churned in the pit of her stomach together with the fear about Monica and Oscar's safety and the worry about her own situation. Then again, maybe it was simply morning sickness returning and she was overthinking it.

While she waited for her nausea to subside, she tapped her earpiece to check her messages and nearly burst into tears of relief.

They're both okay. We leave tonight. I'll pick you up early afternoon, be ready. Signed, 'P', from an unrecognised number.

I'll be ready. Not from here, though. She tapped out the address nearby that she planned to visit that morning. Richard White's home.

Opening the bedroom door and peering over the banister, Alice saw that Mary was sound asleep on the sofa, curled in a foetal position with her arm wrapped protectively around her tablet. She closed the door quietly and started looking through her wardrobe for suitable non-work attire, preferably with an elastic waist. The pants she had been wearing yesterday had become a little tight over her expanding belly. Settling for a pair of monochrome kaftan pants and a black top, she slipped on a pair of sandals, ran a brush through her hair, and popped the flash drive into her pocket.

Picking up her earpiece from the bedside table, Alice peeked out again at her lady-baby-sitter. Mary hadn't moved. She trod quietly through the apartment to the door and left. Inside the lift, she pressed the button for the car park and waited. She closed her eyes and saw Oliver's pained expression. It was a hopeless choice: stay with Oliver and give up their baby, or leave Oliver and keep their baby.

Come on Alice, she berated herself. *There have to be more options, throw the chips up in the air again and see where they land.*

In her mind she laughed as she remembered herself as a child with her own mother, dancing in the rain.

"Free your mind, Alice, let it all go!" her mother had shouted, spinning faster and flinging the raindrops off the end of her fingers.

By the time her fellow passengers alighted from the lift in a single file and streamed off to their respective routes, she felt inexplicably exhausted, yet elated. The chips had not only landed, they had slotted into place to form a new plan.

She drove across the city to the house of a man who was another renowned early riser. A man whom she knew to have interests aligned with her own, though for an altogether different reason. A man who could provide her with what she needed in exchange for information that he could use to get what he wanted.

CHAPTER 40

RICHARD WHITE LOOKED up briefly as Alice approached him, just long enough to register her presence, before he dug into the soft earth with a small green fork and plucked out another weed, roots and all. He dropped it onto a small pile next to him and sat back on his heels, stabbing the fork upright into the garden bed.

Alice mused that gardening seemed a strange hobby for one of the most powerful men in the country. If the rising unpopularity of the current government continued, it was widely expected that the Honourable Richard White, Leader of the Opposition, would become Prime Minister Richard White after the forthcoming election.

Alice shuddered, realising she had more in common with this man than she would have liked. Strong-willed daughters who knew what they wanted and would stop at nothing in their pursuit to get it. She desperately hoped that Monica wouldn't be quite as stubborn as Charlotte White, if it came to it. But she was here today to make sure that Monica wouldn't need to. At least she knew her daughter was safely with Pete, for now.

"Well, well, Alice Mooney. You really are causing quite the stir behind highly placed doors in this fine country of ours. I'm sorry to hear about your daughter."

"Thank you. I have faith that she will be found soon, alive and well." She paused. "But that's not why I'm here."

Mr. White nodded. "To what *do* I owe the pleasure of your visit today?"

Alice stared at the gardening fork and bit her lip. She cleared her throat and sat down on the stone bench nearby.

"I'm so sorry for your loss, Mr. White," she said.

He opened his mouth, then sighed and turned back to the garden, swiping at the soil with his meaty hand to smooth out the gashes his extractions had left.

"She was a wonderful girl, was Charlotte." He patted down a mound of dirt. "But very stubborn and idealistic. She believed her death would be enough to shake up the system; shock the nation into action." Mr. White picked up the fork and stabbed around the roots of a large broad leaf weed, using his leverage to lift it up further. "She overestimated her own importance and underestimated this country's political capacity for sweeping inconvenient events under the carpet."

There was something soothing and cathartic about watching one of the nation's leaders getting his hands dirty to tame his own backyard.

"Your former gardener."

Mr. White paused mid-strike, then re-grouped, sliced the fork into the roots and hefted the whole plant out of the earth, sending it flying into the pile next to him.

Alice swallowed and pressed on. "When we interviewed him, he said Charlotte had found something in your study. Some papers."

Mr. White placed the fork on top of the weed pile and stood. "Shall we head inside and have this conversation? That stone bench is none too comfortable and manual labour is thirsty work for a desk-bound man."

Alice settled in at the kitchen table, waiting for the kettle to boil and watching Mr. White scrub the dirt off of his hands at the kitchen sink. So far, he'd made small talk about nothing in particular. Alice smiled and nodded politely where required, allowing the white noise to wash over her. Eventually he stopped chattering, poured two mugs of tea and sat down opposite her.

"Our gardener had convinced Charlotte that there was a government conspiracy to create an obedient underclass to serve the overlords by fiddling with their genetics." He stopped and shook his head, laughing. "Believe me, if there was some sort of injection I could administer to people to get them to act in their own best interests, I'd fully support it. But that's not how the human psyche works. You know, whoever first based economic systems on the assumption that humans are rational ought to be taken out and shot. It's such a ridiculous notion." He paused to lift his tea to his mouth, gazing at the fernery outside the full-length window at Alice's back.

"What did Charlotte find in your study?" Alice prompted gently.

"Proof. Or so she thought." He looked at Alice intently then. "Is this an official inquiry? I thought that was closed."

Alice shook her head and drank from her own cup. "Not official. Just me. I need to know." She placed her hand on her stomach. "I need your help. And I think I can help you, too, but I need the full story."

Mr. White nodded. "Okay. Well, her gardener and his band of radicals are partly correct. We realised some time ago that if we could gain control of the genetic make-up of babies before they're conceived, we could positively influence the health and wellbeing of society. Your usual standard genetic diseases were easy to test for, but as we gained the ability to test for more rare diseases it became more expensive—and more contentious—to try and figure out what to do where an anomaly was found in the embryo post-implantation.

"Hence the bi-partisan support for the Genetic Diversification System. Not that the Equality Party has really needed our support for the past twenty-odd years."

"Public opinion is shifting," said Alice quietly.

"Yes, it does feel that way," he eyed her curiously, but went on. "The G.D.S. has made it easier to ensure brothers weren't accidentally breeding with sisters through egg and sperm donation. Easier to screen genetic material for known diseases prior to implantation. But, as you know, there's been a great amount of push back from the romantics of society who can't separate relationships from reproduction." He stopped abruptly and sipped his tea, as though he'd finished his story.

"But that's all public knowledge," said Alice impatiently.

Mr. White smiled. "Ah, but then the government got cocky. Their think tank finally managed to genetically engineer certain personality traits such as rationality. Ambition. Subservience. They'd figured out a way to breed and raise a population that was deliberately split into the masses who would meekly serve and a minority who would rule them." He peered into his half-empty mug, lifted it to his lips and downed the remainder. "My inside sources found evidence that the government was planning to tweak quite a few more genes than the ones controlling congenital and mental illnesses. *That's* the evidence that Charlotte found in my study."

Alice nodded. It was true, then, what Mary had uncovered at the laboratories.

"So, you support this policy, then?" she asked evenly.

"I wouldn't call it a 'policy', that's a little too official, don't you think? And no, I don't support it. Just think what we'd lose if everyone started behaving in an entirely predictable manner." He gestured towards two works of art on the wall opposite. "The man who painted those left his family, quit his job and lived in a shed in his patron's backyard, spending his welfare payments on paint. Why? Because he wanted to see how living away from people would affect his art—sort of a before and after shot." He pointed at the first picture, a landscape of broad brushstrokes, sweeping gums, a fiery sunset behind the hills and a couple sitting on their front porch, sipping tea while watching sheep graze on green pastures. "That's the 'before' shot, while he was living with his family." He nodded at the second painting, an orange-yellow sphere surrounded by a dizzying mess of spots, dots and spirals. "That's the 'living-in-a-shed' art."

Alice raised her eyebrows. "And your point?"

"A purely rational mind does not create great art." He leaned forward. "And what point is there to life without great beauty and wonder?"

Alice frowned. "But it makes no economic sense. The artist presumably left behind a traumatised family and failed to contribute substantially to society."

"Ah," said Mr. White, holding up a forefinger. "But think of the calming benefits of beauty to the minds of the many beholders of his artwork over the past century. And what of the livelihood of the paint manufacturer? The canvas retailer and the art gallery owner? The esoteric satisfaction of his patron, who had no skill himself, in knowing that he was contributing to the creation of great art?"

Alice brought her teacup back to the table too quickly and jumped at the clatter of ceramic on glass. "But does all of that outweigh the sorrow and anger of the children he abandoned, or the extra financial, emotional and physical burden he left to their mother?"

Mr. White shrugged and sat back in his chair. "And so, the argument goes around again. At the end of the day, I don't believe we should be messing around with the personalities of an entire species. But sadly, I've yet to find a way to stop it from happening which doesn't rock the people's faith in the rest of the system. Because, after all, the rest of the system is working quite well."

"For some," added Alice.

Mr. White nodded. "For most, I'd say, especially the children who are able to enjoy safe and happy childhoods. So, Ms. Mooney. You sought me out on a Sunday for an urgent reason, yes? This sort of existential chat could have waited until office hours." He stretched out his arms and laid his palms flat on the table. "What is it that you want?"

Alice stared at his hands for a moment and ran her tongue around the inside of her teeth. She raised her eyes to his. "I can give you evidence which will help you discredit the G.D.S. *and* the Equality Party, paving the way for your party to win the next federal election."

Mr. White pressed his fingers into the glass. Small outlines of condensation appeared.

"I see. You consider yourself quite the king-maker, then. And what can I do for you in return?"

Alice pulled out duplicate contracts and a pen. She placed them on the table and slid them towards him.

"This. I want you to guarantee the safety of my family—now and into the future."

He read it slowly. "That's quite some evidence you've got there. And it's from a reliable source?"

"Yes."

"And this is all you're asking in return?"

Alice nodded. "Can you make it happen?"

Mr. White shrugged. "Of course, I can pull some strings if you keep up your end of the bargain. But I think you should know, I feel like I'm getting the better deal."

He picked up the pen and signed both copies. She slid the flash drive across the table and took one of the signed contracts.

"You'd better start reading up on how to run a country, Mr. White. It's time for things to change." Alice smiled wryly and showed herself out.

Pete was waiting for Alice at her car in front of Mr. White's house. His long body leaned against the driver's door, his arms crossed.

"Is it safe for you to be standing out in the open like that?" she asked nervously.

"It's safe for now, but we should go. Monica and Oscar are both fine. I had to modify our plans because of the fire, but I got them out. They're at a safe house a few hours outside of the city."

Alice stared at him coldly.

"They're fine," he repeated.

Alice didn't trust herself to speak. She couldn't tell if she was grateful to Pete for rescuing her daughter or furious with him for lying to her when she'd asked for his help to find her. Mostly she was simply relieved. And tired. She waved her hand at him, trying to swat him away so she could open the locked car door.

Pete glanced at her car and shook his head. "Not that one." He pointed down the street to a black SUV. Alice followed him.

"We'll head out to the suburbs to pick up Ollie, then head west, to the safe house."

"Ollie's not coming," said Alice flatly.

Pete stopped, his hand on the car door. "Are you sure?"

Alice nodded and got into the car. Pete stared across the car roof at where Alice had been standing. After a moment he frowned, lowered himself into the driver's seat and started the engine.

"Did something happen? You want to talk about it?" he asked.

"No."

They drove silently past the bustling cafés serving early morning lattés and breakfast bruschetta. On through the central business district and across the Yarra River to join the freeway. From there they merged into the traffic heading out of the city, heading west, past the smokestacks of the industrial inner west, over the Westgate Bridge. Soon they were leaving the skyline of the city far behind and green space started to appear again.

CHAPTER 41

WHEN MONICA WOKE the next morning, her breast felt cold and her shoulder was stiff where she had lain on it, her arm stretched out across the pillow, her body forming a protective curve for her sleeping son. His face was still and turned slightly towards the window, both arms flung above his head in trusting abandon. Bright light streamed in through the thin curtains. She leaned over and flicked one up, peering out. The sun was high overhead, she'd slept long and deeply. Not wanting to wake Oscar, Monica lowered her head back onto the pillow. She watched his round belly, its slight movements as it rose and fell with each irregular baby breath.

Oscar snuffled and issued a warning cough, then sneezed. Monica reached for him before he started to fuss and, with a practised hand, had him positioned at her breast within seconds.

Twenty minutes later Monica carried Oscar out of their room, down the hallway and out the front door. Standing outside on the porch felt strange, there was nothing to see but empty fields. It was as though the whole world was deserted. There was no sign of the dusty black SUV that had brought her here last night—clearly Uncle Pete had gone out. She allowed herself a brief moment of panic as she imagined her mother and uncle had conspired to abandon her and Oscar in the middle of nowhere.

"No," she told herself firmly. "She always comes back."

Stepping carefully down the rickety porch steps, she sat down on a small area of lawn and lay Oscar down on it. He burbled happily to himself and rolled on his stomach, his heavy head bobbing as he surveyed his new surroundings. Monica shivered a little in the chilly air, reconsidering her plan to wait outside until her uncle returned.

She cried out as something swooped, narrowly missing her, and alighted on a shrub behind her. A small, brown-feathered bird dropped tiny meals into the mouths of its two babies huddled together in a nest. Monica smiled. It looked a little cramped in there as the siblings tried to climb over each other. As she watched, one baby stood, turned and puffed up its feathers. From its rear end it released a small, white globule, which the mother took into her mouth and immediately flew away with.

"Gotta keep the nest clean somehow," said a voice behind and above her. Monica looked up, startled, and saw a head poking out of the open window. "The things we do for kids. I'm Cain, by the way."

Monica blinked warily. "Where's Pete?"

"Gone out for a while. Do you want some breakfast? I've got granola if you're hungry. Is the little guy on solids yet? There's some yoghurt and maybe a cracker."

Monica nodded silently. She scooped up Oscar and followed Cain inside. He ushered her in, visually sweeping the landscape before closing and locking the door behind them.

Oscar sat in an old-fashioned highchair with a metal frame and vinyl padded cushions boasting gaudy, gingham flowers in red and yellow. Monica sat next to him while he gnawed on his cracker, ready to catch him should he start to slide out beneath the moulded plastic tray.

"Sorry about the, ah, vintage equipment," said Cain, flipping over an omelette in a small electric skillet. "The bonus is the eggs are completely fresh."

"It's fine, thank you."

She'd barely taken her eyes off the gun he wore so openly strapped to his hip, uneasily wondering why he felt he needed the weapon so close to him at all times. Now she forced herself to look around the kitchen at the yellow cupboard doors and Formica bench tops. It seemed as if the place had been suddenly abandoned decades ago and never updated since. The only concession to the twenty-first century was a jumble of electronic devices arrayed on a makeshift desk in the corner. At least the house was bright and clean, she thought.

Her eyes rested on a collection of framed photographs on a long, low sideboard. A woman held a baby in one arm and wrapped her other arm around a man. The man rested one arm around the woman's shoulders and pressed his cheek to the top of her head while three children stood in front of them—a boy and two girls—cascading in height from the man's waist to the woman's knee. They all faced the camera, smiling.

This must be a pre-Home system family, thought Monica in wonder.

The woman looked tired, but happy. Imagine being responsible for all those children, alone, while the man went out to work during the day, she mused. How did they do it? She noticed that all the children looked similar, with golden brown hair, blue eyes, long noses kicking up slightly at the end. The boy had clearly inherited his father's sticking-out ears, while the girls had neat, flat ears, just like their mother. Monica looked at Oscar, wondering if he had her ears or the ears of his genetic father. Would people see her and Oscar walking down the street in Sweden and instantly know they were related?

She looked back at the woman in the photograph. If she had managed three children by herself, with no formal qualifications in child-rearing and no state directives, surely Monica could manage one?

"Here you go, eat up."

Cain placed a plate full of toast, omelette and bacon in front of Monica, making her stomach rumble. She hadn't eaten since the day before and shovelled forkfuls of hot, salty food in as quickly as she could with one hand, making sure to keep hold of Oscar with her free hand.

"Pete should be here soon with your mum and her husband," said Cain, sitting down opposite her and blowing on his coffee.

Monica looked up and stopped chewing, glanced at the gun reflexively. Cain followed her gaze and smiled. He pulled the handgun out of the holster and placed it gently on the table.

"Guess you wouldn't have seen one of these before, hey?"

"I've seen them plenty, online. Forensic ballistics is a fascinating science," she retorted.

Cain shrugged and re-holstered the weapon. "You're making a huge mistake, you know."

"Oh?"

"Trying to take your kid away," he nodded at Oscar, who dribbled chunks of cracker down his chin. "You have no idea how good he's got it here, compared to kids in other parts of the world."

"Kids get to stay with their families in other parts of the world."

Cain shook his head adamantly. "Australian kids have families, too. You just don't want to see it. What do you think is going to happen if you leave?"

"I'll get to raise my own son," said Monica, tensing her shoulders.

"The system works, Monica. Sure, the G.D.S. is a step too far, but the monitors are seeing to it, we're trying to fix it." He handed Oscar another cracker.

"The system works great—for kids. When you stop being a kid, life ain't quite so grand anymore," said Monica defiantly.

Cain slammed his fist down on the table. Oscar dropped his cracker and turned down the corners of his lower lip, waiting to see if he should cry or not.

"If you and your bloody selfish mother leave, you'll jeopardise the integrity of the whole system. Thanks to Charlotte White and those pamphlets there's already serious unrest. Then your mother's pregnancy and her pig-headed refusal to terminate it, and now you." Cain stood suddenly, scraping back his chair and knocking it over. He leaned over so close that Monica could smell the perspiration on his forehead. "You'll destroy what we've spent decades protecting, just because you can't find it in yourself to make a few sacrifices for the sake of your own child."

"You're scaring Oscar," she whispered, shaking.

On cue, Oscar wailed loudly. Monica stood to go to him, pausing momentarily while Cain blocked her way, his hand resting lightly on his holster.

She bowed her head. "Please, let me go to him."

He moved aside. She grabbed Oscar and walked quickly to their bedroom, shutting the door behind her, willing Uncle Pete to arrive quickly.

CHAPTER 42

A LICE LAID HER hands on her lap and fixed her eyes on the simple country road, devoid of painted lines and gutters.

"So, are you going to tell me why you decided it was a good idea to try to incinerate my daughter?"

Pete glanced sideways at her. "The fire wasn't part of the plan. I was already there scoping the Birthing Home security. I took the opportunity to get her out, but I don't know how the fire started."

Alice felt the cold fingers of fear creep up her spine. "Mary said there are rumours that the sprinkler system was disabled remotely. That wasn't you?"

Pete gave her a hurt look. "Of course it wasn't. I'm trying to help you, Alice. I would never take that kind of risk with Oscar's life."

"Or your niece's life," Alice added, pointedly.

"Or my niece's life."

"So where is she now?"

"There's an abandoned farmhouse, three hours west of the city."

"And she and Oscar are safe there for now? You're sure?" asked Alice.

"Yes, they're safe. It's equipped with high-tech surveillance. Cain, one of our monitors, is keeping an eye on her. Don't worry, he knows what he's doing." He paused, waiting for Alice to respond. "Let's just get there as quickly as we can, okay?" He pushed down on the accelerator.

Alice watched the needle creep to the right on the speedometer and hooked her thumb under her seatbelt, gripping it in her fist.

"How could any mother do this to her children?" she said quietly.

"Do what?"

"Sign away her bloodline to be lab rats? And then abandon them. How could Mum do that to us?"

Pete stared at her incredulously. "For the sake of the children, Alice, I thought you understood that. She was very sick. If you suffered from a severe mental illness and were told there was a way you could spare your own children—and the children of others—from suffering, wouldn't you do it, too? She had no way of predicting how the experiment would be abused by the Equality Party."

"She wasn't always that sick, though. She was fine when we were kids. Maybe with medication and therapy she could have—"

"Alice, stop it. Stop rewriting history. Jesus, you always do this."

"Do what?"

'Whitewash the past. Mum was never quite right, and she only got worse as time went on. Don't you remember?"

"She came every Sunday. She came for us." Alice insisted.

"Yes, but she became so erratic, she wasn't allowed to even be alone with us, remember?" he said quietly. "She stayed at the Home with us most Sundays. Her visits became shorter as her condition worsened. Then they were supervised. Then they stopped altogether." Pete glanced sideways at her and frowned.

Alice dug her thumbnail into her ring finger, hard. Pete checked the rear-view mirror, then Alice, then shifted his eyes back to the road.

"You remember the last time she took us out? She brought us back soaked to the bone and nearly hypothermic," said Pete, trying to unlock her true memory.

Alice smiled. "She took us dancing in the rain. It was wonderful."

"She forgot to feed us."

"We weren't hungry," she whispered.

"Oh, Alice," he sighed. "She was sick, they decided she'd become a bad influence on our mental and emotional development and that we'd be better off without her in our lives. And she agreed."

"I wanted her there. I didn't care how broken she was. I just wanted her to think of me instead of the goddamned *greater good* for once." Alice shut her eyes and shook her head, shaking the memories back into their box. "I needed her, Pete. After the baby..."

Pete glanced at her. "She tried, Alice. You could have gone with her."

"I couldn't leave!" she shouted. "I couldn't leave my baby and she should have stayed."

"Alice, your baby died," said Pete quietly. "You couldn't have changed that. But you could have left. You can't blame Mum for your decision."

"I couldn't leave," she whispered again, staring out the window and seeing her tiny, lifeless infant with her mind's eye. Monica and Oscar's safety was all that mattered now. They would make it out of Australia. She would give her daughter the gift of freedom that she had failed to accept from her own mother.

CHAPTER 43

MONICA SPENT THE next few hours tensely watching the driveway out of her bedroom window, waiting for her uncle and mother. Finally, a black SUV pulled up just a few meters from the front porch. Cain appeared at the front door and Alice burst out of the passenger door of the SUV. Monica gathered up Oscar and went out to join them. She stood hesitantly on the porch, away from Cain, and allowed herself to be hugged tightly, frowning slightly in surprise at such a rare physical display of affection from her mother.

"You're okay," said Alice, standing back and looking her over as though to check for any lasting damage from the fire, even though she knew there was none.

"Yes, I'm fine," replied Monica impatiently, watching over Alice's shoulder as Pete emerged from the driver's side door. He nodded to her, unsmiling.

"You're safe now," said Alice. "Pete has arranged flights to take you and Oscar to Stockholm, leaving tonight. We don't have much time."

Monica turned back to Alice, confused. "Where's Ollie? We can't leave without him."

Alice swallowed and took both of Monica's hands. "He's..." she faltered and looked at the ground, resting her eyes on Oscar. "He's not coming."

"You're leaving him? To come with me?" Monica's expression bore a mixture of shared pain at Alice's loss, and elation at her mother's sacrifice.

Alice looked at Pete and Cain, then back to Monica. "We should go inside, let's talk in there."

"Pete, I need a word with you upstairs," said Cain, flicking his head toward the house.

"We need to leave as soon as possible. It can't wait?" Pete asked impatiently.

"No. It can't."

Pete nodded and followed him into the house and up the stairs.

"In here." Monica led her mother through to the kitchen.

They sat around the cold, Formica table, Monica clutching Oscar tightly to her. A broken piping on the seat stabbed at her thigh and she shifted uncomfortably.

"Mum? What's going on?"

Alice put her hands on the table and stared at them for a moment.

"Pete has arranged for you and Oscar to fly out to Sweden from Adelaide. It's a five-hour drive from here, but it's a small airport and they won't be looking for you there. You'll travel on British passports. If anyone asks, you'll say you came to Australia so that your baby could have medical treatment here and now you're returning home to Europe."

"And what about you, Mum?"

"I'm staying here."

Monica tore her hands away from Alice's, scrambling up from her chair and backing away from the table. "I... I don't understand. I can't do this alone, Mum."

"Yes, you can. And you'll have Monique, my Mum," Alice held out a hand, pleading with Monica to understand.

"You're abandoning me to the crazy mother who abandoned *you*?" said Monica bitterly. "I should have known, I should have known you would do this!" Her face contorted with fury.

"I'm sorry, Monica. I can't leave Melbourne, not now. The G.D.S., it's worse than any of us realised. I have to help stop it."

"You always do this, you never stay. There's always something more important." She kicked the sideboard in frustration. "Why do you never choose me?"

Alice, now wary of her tempestuous daughter, took a sharp breath and started to throw out details like olive branches. "My mum—your grandmother—lives in a small apartment just outside of Stockholm. It's a basic setup but it's a beautiful area. Pete and I will make sure you have enough money to keep you and Oscar fed and clothed. After three years you'll be able to apply for citizenship, which means you'll get access to childcare and will be able to continue your studies."

Monica continued to stare at the photograph. She could hear low voices upstairs. They sounded tense, angry.

"It's not too late to change your mind. You could stay here, go back to the Birthing Home," said Alice, dropping her hands in her lap.

"Gah!" exclaimed Oscar, suddenly arching his back and trying to look into Monica's face, upside down.

Monica stared at him, unseeing. Then she blinked, smiled back at him and gently turned him around.

"I don't know if it's hormones, or biological imperative or an irrational psychological attachment," she said, transfixed by Oscar's eyes. "I didn't want a baby in the first place, but I was told I had to, and I did. And now I can't—I won't—just hand him over and go back to my other life like some freaking mindless drone." Monica looked back at Alice, a pained crease between her eyebrows. She shook her head. "I'm leaving this hell-hole tonight and I'm taking my baby with me." Her eyes flicked down to Alice's abdomen. "And, quite frankly, I don't understand how you can even consider raising another child in this broken, inhumane excuse for a society." She spat these final words at her mother through a locked jaw.

Alice sat back and smiled wryly. "That's my girl," she said quietly.

Monica glared at her.

"I'm going to tell you something that my mother told me when I was about your age. I didn't understand at the time and I hated her for it. Hopefully you're smarter than I was."

Monica focused her attention on Oscar, bouncing him on her lap. She pretended to ignore Alice while biting down on a trembling lip.

"First of all, you are perfectly capable of living your own life and making your own decisions. You'll always be my baby and I'll always be here for you whenever you need me. But I also need to consider myself and what's best for me. If I can't live with my own decisions, I can't support you to act on yours."

Monica looked up at Alice at that point and rubbed quickly at her glistening eyes, then shook her head and looked away.

"I'm pregnant, Monica. This baby will be your brother or sister, it'll be Oscar's aunt or uncle. But this baby is also Ollie's son or daughter. I can't take Ollie away from his children—from Ellie and Tom. And I can't take this baby away from Ollie. But I can still help you."

"How? How can you help me if you won't come with me?" Monica's voice broke and her breath came in gulps.

Alice leaned across the table and put her hand over Monica's. "I can take my own mother up on the offer she made to me twenty years ago. I can send you to Monique and she will care for you and Oscar just the same as she would have cared for me if I hadn't been so stubborn."

Monica didn't withdraw from her mother's touch.

"But what about *your* baby?" she asked. "Will they let you raise her? Or him?"

Alice smiled sadly. "My baby will be raised by its father. I've arranged for him or her to be placed in Ollie's Home after the first six months. I've made a deal with someone who can make it happen." She shuddered involuntarily at the vision that popped into her mind of the sickening images she'd handed over to Richard White. "I'll be able to visit my child whenever I want, I'll still be a part of its life. The system isn't broken, Mon, it just needs a few... adjustments. There's so much more I can do here." She paused, willing Monica to understand, to forgive her.

Monica nodded and wiped at her tear-stained face, embarrassed. Oscar's lower lip began to tremble again. She forced a smile.

"It's okay, Oscar."

Oscar watched his mother's eyes, waiting, lip still puckered. He reached out his tiny hand to grab her nose. She took his hand, traced her finger around his palm and smiled as he giggled.

"It's going to be okay," she told him again, adding a brighter tone to her voice. "We're going to Sweden to visit your great-grandma." Monica sniffed again, her breath catching in her throat as she heard heavy footsteps on the stairs. She looked up as Pete appeared in the doorway, his palms resting on the top of the doorframe. He leaned forward, flexing his arms and shoulders, and stared at Oscar intently.

"We're ready," Alice prompted, standing and taking a step towards Monica.

Pete shook his head slightly and looked at Alice as though he'd only just realised she was there.

"Let's go, then."

"Pete, is everything okay?" said Alice quietly, sensing the tension as Cain descended the stairs and came to rest against the wall immediately behind Pete.

"Everything's fine, we'll just have to be careful," he said evenly. "Come on, we need to go. We've got a long drive ahead of us." Pete avoided meeting his colleague's eyes as he turned and paced down the hallway.

Monica nodded and allowed Alice to lead her and Oscar back through the house, out the front door and into the waiting SUV.

"Passports are in the glove compartment, luggage is in the back seat," Alice muttered to herself as she closed her own door and started ticking off a mental checklist. Monica sat in the back seat with her hand on Oscar's back as he leant against her and flicked the suitcase wheels that jutted out towards him. He giggled in delight as they spun.

"Mum, is Uncle Pete in trouble? Will they come after us?"

"No, I don't think they will," said Alice, watching Pete as he circled the outside of the vehicle, checking the tyres and peering underneath. She wasn't sure whether either of them were referring to the government or the monitors, but her statement held true for both.

"Pete doesn't exist as far as the authorities are concerned. And the monitors won't want to alert the government to their presence." She turned around to face Monica as Pete slipped into the driver's seat and gave the car its instructions. "Right now, we just need to get you, Oscar and Pete on that flight and away from here."

Pete stared straight ahead at the road, clearly not in the mood for chatting. Oscar started to wail; Monica settled in to feed him. Alice picked up her tablet and tapped out a message.

Monica and Oscar are safe. You can send the first media release.

She eyed her brother before hitting *send*, silently apologising to him for what she was about to do.

After a minute or two the reply came from Mary: *Done—first round sent to journos. Package to cops scheduled to go in 20 mins. Should be enough time for media to get there and film the arrests...*

Alice had promised Pete she would keep the incriminating photographs he gave her away from the public eye. She'd assured Monica she wouldn't get Pete into any trouble. She may have just disappointed them both. At least Pete was leaving the country tonight.

As the night descended and the adrenaline wore off, Monica and Oscar slept. Eventually Alice's hands stopped shaking and Pete pulled over at an isolated recharging station. While he charged the car's battery, and scraped the suicidal bugs off the windscreen, Alice headed inside to settle the bill and buy a few snacks. Inside at the counter, she caught the tail end of a breaking news item on the attendant's wall screen.

"Confirmation just in: Graeme Smythe, Secretary of the Department of Genetics and Reproduction, has now been arrested on suspicion of three counts of... paedophilia," said the newsreader, bowing her heavily made-up face at the last word. "Leading figures around Australia have expressed shock and dismay that this monster, the figurehead of the G.D.S.—a program so intrinsically linked with the safety and wellbeing of our children—could have been allowed to go unnoticed for so long."

The screen cut to footage of Richard White, sitting at his desk and holding a photograph of his deceased daughter, Charlotte White. He wore a grave expression. A caption appeared at the bottom of the screen: *Richard White, leader of the Conservative Party, calls for immediate suspension of G.D.S. over child abuse charges.*

"We, as a nation, have the right to feel betrayed," said Mr. White. "At best, this is reprehensible incompetence on the part of the Equality Party. At worst, criminal negligence of the safety of all of our children." He paused for effect and touched Charlotte's photograph. "I call upon Barbara Mathers, Minister for Genetics and Reproduction, to resign immediately. I call upon the government to cease implementation of the G.D.S., pending a full review of Smythe's involvement. And finally..." He leaned forward and stared directly at the camera. "I call upon the Equality Party to take a good hard look at themselves and consider asking the good people of Australia for their forgiveness for letting this happen."

"Mr. White," said a reporter off-screen. "Do you think the Equality Party should call an early election?"

Richard White shook his head sadly. "I can only hope that the Equality Party will do as their conscience guides them."

Alice smiled. "He's good, I'll give him that."

CHAPTER 44

MOTHER, DAUGHTER AND grandson arrived at Adelaide airport with minutes to spare. Monica and Oscar had slept for most of the long drive. In the end there was just enough time for the practicalities and a final, tight hug while Pete unloaded their luggage from the trunk.

"Here's a bank card, there's enough money on it to get you through a few weeks. Pete and I will make sure it's reloaded regularly. Take care of yourself and... give my love to Mum, won't you?"

Monica nodded. "Come and visit us some time soon?"

"Maybe. I hope so," said Alice.

Monica smiled, a pained expression on her face. Alice bit down on her lip, hard, as she watched her daughter turn and walk away. Holding Oscar in one arm, Monica pushed their hand luggage on wheels with the other while Pete wheeled two large suitcases ahead of her.

Alice abandoned the SUV in the airport parking lot and headed towards the bus depot. A bus and then a train back to Melbourne wouldn't require identification, unlike hiring a car or catching a flight. It was best not to leave a trail, she figured, even with her protection in place.

An hour later, Alice settled down into her train seat and hooked her earpiece over her ear.

"Hey, lover," she said softly when he answered.

He replied gently, a smile in his voice: "Hey, lover."

She paused, her eyes closed, listening to him breathe.

"You're not on a plane, are you?" he said finally.

"No, I'm not."

"It's been a big news day. I've had the screen on at our apartment all afternoon. I guess you'd know a bit about that?"

"Monica and Oscar have left for Sweden with Pete," she said.

"That must have been very difficult for you," said Oliver carefully. "And you? Where are you going now?"

"I'm coming home," she said. "You and Margery are going to raise our baby. I've arranged it all."

"Thank you, Alice," he breathed. "You won't regret it, I promise. I'll make sure of it."

"I hope so, Ollie. I really hope so." She covered her mouth and a ragged sob. "I love you so much."

"I love you, too."

Alice ended the call and stared out of the window, allowing her tears to run freely down her face as her baby started to kick and flutter in her belly.

It didn't seem like a sensible solution, to send her daughter halfway across the globe to live with a grandmother she'd never met; to hope that her unborn baby would arrive healthy against all the odds, only to give it away. The pain of her immediate and future losses hurt so much right now, but in her heart, she knew she'd made the right choice. It was the best she could do, and it would have to be enough, for now.

Acknowledgements

Writing a novel is a marathon where each stop contains a tempting couch, wide-screen television and a sign saying, "Are you *sure* you want to keep going?"

Thank you to everyone who believed I could start, helped me prepare, simply assumed I would keep going or actively pushed me off the couch and back onto the track.

To my parents, the first to foster my imagination. To all of my English teachers, especially the one who refused to give me another top grade until I actually put in the effort and improved.

To my husband who said, "Why not?" when I told him I would never write a novel; and to my children who both inspired me and put up with me disappearing for periods of time to "do writing".

To my early readers, thank you for asking for the next chapter, for reading draft manuscripts and providing invaluable feedback: Caitlin Hurse, Freda Moloney, Angela Perryman, Kylie Laughlin, Linda Wilson, Jess Newman, Amy Wakley-Ahearn, Melissa Sorini and Gary Wilson.

To the incredibly generous folk of the writing community for your encouragement and advice throughout the years.

To my wonderful agent, Lauren Bieker of FinePrint Literary Management, for her editorial feedback, enthusiasm and for never giving up on this book.

To the 80 people who generously provided funding support to bring this book to life - thank you so very much. And thanks to Lisa Shearon for showing me what was possible. In particular, thanks to the following major sponsors: Linda Wilson, Gary Wilson, Geoff van der Meer, Rowena Hallam, Kylie Laughlin, Chris & Yvonne Bowyer, Susan Cowan, Joy Sankey, Irene & Barry Bowyer, Jo-Anne Bowyer, Laura McDougall and Andrew & Yoshiko Bowyer.

Last but not least, thank you to all the readers and writers of stories who together create the most brilliantly endless cycle of imaginative creation.

About the author

Rebecca Bowyer lives in Melbourne, Australia with her husband and two young sons. When not at her day job, making school lunches or supervising visits to the skate park, she can be found writing about books, reading and writing at storyaddict.com.au.

Rebecca's articles on writing, feminism, parenting and the history of parenting have been published widely, including on Women's Agenda, Ripen the Page Literary Magazine, Kidspot, Essential Kids, Mamamia, Seeing the Lighter Side and more.

Maternal Instinct is her first novel.